Death
Gone A-Rye

Books by Winnie Archer

Kneaded to Death

Crust No One

The Walking Bread

Flour in the Attic

Dough or Die

Death Gone A-Rye

Death
Gone A-Rye
Winnie Archer

5/2021

KENSINGTON
PUBLISHING CORP.

www.kensingtonbooks.com

KENSINGTON BOOKS are published by

Kensington Publishing Corp.
119 West 40th Street
New York, NY 10018

First Kensington Books Mass Market Paperback Printing: May 2021

ISBN-13: 978-1-4967-3354-2
ISBN-10: 1-4967-3354-1

ISBN-13: 978-1-4967-3357-3 (ebook)
ISBN-10: 1-4967-357-6 (ebook)

10 9 8 7 6 5 4 3 2 1

Printed in the United States of America

For Monica Palla
Thanks for being there

Chapter 1

The sky was a periwinkle blue dotted with cotton ball clouds. The sound of waves crashed along the surf, intermixed with the occasional squawk of a sea gull. The light April breeze might have made the late afternoon too chilly for an outdoor wedding, but the stars had aligned and the weather was a temperate sixty-eight degrees. It couldn't have been more perfect if we had dialed in an order to Mother Nature herself.

My brother, Billy Culpepper, stood with his back to the Pacific Ocean wearing a cream-colored lightweight suit, turquoise tie and boutonniere, and a stupidly beautiful and nervous grin. His hazel eyes seemed to almost glow with the backdrop of the Pacific Ocean behind him. His best man, Terry Masaki, stood next to him in a similar linen suit, a slight wave in his fine black hair. It was parted in the middle and gave him a movie star look. The sole groomsman was Emmaline's brother, Efram. He was wider than both Billy and Terry, had a nearly shaved head, and had cheekbones that sliced across his face. He was half tank, half man, and, from my experience with him, was the biggest teddy bear on the planet.

The three men stood in front of the unbelievably gorgeous wedding arch Billy had built in his garage. He had used over thirty pieces of driftwood that he'd gathered from coastal shores during the last several months. He'd designed the arbor to be self-standing with the two support poles, two sides, and a top piece wound together from the wood. While Billy and Em were on their honeymoon, Terry and Efram would disassemble it and put it up in their backyard. From wedding arch to backyard arbor, the piece would be a constant reminder of Billy and Emmaline's special day.

Emmaline hadn't seen the arbor yet. Billy was full of surprises for the love of his life. They'd spent years at different crossroads, always missing each other. She'd been attached, and he hadn't. Or he'd been seeing someone when she was single. Finally, though, they'd gotten together, and now they were getting hitched. Everything was as it should be.

A cluster of greenery and flowers cascaded down from the top left of the arbor, with another bouquet on the right side. White tulle had been wrapped around the frame, the ends now billowing in the gentle wind. It was magical.

The outdoor patio of Baptista's Cantina and Grill had been transformed from a dining area to a wedding venue and Miguel, who happened to be the love of *my* life, had closed the restaurant for the occasion. The moment the ceremony ended, he had staff ready to move the chairs that currently faced the altar, set up tables, and serve the food that was being prepared in the restaurant's state-of-the-art kitchen, which Miguel had recently renovated.

My brother's wedding to my best friend was one for the ages. Everything was perfect.

A string trio with a violin, a viola, and a cello sat on white slipcovered chairs, music stands holding the sheet music. They played while the guests trickled in. Traditionally, the groom's friends and family sat on one side while the bride's friends and family sat on the other. Billy and Emmaline had grown up together, so, for the most part, they shared the same friends. Those friends seated themselves on either side of the aisle, while Emmaline's family took the front row seats on the left. My dad, two of my cousins who'd up come from Los Angeles, and Olaya Solis and Penelope Branford, who were the women I'd chosen to be part of my family, sat on the right with Olaya next to my dad, Owen, and Mrs. Branford on his other side. They were bolstering him with silent emotional support, I knew. There was a hole in all of our hearts because of my mother's absence. I looked up at the sky and closed my eyes. She might not be here with us physically, but I could feel her presence.

I met Billy's gaze and raised my eyebrows. He was marrying his soul mate, but I understood his nerves. Marriage was a big step. I knew. I'd been there once. If and when I ever did it again, it would be forever.

He flipped his wrist and glanced down at his watch, then back at me. I got the message. My heart fluttered. It was time.

I scurried around the chairs, noticing people I recognized as members of the Santa Sofia sheriff's department, which Emmaline Davis ran, huddled together. Some of her staff were manning the office and streets, but a handful of them, including the captain, a new position within the department, were here to celebrate her wedding.

Emmaline had stepped into the role of sheriff after her predecessor found himself in a heap of trouble. He'd run a bare-bones operation with minimal manpower to fill the typical positions within a department. Em had changed all that. She'd established a hierarchy, which included a captain who was over the criminal investigation division, freeing up Emmaline to run the department, which oversaw the county jail, policed the unincorporated areas of our county, served warrants, and secured the courthouses. It was a big job, but she was a strong woman and more than capable of handling it all.

The new captain was a tall, thin man with long sideburns and feathery blond hair. All he needed was a black turtleneck and a brown leather blazer and he could have played David Soul's part in a *Starsky & Hutch* reboot. As I scooted by, he withdrew his cell phone from the pocket of his lightweight jacket and peered at it, but the sudden movement of his department people drew his attention away from his screen. As if they'd received some sort of subliminal message, Emmaline's subordinates moved as a group toward their seats.

I slipped through the patio door leading inside the restaurant. The second Emmaline laid eyes on me, she screeched, all her sheriff composure out the window. "Ivy, where have you been? I'm so nervous. I think my knees are going to buckle."

I rushed over to her. "You and Billy have been waiting for this day since you were kids. Come on, you're fine."

Em's mother and father had stepped back, allowing me room to wrap my arms around my best friend and give her a squeeze.

"He's a great guy," she said.

I might be biased because he's my brother, but I

agreed with her. Wholeheartedly. "He definitely is a great guy. Better than great. And you are perfect together."

She lifted her chin slightly, her lips curving up. "I really thought this day would never come."

From the patio, the string trio finished the song they'd been playing. A silence fell. I squeezed Em's hand. "But here it is," I said just as the string instruments began playing Pachelbel's Canon in D.

"Ready, love?" Emmaline's mother had stepped forward next to her daughter.

Em nodded, her eyes already glistening.

Miguel looked dashing in beige linen pants, boat shoes, and a black guayabera decorated with satin stitching on either side of the buttons. His years in the military, coupled with his daily bike rides and runs along the beach, meant he was lean and mean and wore his clothes well. Enrique Iglesias had nothing on Miguel Baptista. He whispered something to the little flower girl, who was Terry Masaki's four-year-old daughter, Hana. She giggled and bit her lower lip as she got ready to skip toward the groom. She looked like a fairy in her pale turquoise sheath, her satiny black hair dusting her shoulders, and a wreath of daisies like a halo encircling her head. She waved at her daddy, who stood next to Billy, then at her mom, Mei, who snapped pictures of her little girl with her phone. Miguel urged Hana forward and she started down the aisle. She carried a sweet drawstring satin bag, digging her hand into it, pulling it out with a fist full of satin silver, aquamarine, and turquoise rose petals, and tossing them on the white runner leading to the altar.

Emmaline's cousin, Vonnie, went next. Vonnie was shorter than Em. They had the same perfect dark skin, but while Emmaline was slender, Vonnie was curvy. She had a weave done for the wedding and today her black hair had a million kinky curls, the volume of it framing her face. Emmaline generally preferred natural, but for the wedding she'd gone with braids woven into an intricate updo.

Emmaline had wanted a small wedding party with her one bridesmaid—Vonnie—and me, her maid of honor, looking beachy and radiant. Her life was all order amid the chaos of crime. In contrast, she wanted her wedding to be relaxed and effervescent. So far, so good. Vonnie glided down the aisle, holding a small spray of daisies tied together with a length of white ribbon. When she was halfway to the altar, I straightened my dress. The shade of turquoise was paler than Vonnie's. It draped over one shoulder, reminiscent of a Greek goddess, and fell effortlessly, flowing behind me as I walked slowly down the aisle.

When I reached the halfway mark between the restaurant and the altar, the Pachelbel faded, and the traditional wedding march began. The guests rose in unison and all eyes turned to face the bride. I reached my spot next to Vonnie. We smiled at each other and as I looked at Emmaline, flanked on either side by her parents, gliding toward us, my eyes filled. My best friend was getting married. To my brother. I couldn't have dreamed up a better day for them.

Beneath her veil, I knew Em's eyes were glistening. From the driftwood archway to Vonnie and me, to the Pacific Ocean as a backdrop, and then to Billy, standing next to Terry and Efrem, a goofy grin on his face, this was the day she'd been looking forward to.

She reached the front altar. Her mom lifted Em's veil, arranging it so it hung neatly behind her. She bussed her daughter's cheek. Em hugged her mom, then her dad.

They retreated to their reserved seats while Em handed me her bouquet of fresh daisies.

As Billy stepped next to her, she pointed at the archway, whispering something to him. He nodded, and this time, her eyes filled and her lower lip quivered with emotion. She wove her arm around his and moved closer.

As the pastor led the ceremony, I felt a pair of eyes on me. I scanned the guests. Everyone's attention was on Billy and Emmaline. Everyone except one man. Miguel sat in the back row, ready to jump into action once the ceremony ended. But for now, he was intent, not on the wedding couple, but on me. As I met his gaze, one side of his mouth lifted in a saucy smile and his eyebrows raised slightly. What was his unspoken message? I couldn't exactly say, but I liked that he was thinking about me in this moment. Miguel and I had been through a lot over the years, but we'd found our way back to each other and it was nothing but bright roads ahead for us.

I smiled back at him, then returned my attention to the ceremony. Billy and Em had chosen to write their own vows, something I wasn't sure I'd have the courage to do and speak aloud. Emmaline was finishing hers, speaking through her tears. "Things have a way of falling into place at the right time. It took a while, but we were finally in the right place at the right time. You are my soul mate, Billy, and I love you. I love the way you show your love for me. I love how I still get butterflies whenever I lay eyes on you. I love how you take care of me, but also everyone around you. I love that we are, above all, best friends. I'm a strong woman, and you admire and respect that. Being with you has made me a better woman. You, Billy, have my heart forever and ever. I promise always to love you, respect you, and stand by your side."

Next to me, Vonnie sniffled. I'd been smart enough to tuck several tissues into the bodice of my dress. I artfully removed one now, handing it to Vonnie. Meanwhile Billy held Emmaline's hands in his and gazed at her with such love I thought his heart might actually burst.

Mine felt like it was about to.

"Em," he began. "I have loved you since we were little kids running around barefoot on the beach. I don't know how many people can say they are marrying the love of their life, but for me, that is the absolute truth. I've wanted you to be my wife for as long as I can remember. Now it is finally happening. I am blessed that you choose me to spend your life with, and I choose you. I'll always choose you. Today we may be starting a new chapter, but we're already a book. I already belong to you. Falling in love with you has been like walking into a house and knowing you're home.

"Em, I promise to stand by your side, always. To continue to learn from you, to always make you your favorite green smoothies, to keep my eyes open and to see clearly with you by my side, to binge-watch *Parks and Rec* with you after a tough day, or maybe *The Office*, but most importantly, today, in front of our friends and family, I promise to love you, respect you, and cherish you forever."

There were some chuckles, and there was not a dry eye in the house.

Except, maybe, the sheriff's department's captain. Even from where I stood at the altar, I could see him cradling his phone in one hand, his focus fully on his screen.

Somehow, I resisted a grimace. The pastor pronounced Billy and Emmaline husband and wife. The newly married couple kissed, and then Em turned to me and we fell into a hug. "Real sisters at last," she said with a happy sigh.

We'd been sisters of the heart since we were kids, but now it was official. I squeezed her, then let her go so she and Billy could walk up the aisle as Mr. and Mrs. Culpepper. Although I knew Em was going to stick with "Davis" professionally. She was sheriff, after all. Keeping her maiden name at work seemed easiest and best.

I held on to Terry's crooked arm and followed Billy and Em back toward the restaurant, Vonnie and Efrem behind us. Miguel had already gotten the ball rolling on his end of things. As the guests stood and began milling around, his staff swept in to fold up the chairs. They set up the round tables, redistributing the chairs around them. As much as I wanted to find Billy and Emmaline again and give them both rib-crushing hugs and sloppy congratulatory smooches, I let the rest of the guests have their turns. I skirted around the tables and slipped inside, stopping when I saw the spread that had materialized between the time the ceremony had started and now. Buffet tables overflowed with the food choices Em and Billy had selected. Fancy shrimp quesadillas; crab and shrimp cocktail spooned into straight clear glasses and topped with chunks of avocado and lime; and corn cakes, each covered with a healthy dollop of a chopped shrimp, avocado, tomato, and cilantro mixture, a drizzle of tomatillo cream on top. And these were only a few of the offerings.

Another table, perpendicular to the buffet line, was mounded with bread from Yeast of Eden. Billy and Em couldn't get enough of the bread shop where I worked alongside the owner, Olaya Solis. I was her apprentice, of sorts, but had worked for her almost since I met her. I would have done it for free, I loved it so much, but Olaya insisted on paying me. Since my savings were running low, I was glad for the steady paycheck. I was a good student and worked hard, both at the shop and in my own kitchen. Thus, my collection of bread recipes had grown from zero to about ten. These were the ones I could make without a recipe and that almost always turned out well.

Olaya had at least two dozen more in her head. Maybe one day I'd have a fraction of those in my repertoire. What I saw before me today, though, was like nothing Olaya had ever made before. Or at least not like anything I'd ever seen from her. There were mounds of popovers and traditional dinner rolls, but one of the standouts was a basket of beautiful buns that looked like the dough had been swirled with a vibrant purple. I knew she'd used butterfly pea flower to get that deep color. "It is used in ancient Chinese and Ayurvedic medicines," she'd told me when I'd first seen her bake with it. "It does not change the flavor, but has healing properties."

But what really made me gasp were the focaccia breads that looked like pieces of art. They could be van Gogh paintings. There were eleven focaccia loaves in all, each with a different floral design. One was of sunflowers and poppies with the design made from Kalamata olives, the stems and leaves made from fresh herbs set into the dough, yellow peppers for the sunflower petals, capers for the seeds in the center of each bloom, and grape tomatoes adding pops of color. Several of the focaccias were heart shaped, with herb stems and baby bell pepper slices, grape tomato or olive flower tops. Little slices of red onion created an illusion of the earth beneath the flowers. The dough palettes were gorgeous and inspiring and filled with the love Olaya had developed for Billy and Emmaline. I had become a pseudo-granddaughter to Olaya, as she had become the family I had chosen. My own family, which meant my dad, my brother, and now Em, had become like family to Olaya, too. This display of breads was her way of showing that affection.

An arm slipped through mine and suddenly there she was at my side. I was a bit taller than she was and, with my heels on, even more so. I tilted my head to hers, the spiraled tendrils of my ginger hair cascading over her short, spiked iron-gray strands. She had traded her typical caftan for a slightly fancier flowing dress. Olaya was a free spirit with an incredible business mind and creativity that flowed from her core into the bread she baked. "This is absolutely amazing," I said.

"*Sí.* They are an amazing couple," she said.

Miguel appeared at my other side, complimenting the display of bread just as I had. "I've never seen focaccia art," he said.

"It is Instagram-worthy, do you not think?" Olaya winked at me. I knew she did not have Instagram or any other social media for that matter. I ran the website, the bread shop's Facebook page, and its brand-new Instagram account. Those tasks took me out of Yeast of Eden's commercial kitchen, but they still kept me connected to Olaya's bread, which had magical elements that no one could explain. Whatever ailed you, Olaya had a loaf of bread that was healing.

"Are those sourdough?" Miguel asked. He pointed to a cluster of dinner rolls. Instead of having a rounded top, each looked like the dough had been rolled into a strand, then knotted and sprinkled with white and black sesame seeds.

"Yes. Made with fresh-milled local rye, spelt, and, *por supuesto*, wild yeast."

"Of course. Only wild yeast," Miguel agreed with a smile.

"You laugh, but it makes a huge difference," she said.

Miguel threw up his hands. "I am not laughing. I know the importance of your traditions and the best ingredients."

Olaya nodded her head, just once. It was her acknowledgment that she knew Miguel understood. She released my arm, took up a napkin, and used it to rearrange a few of the rolls to better balance the display. Miguel slipped his arm around me, pulling me close. "You look beautiful," he said. With his free hand, he played with the loose strands of my hair. "I like the updo."

I gingerly patted the back of my head. My hair tended toward unruly, but the clips and bobby pins were keeping it controlled at the moment. My coquettish reply was stalled when the door from the patio flung open and a man stepped through. It was David Soul's look-alike. He had his phone in his hand again, but this time he held it to his ear. "I'll tell her, but she's leaving on her honeymoon. Don't worry. I'll handle it."

Miguel and I looked at each other. This was the captain in the sheriff's department, and he was clearly talking about Emmaline. "Will do," he said into his phone. He snapped the device onto the phone clip strung onto his belt, then looked up, noticing us for the first time. A wee bit concerning for a crime investigator. I thought spacial awareness and observation would be key to his position.

"Sorry 'bout that," he said. He looked at me. "You're Ivy, right? Culpepper? Sister of the groom?"

I nodded. I'd originally placed him in his late forties, but up close, he looked younger. Maybe forty or forty-one. His skin was tanned, and with his blond hair and white teeth, he wore his age well. I wondered how he felt about having a female boss who was younger than him, hoping he was the progressive sort who celebrated women in power.

"The sheriff has mentioned your, um, contributions to the department."

Contributions. That was one way to put it. Crime solving was another. I was an apprentice baker at Yeast of Eden, but I had also found myself acting as a Santa Sofia sleuth lately. "She's mentioned you, too. She was thrilled to steal you from San Luis Obispo."

He nodded but didn't continue the chitchat. "There's been a . . . an incident. Good to see you." He nodded to Miguel, acknowledging him, although they hadn't formally met, before turning on his cowboy-booted heel and heading back outside.

From his conversation on the phone and his demeanor, I knew he didn't want to burden Emmaline with whatever incident had happened, but she was the sheriff and I knew he had to. I pulled away from Miguel. "I'll be right back," I said, and started after him.

"Stay out of it," Miguel called after me.

I couldn't promise that until I knew what *it* was. I looked over my shoulder and smiled. "I don't know what you're talking about," I said, and before he could tell me exactly what he was thinking, which was that I didn't need to get wrapped up in another murder, I was back on the patio and making a beeline for Em and Billy.

By the time I reached the newly married couple, the captain had already pulled Emmaline aside. With her hands on her hips and her face tight as she listened to him, she had shifted from blushing bride to badass sheriff. She glanced at me as I came up next to her. The captain looked hesitant and stopped speaking. "Ivy, this is Captain Craig York. Craig, my best friend, Ivy Culpepper." She didn't wait for either of us to acknowledge the introduction, instead rolling one hand in the air, telling him to keep going.

"It's a local school board member," he said.

Her breath hitched. I don't think the captain noticed, but I'd known Emmaline Davis for nearly my whole life, and I knew what that response was about. The Santa Sofia school board was made up of five people. One of them, Candace Coffey, had been in high school with us. Now she was a mother of three and served as vice president of the board. "Dead?" Em asked, and I knew she was hoping against hope, just like I was, that it wasn't Candy.

York cupped one hand against the back of his neck before saying, "Murder."

"Who?" Em asked.

"Nessa Renchrik. School board president."

Em and I both sighed in relief, although only mine was audible. *Not Candy, thank God.*

"I'll handle it," York said. "I'll keep you updated."

I could see the internal battle Em was going through. How could she leave town when a murder had just happened? But it was her honeymoon.

She proceeded to give him precise instructions on how often he was to be in touch with her, and emphasized the high priority of the case. A school board member was a political figure in a community. The people of Santa Sofia would demand answers and justice.

"Will do," York said. He gave one succinct nod to both of us before walking away.

The second we were alone, I took Emmaline's hand. "It's going to be okay. He seems on top of things."

She grimaced. Not the most desirable expression for a bride. "He's new."

"You wouldn't have hired him if he wasn't qualified. He can handle it."

"It's not Candy," she said, hands on her hips again. "Thank God."

"Do you know this woman, Nessa?" I asked.

"No. But school board president. That's not good."

Billy sidled up behind her and snaked his arms around her waist. "What's going on, Mrs. Culpepper?"

"Murder," she said.

His face fell. "Uh-oh."

She put her hands on top of his. "And it's a high-profile one."

His hold on her tightened. "You have people to handle it, though. We have a flight to catch in the morning, and, you know, a wedding reception with all our friends and family."

She turned to face him, tilting her head to look up at him. "And we're going to enjoy every second of it. Captain York is handling the investigation. He'll update me, but he's in charge."

Billy nodded. "Good to hear. Now, let's round these folks up and head inside for the food."

Craig York's words came back to me then. I'd made contributions to the department with my sleuthing skills. There was no reason I couldn't help out again. Miguel had told me to stay out of it, but I just couldn't. And since I had an in with Candy, maybe I'd be able to get information York couldn't.

The next few hours would be filled with food and dancing, but in my mind, I'd be formulating a plan on how to solve a murder.

Chapter 2

The reception after Emmaline and Billy's wedding had been perfect, if you didn't count the pall of a murder hanging over the sheriff. Em had done a good job of staying in the moment, though, and she'd only excused herself a handful of times to check in with Captain York.

By the time I got home, I was exhausted. I showered, dressed in lightweight PJs, and climbed into bed. Next to me Agatha, my brindle pug, snored and gurgled. She sounded as if she had a head cold, but it was just her smoosh-faced pug-ness coming through loud and clear. I reclined on my bed, laptop open, knees propped up at an angle, my back supported by three pillows. Agatha lay stretched out beside me, her head at my foot, her backside at my hip. I moved my computer enough to lean forward and nudge her head. She let out a complaining sigh but readjusted herself, giving one big snore before settling down again, quietly this time.

"You are too much," I said, laying my palm on the side of her belly. Agatha had been a rescue. Now she was my bosom buddy. "And I love you."

This time Agatha gave a deep contented sigh. She loved me, too.

I went back to my Internet search. Emmaline didn't entirely trust Captain York yet, so I told her I'd be keeping my eyes and ears open while she was gone. Of course me keeping my eyes and ears open was not a passive thing. It meant that I'd be actively searching and listening. I'd be doing my best at getting to the truth of the matter. Not only was I helping Em; I was also satisfying my own curiosity, given that I actually knew a school board member. Calling Candace Coffey was first on my list of things to do in the morning.

I typed Nessa Renchrik's name into the search bar on my computer. A series of photos came up first, followed by links to her Facebook page, several interviews she'd done with the *Santa Sofia Daily*, the local newspaper, her LinkedIn profile, and her Twitter handle, which was @RenchrikinSS. She was attractive. Blond shoulder-length hair that looked a little wispy in a few of the shots. It was pulled up into a formal style in another and she looked elegant. She had fine facial features with a narrow nose, lips on the thin side, and wide-set hazel eyes. I read about her background, discovering that she was forty-two years old, was the mother of two, and had been married for eighteen years. She'd been school board president for the last year. She was in the middle of her second term.

It's amazing what you can glean from Google. All that was missing was her shoe size and whether she preferred her husband in boxers or briefs.

I went back to the top of the search page and clicked on the first entry, which was the *Santa Sofia Daily*'s post about Nessa's death.

Vanessa Renchrik, 42, a longtime member of the Santa Sofia Board of Education, was found dead earlier today in the school district's boardroom. Mrs. Renchrik has served as Secretary, Vice President, and was currently President of the school board. She was a visible member of the community and has led the district through tumultuous times during her tenure, including leading the district through layoffs, budget cuts, tax increases. She is survived by her husband, Cliff, and their two children. The sheriff's department's criminal investigation division is pursuing a series of leads.

Ah, so her first name was actually Vanessa. Nessa for short. It went on to give the information about the celebration of life service that would be held later in the week. I marked the time and date in my calendar before logging on to Twitter. I didn't have a personal account, but I did run the bread shop's @yeastofedenSS account. It was a new account and had only 150 followers, but I was slowly working to build it up, along with the bread shop's Instagram account. That was much more successful. The photo of the Vincent van Dough focaccias Olaya had made for the wedding was racking up the likes. Instagram was where it was at for a baker.

I typed in Nessa's Twitter handle and her feed came up. It was instantly obvious that she was not an active tweeter. One tweet, posted two days prior, said: *No decision I make is based on emotions.*

I sat up straighter and grabbed a sheet of paper from my nightstand and jotted down the date and time of the text, as well as what Nessa had said in it, followed by a few thoughts that had instantly come to mind. *What decision was she talking about, or was it a blanket statement? No one was tagged on the post, but it felt like a subtweet. But to whom, and about what?*

Agatha stirred and lifted her head. A second later, I heard the front door open with the light jiggling of keys followed by the click of it closing again. Miguel's voice called out. "Ivy?"

"In the bedroom," I called. I'd offered to help clean up after the wedding reception, but Miguel had insisted I go home. "I have a crew of people. It's what I pay them for," he'd told me.

Agatha looked at me, tilting her head when she heard Miguel's voice. Her eyelids grew heavy over her bulbous eyes and she settled her head back down on her blanket. Miguel was old news to her. Not worth barking at.

The man himself appeared in the doorway a few seconds later. From planning the menu, prep and set up, to the event itself, to breaking it all down and cleanup, hosting a wedding and reception was not for the faint of heart. He looked worn out. "My hot-water heater went on the fritz yesterday," he said. "I didn't have a chance to call for service, and a cold shower won't cut it right now." He dragged his hand over his face as he leaned against the doorjamb.

"Shower here," I said.

He cupped his hand behind his neck. "Thanks. Not enough time in the day lately."

He could say that again. Between building up my fledgling photography business, working part-time at Yeast of Eden, and doing the crime solving I'd somehow fallen into, the days zoomed by. There were periods where Miguel and I didn't see each other for a stretch of three days. Neither of us liked that.

"The wedding was beautiful, though," I said, "and the food was incredible."

"Thanks." He smiled. "Billy and Em looked happy. Crazy about that murder, though. I hope Em can hang up her sheriff hat long enough for to enjoy her honeymoon."

"Oh, she definitely will," I said. "It's Costa Rica."

For the first time, he registered my laptop and note-book. His eyes narrowed. "What are you doing there?"

"Shower first; then I'll tell you all about it."

He hesitated, looking like he was going to say some-thing, but he seemed to reconsider. He nodded, then dis-appeared into the bathroom. A moment later, the pipes creaked as the water turned on. My old Tudor house was quaint and oozed charm, but its age was showing.

"Did you know Nessa Renchrik's name is really Vanessa?" I called.

Miguel gave a low moan from the shower. The hot water felt good.

I went back to my research, somehow managing to ig-nore the fact that Miguel Baptista was alone and naked in my shower. Helping out your best friend so she could honeymoon in peace took great sacrifice. And restraint.

I searched Twitter and Facebook, jotting down more notes as I found out things about Nessa Renchrik thanks to social media:

She was in the middle of her third term.

Her husband said she'd been out running errands. She hadn't told him she was going to the district office.

The tweets and Facebook responses about her death were varied. Some people expressed their condolences to the family. *Poor kids.* #mourningmom *What will the husband do now?* #copingafterlosingalovedone *What a loss for the school board.* #forthekids

Others were not so favorable. *She deserved it.* #liar *Her kids are better off.* #nomoremaleficentmother *Ding dong, the witch is dead.* #dingdongthewitchisdead

"Listen to this," I said as Miguel came out of the bathroom. I read him the responses to Nessa's death, finishing with, "Hashtag, ding dong, the witch is dead. Crazy, right?" I said, finally looking up.

Miguel was rubbing his damp hair with a small white towel. He was bare chested, another white towel wrapped around his waist. I loved seeing him here, comfortable. Playing house. We'd gotten closer and closer. Who was I kidding? I loved this man. I wanted nothing more than to have him here in my house at bedtime and to wake up next to him every morning.

I'd been married—and divorced. If I married again, it would be forever. Miguel and I were a long way from taking that step, but the romance of Emmaline and Billy's wedding had gotten to me. As I looked at Miguel now, any future I imagined had him in it.

"Wow. Mixed reviews on her, huh?" Miguel said as he moved to the dresser and pulled out a pair of pajama pants from the drawer of stuff he kept here. They were pine green and cotton. I'd looked down at my notes, and when I looked back up, he'd slipped them on, had tossed the towels onto the chair in the corner, and was halfway to stretching himself out beside me. I swallowed, the love I felt for him bubbling up. Or maybe it wasn't exactly love at this precise moment. There were no mixed reviews on him.

Agatha moved her head and let out a squeaky stretching sound. She looked at Miguel, hauled herself up from repose, and plopped down next to him, her body right alongside his. He scratched her belly, lay back, and propped his other hand behind his head. "Did you find anything else?" he asked.

"Not yet, but do you remember Candace Coffey?"

He closed his eyes and for a few seconds I thought he had drifted off, but he opened them again suddenly and said, "Didn't she used to be Candace McIntyre?"

"Right. She married Maxwell Coffey." I rolled my eyes. "*What* were his parents thinking when they named him that?"

Miguel laughed. "God. Good question. Very good question."

I swallowed my laugh. "Candy is on the school board, too."

"One of the schools has a Spring Fling coming up next weekend. Someone there did hit me up to sponsor it."

"Are you going to do it?" I asked. The Spring Fling was a big fundraiser for one of the elementary schools. Some schools did fall festivals. Others held holiday events. Chavez Elementary capitalized on the temperate weather and spirit of new beginnings, holding theirs in April. Olaya had been asked to sponsor a booth, so Yeast of Eden would be selling bread there.

Miguel's eyelids fluttered to half-mast. "I can't. We have a big event that weekend. I need to find that message," he murmured.

I went back to Candace Coffey. "Candy was elected two years ago. Board members serve four-year terms."

"Mmm."

I was losing him, and it was no wonder. Restaurant work was hard. The guy was exhausted after a long week followed by catering the wedding.

I scanned back over the search results for Nessa, zeroing in on her social media profiles. Just like that, I made a decision, moved the mouse, and tapped the touchpad on my laptop to start an account on Twitter. For the bread shop's account, I'd used the Yeast of Eden info email. For this one, I used my personal email. I paused as I thought of what handle to use. I went with @Ivy_Bakr. Miguel's eyes had drifted closed and before long his breathing grew rhythmic and steady. I finished setting up my Twitter account, and immediately followed the people who'd been actively commenting on Nessa Renchrik's death. Finally, I responded to @MarisasMama, the person who'd said: *Ding dong, the witch is dead,* with the simple statement, *Tell me more.*

I was about to close the tab and sign off for the night when a got a direct message alert from @MarisasMama. It was short and to the point: *Santa Sofia is better off without Nessa Renchrik*

Immediately, I typed: *Why?*

@MarisasMama was just as quick with her response: *She was just another politician. She didn't care about the kids, or anyone for that matter.*

Huh. My fingers flew over the keyboard. *I thought people liked her. Three terms . . .*

She was a liar and she didn't play by the rules.

@MarisasMama seemed to be in the know. I replied with a shocked, *What do you mean?*

You have to practice what you preach, @MarisasMama replied.

I decided to push a little further. See if she would give up some actual details. *Who did she have in her pocket?*

This time, @MarisasMama didn't answer right away. I tapped the pads of my fingertips against the sides of my laptop, waiting. God, I hoped I hadn't scared her away. Finally, after a solid minute, the DM came: *Who are you?*

Shoot. How could I answer that question and keep her talking? I went with a version of the truth: *Just a concerned citizen.*

The police?

No! Ha-ha. I work in a bakery. I grew up here. Just curious. That was all true.

There was another pregnant pause before @Marisas Mama responded again. It was a link. That was it.

I clicked on it, and it took me to a newspaper article about a local ICE sting that had resulted in the arrest of more than one hundred people just outside our county limits. The article detailed the operation, which included the raid of a local trailer park that housed the majority of the immigrants. A few, apparently, managed to escape through something that was being called an Underground Railroad, of sorts, but most had been caught in ICE's net. It was unclear from the article how or why this particular region and location had been selected by the immigration agency.

How had I never heard of this? Why had Emmaline never mentioned it? The neighboring sheriff's department would have worked with the government agency, but surely she would have had information about it. I picked up my phone to text her, abruptly stopping when I remembered that it was her wedding night.

I went back to Twitter and my direct message inbox. Nothing new from @MarisasMama. I messaged her: *What does this have to do with Nessa Renchrik?*

I waited for a response. Crickets. @MarisasMama seemed to be done chatting with me. I clicked on her profile to see what information I could glean about her. Front and center was her photo, which was a close-up of her face, oversized throwback glasses, bright red lips, a sweep of brown highlighted hair, and sparkling white teeth. Her bio information stated that she was a feminist, immigrant daughter, and proud mother of a baby girl. More than that, though, was her name. Lulú Sanchez-Patrick. I highlighted it, copied it, and pasted it into the search bar. The Internet was magic. Just like that, I had more information than Lulu Sanchez-Patrick probably wanted the world to know about her. I clicked, clicked, clicked, writing down in my notebook her name, birthdate, email address, place of employment, and the name of her husband. The Internet was magic, but also scary.

Beside me, Miguel sighed and rolled over, his body facing me. Agatha complained, repositioning herself, her back pressed against his legs. His eyes were still closed, but his hand reached out to touch mine.

I signed off, leaned my computer up against my nightstand, and turned off the light. Tomorrow, I'd see if I could set up a meeting with @MarisasMama, aka Lulu Sanchez-Patrick.

Chapter 3

Miguel's restaurant was closed on Sundays and Mondays. So was Yeast of Eden, and the school district was not open on Sundays, which meant I did not have direct access to any information from the belly of the beast, so to speak. What I *did* have was an email for Candace Coffey, but despite multiple tries, I didn't hear from her until Monday morning.

"Ivy Culpepper," she said when I called her on the number she sent through email. "Getting your message was like a blast from the past. I heard you were back in town, but, God, I haven't heard from you in ages. I was really sorry about your mom."

My mom's unexpected—and far too early—death had initially brought me back to Santa Sofia. Olaya Solis and her bread shop had been one of the key factors in my staying. Bread making, it turns out, is good for the soul.

"Thanks," I said, wanting to quickly change the subject. I couldn't ask her how she'd been during the many years I'd been gone because, as of Saturday, I knew she had been horrible. A murder could do that to a person. "I heard about what happened—"

"It's unreal," she interrupted. "I don't know why she was even at the district office. The board meeting's not till tomorrow." She paused. "You know, when I first found out, I couldn't wrap my head around the fact that she was just here, and then suddenly she just wasn't. Honestly, I still can't quite believe it."

I knew that feeling well, but I didn't want to go there with my emotions. Instead, I redirected. "I'd love to get together for a cup of coffee or something."

She hesitated for the briefest moment before saying, "I'm meeting the detective in charge of the investigation at the district office in . . . gosh . . . thirty minutes, then . . . I don't know; it's a busy day."

I jumped at the opening. "No problem. I can come to the district office. I'd just love to see you and say hi. I'll see you soon!" I spoke quickly and hung up before Candy could discourage me from coming or, worse, tell me not to come at all.

Agatha stood at my feet, looking up at me with her huge expectant eyes. I crouched down to scratch the top of her head. "Sorry, chickadee. No *w.a.l.k.* right now." I spelled it out because she knew the word "walk" and I didn't want to tease her. "We'll go to the beach later. Deal?"

She gave me a slow blink, as if she'd understood everything I'd just said and was communicating her disappointment. She turned her backside to me, trotted to the couch, her little tail curled into a coil, jumped up, and turned herself around until she found the perfect spot to curl up in.

"Okay, then. Wish me luck." I slung on my crossbody bag, took the keys from the hook in the hallway, and went into the garage, pressing the button to open the door. It was an automatic action. I entered the garage, got in the car, and backed out, almost without thinking. Today was no different, except when I put the car in reverse and started back I glanced in the rearview mirror and saw a figure standing smack in the middle of the driveway. I slammed on the brakes and yelled. My hand instantly shot out, my finger depressing the button on the door. The driver's side window slid down and I craned my head out, yelling. "Mrs. Branford! You scared me to death! I could have hit you."

She marched up to the passenger side of the car, swinging her handy-dandy cane, which was more of a prop than an actual necessity, yanked open the door of my pearl-white Fiat crossover, and slid in. "Thankfully you did not hit me. Now, where are we going?"

I rolled my window back up then turned to face her. She'd closed her door and her cane was now lying across her legs, the handle in her right hand, the bottom of it pointed straight at me, moving slightly in a back-and-forth slide. The way she held on to it conjured up an image of a pool cue, with me as the ball.

I shook my head, dislodging that idea. Mrs. Branford was feisty and she wasn't one to easily follow directions if she had her own idea about something, but a pool shark she was not. "We? Where are *we* going? I know where *I'm* going," I said.

"And I know that wherever you are going, it has something to do with that woman's death."

I sputtered in a non-denial denial, but she held up one

gnarled hand. "No need to deny it, my dear. I know you quite well."

That was true. But my suspicion was that she'd also overheard my conversation with Emmaline at the wedding. "I'm just doing what Em asked me to do. You know how she is."

"I do, indeed. She has a hard time letting go of control, even on her honeymoon." She'd hit the nail on the head. "And as you know," she continued, "every good sleuth needs a sidekick. Time to reprise my role."

I finished backing out of the garage, but now the car was idling on the driveway. "Reprise your role?"

"Of course." She left it at that.

When I thought about it, she had practically given me a heart attack a couple of times (poker at a bar called The Library), but she'd also been quite helpful in ferreting out the truth, too (poker at a bar called The Library).

I thought about canceling. Calling the whole thing off. After all, I was not a crime investigator. Miguel's words from the wedding sounded in my head: *Stay out of it.* But it turns out I couldn't. Em had asked for my help, and Mrs. Branford was strapped in and ready to go. "Okay, then," I said. I checked the rearview and looked over my shoulder, then backed out of my driveway.

I started filling Mrs. Branford in on the few details I had. "The victim's name is Nessa Renchrik. School board president. She was found dead in the board's meeting room."

"Dead as in murdered," Mrs. Branford said. Not a question, but a statement. "*R-e-n-c-h-r-i-k?*"

I verified the spelling with a nod of my head.

A periwinkle Moleskine notebook suddenly appeared in Mrs. Branford's hand, along with a black gel pen.

I stared. Where had she hidden that?

She turned to the first page and wrote something. I craned my neck to get a glimpse of the page. In her spidery writing, she'd created a title page that said: "Nessa Renchrik." She turned the page and wrote something else. Presumably the cause of death.

"You're taking notes?"

"I always have. It's the best way to commit things to memory if you are a tactile learner, which I am."

"Have you always taken notes, I mean, of—" I broke off, not sure how to say what I wanted to say. "Our cases" wasn't accurate. I went with, "Of the crimes we've, um, sleuthed?"

"Always. I have a neat row of five little notebooks on my bookshelf."

Huh. It was quite similar to the notes I'd taken during my Internet search the other night. But five uniform Moleskine notebooks was more orderly than I'd been. How had I never known this about her?

"Okay, then," I said again. Mrs. Branford was leaving me a little speechless today.

"Cause of death?" she asked.

"Emmaline texted this morning. She said the victim appeared to have been hit with a chair. Blunt force trauma to the head when she fell against the table on the dais."

"What else do you know? Cops?"

I turned to stare at her. She gained confidence with every crime we encountered. "With Em on her honeymoon, Captain Craig York is in charge." Of course he probably would have been in charge regardless, given his position in the department and the new division Emmaline had created. But I knew her. She liked to have her hands in every pot, and the murder of a school board member was a pretty big pot.

"And Emmaline asked you to keep her posted about anything unusual you happen to happen upon."

Statement, not question. Mrs. Branford knew me well, and it looked like she had a pretty good handle on my new sister-in-law, too.

"The criminal division is investigating. I'm just going to talk to an old high school friend."

At this, Mrs. Branford, with her snowy white curls and the map of wrinkles on her face, turned a side-eye to me. "Any high school friend of yours is probably a former student of mine."

That was true. Mrs. Branford had been an institution at Santa Sofia High School. Both Billy and I had been through her class, as had Emmaline, Miguel's sister, Laura, and most of our friends. "Her name was Candace McIntyre, now Candace Coffey."

She leaned her head against the back of her seat and closed her eyes. "Candace McIntyre. Candace McIntyre. Candace . . . Candy." She sat up and her eyes popped open. "Candy McIntyre. I remember her. On the short side. Permanent smile and rosy cheeks."

"That's her," I said, "although I haven't seen her in years. And given the murder, she's probably not too smiley right now."

Silence fell for a few seconds before Mrs. Branford's voice broke into it, calm and reflective. "'If I should go before the rest of you / Break not a flower nor inscribe a stone / Nor when I'm gone speak in a Sunday voice / But be the usual selves that I have known / Weep if you must / Parting is hell / But life goes on / So sing as well.'"

Ever the English teacher, I ventured a guess. "Walt Whitman?"

"Good heavens, no. Joyce Grenfell. She was not known as a poet, but if the poem fits—"

We drove in silence and I thought about the recitation. It was, I realized, Mrs. Branford's ode to death, though written by someone else. She had no use for sorrow. She lived life as she wanted. Maybe Nessa Renchrik had, too.

"What else do you know?" Mrs. Branford asked after we'd driven a few blocks.

"Forty-two years old. Mother of two. She's been school board president a long time. She was in the middle of her second term."

"And she was found, on a Saturday, in the board-room."

"Yes. The board meeting is scheduled for tomorrow night."

"Did she have a reason to be in the district office?"

That was a question I'd asked myself and of course I didn't have the answer to. Candy didn't seem to think so. "Whether she did or didn't, who would have known she was there?"

Mrs. Branford rolled her cane on her lap. "Who's to say she was the intended victim? Could she have inter-rupted something?"

That was an excellent question. I'd assumed Nessa Renchrik had been the intended victim, but maybe she hadn't been. Figuring out the truth there meant fleshing out Nessa's life. My mind strayed to @MarisasMama. She seemed to think Nessa had it coming. "If we look at her death as accidental—wrong place, wrong time—that definitely changes things. Who else would have been there? What could she have walked in on?"

"Or," Mrs. Branford said, "maybe she had planned to meet someone there and things had gone wrong."

My octogenarian neighbor loved nothing more than to play devil's advocate. "She was elected twice; either she was well liked . . . or respected, or she was a good politician," I said.

"Those things are, quite often, mutually exclusive," she said.

Well-liked and respected politicians. Right. "If she was the intended victim, someone clearly was not fond of her. This case is high profile, Mrs. Branford. Emmaline is worried because it'll be in the news cycle. If we can help get to the bottom of it, fast, she might be able to enjoy her honeymoon. If not, well . . ."

"Enough said, dear. We will put on our thinking caps and we will save your brother and new sister-in-law's honeymoon."

I hit the brake pedal and came to a stop at a traffic light. "Maybe Captain York already has it figured out," I said.

She turned her head slightly, giving me a faint smile. "One can hope."

I'd spent some time on Sunday researching the district's school board. The now four-member board until Nessa Renchrik's seat was filled—consisted of three women and one man. Poor Jerry Zenmark. I didn't envy his role as the one male. Candace Coffey had been vice president to Nessa. Now, I supposed, she was acting president.

I'd had the good sense to add Candy's info to my

Contacts on my phone. Now I pressed the Call button on my steering wheel, which was connected to my Bluetooth. A second later, I spoke aloud. "Call Candace Coffey."

The car's automated voice responded with a robotic, "Calling Candace Coffey."

A woman answered, her voice wary . . . and weary. "Candy, it's Ivy."

The connection was crackly, but Candace Coffey's sigh was unmistakable. She'd been holding her breath—had probably answered the phone before checking the caller ID. When she heard a friendly voice, her relief was evident. "Ivy. Are you on your way?"

"Pulling up in five minutes," I said, circumventing any opportunity for her to tell me not to come. "How are you holding up?"

Another sigh. "As well as could be expected, I guess. I still can't believe it."

"I know what you're going through."

"The whole school board is here and it's a zoo. Some officer has gathered everyone together." She lowered her voice to a harsh whisper. "I think he suspects that one of us did this to her."

Captain York, no doubt. "Hang tight, Candy. I'll be there in a few minutes." I pressed a button to end the call and pressed a bit harder on the gas pedal. The car kicked into gear, surging forward with a burst of speed. Was Candy right? Did York suspect one of the school board members? Did he have a reason to think so? It seemed perfectly plausible, and digging into the relationships with the people closest to the victim was a good place to start. Other than visuals and brief bios, I didn't know anything about the other school board members. Any one of them could have had a beef with Nessa, though, and it would have been easy for them to arrange a meeting at the boardroom in the district office. Too obvious, though? If it was a board member, wouldn't they have gone to great lengths to distance themself from the connection to the board?

"Earth to Ivy."

Mrs. Branford's voice brought me back from my musings. "Did this Nessa Renchrik have political aspirations beyond the school board?" I asked.

"I assume you're posing that as a rhetorical question, correct?" Mrs. Branford asked.

"It was more of a wondering than a question," I answered, "but rhetorical nonetheless."

"What are you thinking?"

"Just considering possibilities. School board member. Political opponent? Someone who had something to gain politically by eliminating Nessa Renchrik? And, of course, we have to look at her family members. Her husband?"

"Sadly, it is often the husband." Mrs. Branford had jotted down information but now closed her notebook as we turned into the parking lot for the Santa Sofia district office. The building was a low squat brown structure that lacked windows and personality. It felt oppressive. Like a murder had happened here and the building was keeping the secrets.

Which was actually the truth.

I tended to see the best in people and I wanted to believe that Nessa Renchrik was a good person, but there was an equal chance that she was horrible. Someone had killed her, after all.

I had scarcely parked when the passenger door flew open and Mrs. Branford, moving as if she were in her

twenties instead of her eighties, bounded out of the car. I
caught up to her. "You're speedy today," I said, catching
up to her. She swung her cane, rather than using it for
support. Her orthotic white sneakers were pristine. Not
for the first time, I wondered if she had white shoe polish
and cleaned them after each wear. There was nary a scuff
on them. She had on her daily uniform, which consisted
of a velour tracksuit. Today's color was periwinkle. She
was Sporty Spice, the senior generation.

"No time to waste," she said as we approached the
building. She clasped hold of the door handle and gave a
yank. I grabbed hold of the door over her head and let her
pass through first. If the outside of the building had been
nondescript, the lobby was no better. It was a study in
beige. Tan walls, uncomfortable-looking wooden chairs
with brown upholstered seats, and beige carpet. The designer term might be "neutral tones," but to me it was
plain boring.

The receptionist looked to be in her early thirties. She
had dirty-blond hair pulled back into a ponytail, with
long strands pulled out in front framing her narrow face.
Her lips, which were a rosy pink, drew all the attention.
They popped compared to her light eyebrows and equally
light eyelashes. I smiled and said, "Hi. I'm here to see
Candace Coffey."

"I need a photo ID," she said, barely acknowledging
my presence. I considered giving her a good chastisement
about her lack of customer service, but of course, she was
probably in shock. It wasn't every day that the school
board president was found dead on the dais.

"Sure." I handed over my California REAL ID.

She took it, looked at it, then finally looked up at me.

Her eyes narrowed as she studied the license again. "This is you?"

Granted, it wasn't a great picture. My hair was untamable on a good day. That *hadn't* been a good day. I'd ended up pulling my hair into a topknot to keep it out of my face, my freckles were out in force, which I generally liked, but in the photo they didn't quite work, and, well, did anyone ever look great in a driver's license photo? I gave her a tilted nod and equally tilted smile. "It is."

She shrugged, then turned away to enter my name into whatever system the school district used.

"Candace was a student of mine at the high school," Mrs. Branford said. If she thought being amiable was going to get her a green light to bypass the district's protocol, she was mistaken. The woman behind the desk went through her spiel again, asking for Mrs. Branford's picture ID. Mrs. Branford pulled a little change purse from her tracksuit pocket and retrieved her license, holding it out. I strained to see catch a glimpse of her photo, which I'd never seen. I wondered how old it was. How often did you have to have a new driver's license photo taken, anyway? The woman behind the desk snatched it from between Mrs. Branford's fingers before I could get a look. It took several minutes for her to do whatever it was she did. We lifted our eyebrows at each other in a silent communiqué but waited patiently. Finally, she returned our licenses to us. We each tucked ours away as she gestured to a small kiosk in the corner with a monitor and a card-reading device connected to it. "Sign in, please."

"Candace knows I'm coming—" I started to say, but the receptionist's cold stare froze the words on my lips.

"Everyone has to sign in," she said.

"Right. Thanks." I was pretty sure nothing I did or said would improve the young lady's attitude. I smiled anyway as I stepped up to the kiosk screen, tapped it to bring it to life, and typed my name in on the digital keypad. It wasn't until after I was done that I realized I could have simply laid my driver's license on the card reader.

Mrs. Branford stepped up after me, also realizing too late that she could have used her license. I'd started to tell her, but she was halfway done typing in her name. "Next time," she said.

Once we were both signed into the system, the receptionist came around and opened the door for us, leading us down a hallway, around a corner, and to a large room, the door crisscrossed with yellow crime scene tape. The placard read: Board of Education Meeting Room. Mrs. Branford ignored the police tape, ducking under it as easily as if she were in a limbo dance competition. I followed right behind her, completely in awe, as I often was with her. I wanted to *be* Mrs. Branford when I was in my ninth decade.

A group of people were clustered in the corner of the boardroom, sitting on chairs it looked like they'd dragged over there. I spotted Captain York right away. His voice suddenly broke through above everyone else's. "Is that right?" he asked, but I couldn't see who he was speaking to. He'd had his back to the door, so he didn't see Mrs. Branford and me come in, but now, as if he felt a shift in the air, he stopped and turned. He looked right at me, acknowledged me with a slight nod, then went back to the conversation he'd been having.

Mrs. Branford and I stopped for a minute in the entrance and I took in the details of the room. Two long rectangular tables were pushed up against one of the side walls. A bunch of folding chairs were open and lined up in rows facing the dais where the school board held court. The American and California State flags hung from flag-poles on the left side of the dais.

It was another nondescript space in this nondescript building, but this room had a secret, because there, in the center of the room, was a big empty space cordoned off with crime scene tape. I used my novice investigative skills to deduce that the marked space was where the board president's body had been found. Whatever chair she was hit with was probably now in possession of the regional laboratory services operation.

I spun in a slow circle, cataloging the details in the room so I could report everything back to Emmaline in a comprehensive email. I ended up focusing on the spot where I was sure Nessa Renchrik's body had been. I moved closer to get a better look and saw bloodstains on the carpet. A chill swept through me. There really had been a murder here.

The crime unit had come and gone. If television, the movies, and my knowledge were correct, I'd venture to say that they'd used numbers to mark and photograph every spot of blood, every bit of potential evidence, everything that looked even mildly suspicious. With the exception of the marked place where the body had been found, the scene had been cleared since then.

"What in the world happened here?" I murmured.

Candace Coffey was nothing like I remembered her, although I did still recognize her. She hadn't grown in height, but she'd plumped out quite a bit. Her cheeks

were round, rosy apples and her chin had a chin. I remembered her always being put together with neatly ap-
plied makeup, painted lips, and nicely coiffed hair. Today,
though, she was a hot mess. Her eyes were red rimmed
and her mascara was not waterproof. The murder had
happened a day and a half ago, but she'd been crying
fresh tears, which had left fresh dark crescents under her
lower lashes. The short blunt cut of her tawny hair made
her face look rounder and her cheeks seem fuller. It
looked like she'd started the day with dark lipstick, but it
had faded, leaving her lips looking stained and tired.

It was clear that she was taking Nessa's death hard.

She sat alone. "That's Candace," I started to whisper
to Mrs. Branford, but when I turned, she wasn't there.
Without my knowing, she'd waltzed off and was talking
with a man at the opposite side of the room. I left her to it
and walked over to Candy. With my flattened palm on my
chest, I started to say, "Candy, um, Candace? It's me; I—"
but she jumped up, stopping my words in their tracks.

"Ivy!" She swiped at the smudges of mascara under
her lashes. Her hands held a wad of tissue mashed between them. "I'd recognize you anywhere. You look exactly the same. I'd have recognized you anywhere."

I could say the same about her. We were both older.
Maybe a little wiser. But we still resembled our younger
selves.

"Candy—or should I call you Candace?"

"Candy's good. Reminds me of old times."

"Candy, then. You look great." I gestured to my eyes
and smiled. "Minus the mascara."

She laughed and dabbed at the smears again. "I swear,
I can't get it together. I'm not sure she deserved to die,
but this is a little too close for comfort."

She wasn't sure Nessa had deserved to die. That was an interesting way to put the sentiment, I thought. Maybe she didn't deserve to die, but had she deserved something else? I made a mental note to jot that down later. "Were you good friends?" I asked.

She shook her head. "We've known each other a long time, but we didn't socialize."

"Oh." That surprised me. "When did you first meet?"

She thought for a moment before responding. "She moved here from Michigan before she had kids. I first met her when her daughter, Rachel, and my daughter, Ronnie, were in the same kindergarten class. Now they're seniors." Her lower lip quivered. She paused for a few seconds as she got control of her emotions. "Rachel's not going to have her mom at her graduation," she managed to say through her tears. "It's heartbreaking."

It was incredibly sad. A girl losing her mother at any age was difficult, but as a teenager? Life altering. What struck me, though, was that Candy hadn't said that Nessa wouldn't see her daughter graduate, but that her daughter was the one with the loss of her mother. Would it have been more natural to say that Nessa wouldn't be around to see her daughter graduate? Did Candy's focus on the daughter, Rachel, instead of Nessa mean something, or did it just underscore the fact that Candy and Nessa hadn't actually been friends? I needed to think about it.

After Candy's tears subsided, I swung my arm out, encompassing the group that had gathered in the meeting room, and said, "It's nice that you're all helping each other through this."

Candy looked at the cluster of people Captain York was making his way through. I knew he'd seen me, but thankfully he was completely focused on his task at hand.

The last thing I wanted was for him to chase me out of here for interfering in his investigation.

"People do come together in times of crisis," Candy said.

That was true. I flashed back to not so long ago when Miguel's family had gathered to grieve the loss of a close friend. They'd helped one another through a horrible situation. "It's so sad. Do you have any idea why someone would have done this to her?"

Candy didn't answer right away. I was just about to ask her again when she looked around, lowered her voice so no one else could hear her, and said, "How much time do you have?"

I stared at her, not sure I was getting her meaning. She didn't seem to have any curiosity about why I was so curious about Nessa Renchrik's death. She hadn't asked why I was here, or why any of this was my business. I counted that as a win and just kept going forward with her. "Um, what?"

She stood up, her tears suddenly dried up, her stained lips in a tight line. "Come with me, Ivy."

She started toward the door that led to the side parking lot. The visitor entrance to the board's meeting room? So during board meetings, maybe people didn't have to sign in at the special kiosk. Or maybe this was just an emergency exit for the space.

Either way, I followed her outside, letting the door close behind me. She led me to a bench under a shady tree on the other side of the parking lot. Clearly, she did not want to be overheard.

We sat side by side. I was dying to prod Candace along, so she'd tell me whatever it was she wanted to say, but I bit my tongue. It didn't take long for her to pony up the dirt she had on Nessa. "You'll discover this soon enough, so I might as well tell you."

"Discover what?" I asked.

She lowered her voice, as if she were imparting a great secret. "People didn't like Nessa."

Okay. It probably wasn't a secret, and I wasn't surprised after my direct message conversation with @MarisasMama, but it felt like a bombshell coming on the heels of the woman's death from someone who'd known her for a long time. "Why not?"

Candace glanced around. Not a soul was within earshot of us. "Because she was vile."

I almost fell off the edge of the bench. I don't know what I'd expected her to say, but it certainly wasn't that. "Oh yeah?"

"Is it bad to be speaking ill of the dead?" she asked, but she didn't look overly concerned. Her eyes were dry and she pursed her lips in what I could only describe as a defiant manner.

"If you think it'll help figure out who did this to her . . ."

"But do we want to figure it out?" she asked.

Another comment out of left field. "W-why wouldn't we?"

"Her being gone isn't such a bad thing," she said, sounding rather circumspect.

"But you said inside that you weren't sure she deserved this—"

She waved her hand. "I know. I'm just thinking out loud. She just wasn't a nice person."

"In what ways?" I asked.

Candy looked around again. We were still alone. "We were at a charity dinner Friday night and she was like a pariah."

"What do you mean?" I asked, immediately wondering if someone from that charity dinner could be the killer.

"Let's just say she was out for herself, and she'd mow down anyone who got in her way."

Candace was being incredibly cryptic. I bit my tongue and waited. She definitely wanted to tell me more or she wouldn't have brought me out here away from everyone.

She continued a second later. "Look. Nessa made more enemies than friends. It is not a cliché to say that she would stop at nothing to get whatever she wanted."

"Sounds like she pissed off a lot of people."

"That's exactly what I'm saying."

"Including you?"

"Add me to the end of a very long list," she said with a wry laugh, clearly not concerned that she was giving herself a motive.

What, then, was with all her tears? "You didn't really like her and you weren't friends., but you seemed so upset at her death." If she could be direct, so could I.

As if it was a Pavlovian response, her lower lip started up again and she shook her head. "I honestly don't know. I won't miss her. In fact, I'm glad I won't have to deal with her anymore. But Rachel—"

"Her daughter?"

"Right. I feel for her. I mean she spends the night at our house and when she goes home she finds her mother is gone."

The woman had empathy in spades—at least where Rachel was concerned. "It sounds like you'll be there for her."

Candace squeezed her eyes shut and crinkled her nose for a few seconds, getting ahold of her contradictory emotions. "My daughter and I both will be there for Rachel. For Nessa's children. Poor girls. Poor Tate."

I let that sentiment hang in the air between us for a beat before I said, "Do you know who might have done this to Nessa?" I asked, repeating the question I'd had for her earlier.

Once again, Candace surprised me. She started naming people, ticking them off on her fingers as she went. "Her husband. The superintendent. At least one of our school principals. And I hate to suggest it, but even a few school board members couldn't stand her. Hell, even her hairdresser didn't like her. I don't think they are killers, though."

I raised my eyebrows. "Her hairdresser?" The other people Candy suggested were connected to her role as a school board member. Plus her husband. But mentioning her hairdresser was like looking at one of those picture groupings that asked which one didn't belong.

"Every time Nessa went for an appointment, we all heard about it for days afterward. Gretchen this, and Gretchen that. She had a love-hate relationship with her."

"There are a million hairdressers." I absently touched my hair. I hadn't had a trim in months. "Why didn't she just find someone new?" I asked.

Candace shrugged. "Who the hell knows with Nessa. She liked to complain, so why change—?" She stopped. Thought. Then shook her head. "No, actually that's not it. She was all about power. She would say things like 'She's going to lose her job if she doesn't do better. I'll call that salon owner and I'll have her job. She can't do this to me.' Of course, that's how she was with everyone. Whenever the board disagrees, she sits there and threatens us all. Once she told us we were all idiots for believing the contractor we'd hired and just wait, because it was going to blow up in our faces and she wouldn't lift a finger to make it right."

She really did sound like a piece of work. And from what Candace was saying, the pool of people with a motive to do her in might be pretty big. "Why the superintendent?" I asked.

"Like I said. Power. Basically, she wanted to *be* the superintendent. She wanted to run the school district, and doing that as president of the board wasn't enough because, really, we're not making the day-to-day decisions, are we? We set policy. Dr. Sharma is accountable to us, but she's the expert in education. Nessa didn't see it that way, though. She wanted her hand in everything. She did a pretty good job of alienating people against Dr. Sharma. I've been afraid she'd leave us, but now, well, maybe she'll stay."

Motive for Dr. Sharma. "And the principal?" I asked. "Was she in his—or her—business, too?"

"All of them, but she felt Mr. Davies's school made her look bad. She undermined and she micromanaged. Look, we're elected by regions. Certain schools are in my area; certain ones are in Jerry's; others are in Marge's. You get the gist. Nessa wanted her schools to be the best, as we all do. It's for the kids, right? But it was a competition for Nessa, and Chavez Elementary was a thorn in her side."

Possibly another motive.

Candy continued without prompting. "Nessa didn't care about pissing off a fellow board member by popping into a school in someone else's area, unannounced, then making a big deal out of some problem she observed. She was . . . difficult. But her position made her untouchable.

I mean, we were all at a charity event Friday night and she was up to her usual B.S." She met my gaze. "I honestly can't think of anyone who's going to actually miss her or be sad that she's gone. Besides Rachel and Tate."

"Tate?"

"Her son. He's in fifth grade."

"It's so sad," I said. "Her husband must be beside himself, too."

"I'm not so sure about that." She glanced around, then lowered her voice before dropping another tidbit of gossip. "Between you and me, Tate may or may not have the same father as Rachel. But you didn't hear that from me."

Boy oh boy, Candace was dialed in on all of Nessa Renchrik's drama. If Nessa's husband might not be the father of her son, who might be? That would be an interesting question to find an answer to. And it certainly meant the husband had a motive. In the ten minutes we'd been talking, Candace had provided me with three viable suspects.

"What about her family? Parents? Sibling? Is anyone going to come help with the kids?"

"Her parents are dead. I don't know about siblings. If I had to bet, I'd say, if she has any, they're estranged."

More bridges burned. "So what you're saying, in a nutshell, is that anyone she came across could very well have had it in for her?"

Candace leaned her ample back against the bench. She didn't hesitate before answering. "That's exactly what I'm saying."

Chapter 4

Mrs. Branford could be a study in contradictions. It was something she worked at. In certain circumstances she played the little old biddy. She knew everything that went on in our neighborhood. She was like the quintessential nosy neighbor, only without being annoying. She genuinely cared about the people around her. Everyone sensed that about her and so they talked to her. They shared. Probably they over-shared. Mrs. Branford seemed to know everything about everybody in her galaxy. She was the sun, and the world rotated around her.

If her galaxy was our historic neighborhood, then the universe was Santa Sofia. She'd taught high school English forever and had had multiple generations of families in her classroom. Anytime I was with her out in public, someone made a point of saying hello to her. And I wasn't the only one who couldn't move away from calling her

Mrs. Branford. She'd told me over and over to call her Penelope or Penny, but I just couldn't do it. She'd forever be Mrs. Branford to me. All her former students felt the same.

Sometimes she played the part of the elderly woman in need of assistance. Her cane came in handy in these instances. It was, I'd witnessed as I came back in from talking with Candy, the act she'd put on in the boardroom. She was sitting on a folding chair talking to someone. When she saw me, she tried to stand, using her cane for balance. I saw her lips move and imagined her making a little squeaking sound. The woman she'd been sitting next to quickly stood and helped her up. Mrs. Branford made her way over to me, continuing to play the part of the doddering old woman, but when she reached me, she said, "Ivy dear, hold on to my arm."

I scanned the room, looking for Captain York, but he was nowhere to be seen. Too bad. I wanted to find out what he thought of the suspect pool. I didn't know anyone else in the room by face and it looked like Mrs. Branford needed to leave, so I guided her away from the district building with a hand on one of her elbows. She tottered along with her cane, clearly needing my help, the entire walk back to my car. I helped her into the passenger side and gently closed the door. I always worried that one of these times she wouldn't be acting.

It seemed like that time had come . . . until I got in the car. The moment I shut the driver's side door, she turned to me. No more hunched shoulders. No more clinging to her cane, which now lay easily on her lap. "I had to keep up the part until we were well out of sight. You never know who's watching."

I'd often thought that Mrs. Branford had missed her

calling. She could have had a successful career in the theater if she'd gone that direction. "Well, what did you find out?" she asked.

I didn't miss a beat. "A lot, actually. Candace was pretty forthcoming." I recapped what Candace had told me, ending with, "That's a healthy list of potential suspects."

Mrs. Branford closed her eyes for a moment, processing what I'd said. She opened them again as I pulled out of the parking lot, and said, "It certainly is."

"How about you? Any luck?"

She patted her bouncy white hair and gave me a look that clearly communicated the absurdity of that question. "I found out that our victim had plans to run for state senate. Like you, I also found out that she had no shortage of enemies. That being said, she seemed to be subscribed to the 'keep your friends close and your enemies closer' mind-set."

I directed the car back toward our street before turning to stare at her. She was truly amazing. "In what way?"

"As you discovered, no one seems to have liked her."

"And yet she was reelected and thought she could win the senate seat?" It was a conundrum.

"That is not inexplicable. Manipulation seemed to be the name of her game. She was her own personal lobby, making deals with this person to satisfy that person, then turning around and changing the terms of the initial deal until she got something she wanted."

I gripped the steering wheel, my knuckles turning white. "Mrs. Branford, what are you talking about?"

"Here is an example as told to me by Dr. Sharma, the school superintendent. Not a fan of Nessa Renchrik's, I might add. There is, apparently, a large learning gap between the white student body population and the Hispanic population."

I listened intently as I took another turn.

"Dr. Sharma says she was given the green light to do what was necessary to help the students being underserved. Not an easy task, to be sure. To have the school board's support is crucial. Alas, the full support was not actually there."

We arrived at Maple Street. I breathed easier as we drove down the tree-lined street with its canopy of newly budded leaves. Each house was different from the next. A Craftsman home sat next to a Tudor, which was next door to a Victorian. Next to that was an old farmhouse. The historic area was eclectic—and I loved every bit of it.

When I'd first seen it, I'd thought Mrs. Branford's house was a small Victorian. Since then I'd learned more about the architecture of the old houses in the area and had learned that hers was a Craftsman style. It was ancient—like the owner herself—but she took good care of it. The creamy white window frames contrasted with the warm taupe of the exterior walls. The porch was lopsided and angled toward the street. A marble would roll right off of it. A crooked brick pathway led to the porch steps. It was a little uneven, but it was a bit of character Mrs. Branford didn't want to replace.

"A house can be part of a person, Ivy," she'd told me once. "The Tudor you so love is in your soul in the same way that my house is part of mine. There is history in these old places. It seeps into you in a way that can't really be explained." She'd clasped the railing of her porch and looked up at the thick door trim and the pillars holding up the porch ceiling. "I love this old place."

I knew exactly what she meant. I'd loved my house

from the first moment I'd laid eyes on it. It was like it had called to me, and then it had become mine and I couldn't see leaving it. That simple fact would pose quite a problem if and when Miguel and I got to the point in our relationship where we wanted to share a living space. His house with its view of the Pacific was like a retreat. My house with its brick exterior, dormers, and arches fed my soul.

Now I parked in front of her house and turned in my seat to face her. "Let me guess. Nessa Renchrik wasn't on the superintendent's side."

Mrs. Branford touched the tip of her nose with her index finger. Like in charades, it meant that I'd hit the nail on the head.

"Dr. Sharma crafted a plan with her team," Mrs. Branford went on. "They presented to the board. Each member gave their approval. However, when the plan began to be implemented and there was pushback from some of the school leaders—You know people are reluctant to make change, especially when they don't believe the change is necessary—"

"They didn't think change was needed when so many students were failing?"

At that, Mrs. Branford shrugged. "It is not surprising, Ivy. School politics are just as ruthless as the state and federal brand. When it comes to the success or failure of students, the bottom line is that if the students who look like you are doing okay, that is all that matters."

"So since the white kids who look like Nessa Renchrik are successful, she didn't care about the ones who didn't look like her and who weren't successful?"

"In a nutshell," Mrs. Branford said. She frowned. "A sad reality, but the truth nonetheless."

"Okay. Then some people—like Nessa Renchrik—objected to the superintendent's plan. What happened?"

Mrs. Branford gave a quick and audible exhalation through her nose. "What happened was that—and this is according the superintendent—Nessa did a complete reversal of her stance, withdrawing her support and pulling the rug out from under Dr. Sharma."

My brain started spinning. With Nessa gone, did Dr. Sharma have her green light from all the other school board members to continue with her plan? Combined with Candy Coffey's theory that Nessa Renchrik was a thorn in Dr. Sharma's side because of the former's constant bid for power, the superintendent's motive seemed to grow stronger. I'd barely started looking into what had happened and already Dr. Sharma was rising to the top of my list.

I walked Mrs. Branford to her door, not needing to hold her elbow this time, even on the uneven brick walkway. "I'll be at the ready for when you need me," she said.

"I'll keep you posted," I said with a little laugh and shake of my head. The woman was a master.

Back at home, I let Agatha outside, grabbed my notes from the night before, went to the spare bedroom I'd designated as my study, and found a brand-new journal, then took it all out to the patio table in the backyard. Since I was starting late and didn't have notebooks for each of the crimes I'd helped solve, I made a list of them on the first pages, briefly summarizing who had died and who had done the deed. Once that was complete, I turned a few pages in and wrote "NESSA RENCHRIK" at the center top. Even this small action made me feel more centered and organized.

Agatha had nosed around in the bushes for a few minutes, emerging from a secret spot where she took care of business. She dug into the ground with her front and back paws, like a bull ready to charge, as I started by transcribing my initial notes onto the page. I added all the new information I had next. It took a good forty minutes to get it all down.

I started with a list of names down the left side of the page, beginning with the deceased's husband, Cliff Renchrik. Next, I added Dr. Sharma, the superintendent; and the four remaining school board members: Jerry Zenmark, Margaret Jenkins-Roe, Katherine Candelli, and Candace Coffey. Then I added Lulu Sanchez-Patrick, aka @Marisas Mama. I didn't think she had something to do with the murder, but she was a name and had been the first person to communicate how little Nessa Renchrik was liked by people.

Before I left her, Mrs. Branford had told me that there were eleven school principals. I added them to my list as a single group since I didn't know any names, but wrote down "Principal Davies, Chavez Elementary School" on its own line, as well as "Parents" with a question mark, and "Nessa's hairdresser." There was no shortage of people who seemed to have had a grudge against the late school board president.

On the other side of the page, I drew a box and added Cliff's name, as well as Nessa's children, Rachel and Tate. When I was done, I set my pen down and sat back to think. Agatha looked unworried and blissful lying in a slice of sunlight.

I, on the other hand, felt the opposite of unworried and blissful. There were a lot of people on the suspect list. I didn't know Nessa and I didn't have the excuse of being a police detective to give me a legitimate reason to talk to any of them, yet Emmaline had asked me to see what I could find out. "What to do, what to do," I mused aloud.

Agatha lifted her head to peer at me, then laid her head back down and sighed contentedly.

She was absolutely no help.

Chapter 5

Santa Sofia's Bungalow Oasis neighborhood sat between Malibu and Riviera Streets and was part of the Upper Laguna District, so named by the early residents of the area who'd then formed a neighborhood association. Bungalows were in all the older areas of Santa Sofia, but Bungalow Oasis held the monopoly.

Miguel's stucco-sided house was quaint and welcoming. It sat on a knoll, had a single-car garage down below, and red terra-cotta tiled steps running upstairs on the left side of the house that led to a wrought-iron gate, with the house itself raised and built into the hill. Along with his cooking abilities, Miguel had a green thumb. Bright leafy shrubs bordered the steps leading to the arched front door. Massive pots overflowing with draping flowers and greenery sat on pillars at the top of the steps. The courtyard to the right of the narrow driveway had a single tree and abundant flower beds, and Miguel had recently added a bench. Above the garage was a veranda, which was an extended outside room with a view of the Pacific.

I loved my historic house and I adored my neighborhood, but being at Miguel's house was like being wrapped up in a warm blanket. He'd bought the place as a fixer-upper . . . and had fixed it up. If he ever quit the restaurant business, he could have his own HGTV home show. There was nothing the man couldn't do.

Agatha and I headed to Bungalow Oasis around five o'clock. Miguel's restaurant was closed on Mondays; while I was digging around in Nessa Renchrik's life, he'd gotten his water heater fixed and had messed around in his kitchen, experimenting with new recipes. He had an efficient galley kitchen with a commercial-grade stainless-steel Wolf range. It was a monster with six open top burners, a grill/griddle, and two ovens.

"Indian street food," he said when I walked in.

An array of dishes and ingredients was strewn across the kitchen counters in the kitchen. Whatever he'd conjured up, it had made my stomach growl and my mouth water. "It smells amazing."

The long plank dining table sat outside the long galley kitchen, forming the top band of a letter T. He sat me down and went back to the kitchen, returning a minute later carrying a bowl and setting it on the woven place mat in front of me. It burst with color, shapes, and aromas. "Mexican Bhel," he said. "I wanted to do a little fusion and play off the idea of Indian street food."

I took the fork he offered me, scooped up a helping, and savored the bite. Sweet corn kernels and finely chopped bell peppers were mixed with a perfectly seasoned chipotle salsa, whole pinto beans, small chunks of jicama, and cilantro. He'd tossed it all together with homemade tortilla chips and topped it with a dusting of shredded cheese.

"I'm not sure," he said. "It may be a little too simple. Like a salad bowl without the lettuce."

I couldn't answer him with my mouth full of another bite. Whatever he wanted to call it or do with it, the freshness and combination of the ingredients made the dish sublime. I was about to tell him this when the doorbell rang.

He left me at the table eating the Mexican Bhel. I stopped chewing a moment later when I saw Captain Craig York following him through the living room and into the kitchen. "Can I get you anything?" Miguel asked him, but Captain York shook his head no. York nodded at me. "Ivy."

The nerve of York to call me Ivy. He didn't know me well enough for that. I gulped down the mouthful of bhel, wishing that I had a glass of water. Miguel must have read my mind. He slipped into the kitchen, filled a glass at the tap, and brought it to me. I waited for York to say something about seeing me at the district office earlier, but he didn't. Instead, he said, "Sorry to drop by like this, but I have a few questions for you, Mr. Baptista."

And Miguel was Mr. Baptista. Misogyny much?

Miguel gestured to the table, indicating Captain York should sit, then pulled out the chair next to me and took it. Captain York sat at the end of the table looking far too serious. "I'll cut to the chase. Mr. Baptista, it's come to our knowledge that you had a relationship with the deceased, Mrs. Nessa Renchrik."

Whatever I'd expected him to say, it wasn't that. I felt

the color drain from my face. Next to me, Miguel balked. "What? Where did you hear that?"

But instead of answering Miguel's question, Captain York went on. "I also understand you are sponsoring the Spring Fling event due to your relationship with the deceased."

Miguel leaned forward and his eyes narrowed. "No, actually, I'm not, and I don't have a relationship with the deceased."

I noticed Miguel spoke in the present, as if the woman was still alive. Whether or not Captain York noticed was hard to tell. He continued as if Miguel hadn't spoken. "I understand she contacted you recently."

My mind shot back to Miguel's comment the night before. He'd told me *someone* had reached out to him, then murmured that he needed to find that message. He hadn't mentioned that it was Nessa Renchrik. My body suddenly felt hot and my eyes burned.

Miguel opened his mouth to say something—to respond?, to deny?—but closed it again. "Someone did contact me. I never called back, but I'm telling you I don't know Nessa Renchrik."

"Uh-huh." The captain sat back, folding his arms across his chest as if he just made a move on the chessboard that put his opponent into check.

Miguel sat back, mirroring York.

"That's not what I hear," York said, his narrow gaze steady on Miguel.

"Why don't you tell me what you hear, then." I could tell Miguel was trying to control the snarl that lurked underneath his words. "Because I have no idea what you are talking about."

The Mexican Bhel suddenly felt like rocks in the pit of my stomach. The captain wouldn't be here dropping this little emotional bomb unless he knew or suspected it to be true. How I wished Emmaline was back and in charge rather than soaking up the sun in Costa Rica.

Captain York kept his gaze focused on Miguel as he said, "Vanessa Arnold."

Miguel blinked. Then blinked again. When he spoke, his voice suddenly sounded strained. "What?"

Alarm bells went off in my head. I'd told him Nessa's full name was Vanessa, but he'd been in the shower. Had he not heard me?

"Vanessa Arnold," Captain York repeated. "She goes by Nessa. Renchrik is her married name."

Miguel muttered under his breath. He leaned forward and placed his elbows on the table. "You're saying that Vanessa Arnold and Nessa Renchrik are the same person?"

York's lips twisted into a subtle sneer. "That's exactly what I'm saying, Mr. Baptista. And I think you knew that."

The veins on Miguel's neck tightened. He worked to control himself. "I didn't know that."

York gave his head a little shake. He clearly didn't believe Miguel. He'd weighed and measured him, and found him wanting.

"Look," Miguel said, his voice low. Controlled. "I briefly dated a Vanessa Arnold. That was ten or eleven years ago."

"And you haven't seen her since, is that what you're saying?"

Miguel's Adam's apple climbed up his throat, then dropped as he swallowed. "I saw her last week."

My burning eyes turned blurry and my breath hitched.

York kept his gaze level, his lips a thin line, but his eyebrows lifted enough to show this was an interesting bit of news. "Is that right? After ten . . . or eleven . . . years, you saw her last week? That's a coincidence, isn't it?"

It wasn't really a question.

Miguel's complexion turned sallow, but he kept his gaze level with York's. "I don't know; is it?"

York didn't move. Didn't blink. "I think it is."

I tried to school my expression, seeing Miguel's chest rise and fall in my peripheral vision. "She showed up at the restaurant out of the blue," he said.

"To have lunch? Dinner?"

"She'd placed a To Go order," Miguel said. "She said she and her husband were going out to some party and she was picking up dinner for her kids."

That meant the takeout order had probably been on Friday. The dinner fundraiser Candy had mentioned.

York spoke, sounding smug and patronizing at the same time. "Let me recap. You dated the victim briefly a decade ago. Then just last week, she suddenly shows up at your restaurant. And the next day she's murdered."

I felt the air in the room grow still. Miguel had known Nessa Kenchrik. No, not known. Dated. And seen her the day before she died. Had York come here knowing that fact? Had he been trying to trap Miguel into lying? The obvious conclusion came to mind. He saw Miguel as a suspect. But why? Just because they'd dated ten years ago and she'd suddenly shown back up in his life didn't give him a motive.

Still, I had questions. Had Miguel known Nessa was married when they'd dated? I knew he had a life in between our high school relationship and our rekindled romance. I had no qualms about that specifically, but I did over the fact that Captain York was here talking to Miguel about it and what that might mean.

York rolled his hand in the air. "So you dated ten or so years ago. Go on."

"There's not much to tell," Miguel said. "I was home on leave—"

"Military?" York asked.

Miguel nodded. He didn't elaborate, but I knew the truth. He'd joined when he and I had split up. He'd only recently come back to Santa Sofia to stay—after his father died. Our stories were similar and had brought us back to our hometown, where we'd reconnected.

"I was here for a few months and worked at my family's restaurant. Vanessa used to come into the restaurant pretty frequently—"

"And then not at all in the intervening years?"

Miguel shrugged. "Nope." He went on, ignoring York's skeptical expression. "We got to talking. She said she'd been through a tough breakup. I bought her lunch one day and we kind of hit it off, so we went out a few times."

"You went out a few times." Captain York took out a little notepad. He jotted something down before looking up at Miguel again. "And your breakup with her. Any animosity?"

Miguel scoffed. "There was no breakup. We went on a few dates. That's it."

"Did you know she was married?"

At this, Miguel sat back and ran his hand over his face. "I didn't know when we first started seeing each other."

"But," York prompted.

"I found out," he said. "And I broke it off." Miguel looked at me with a pained expression. "I broke it off."

I believed him, and gave a single nod, encouraging him to keep going with his story.

"We went to Books and More—"

York raised his eyebrows in a silent question.

"The bookstore in town," I said. The place had been around since I was a kid. It was as iconic in Santa Sofia as Yeast of Eden was.

"Right. We were just browsing. She started talking with someone."

"Man or woman?"

"A man. It got a little heated, but they were in the travel section and I was in the fiction area. I couldn't hear what they were talking about. And then he left."

"Did you ask her who it was?"

Miguel nodded.

"And?" York had his pen poised over his notepad ready to write down a name, but Miguel shook his head. "A work acquaintance. That's all she said. I bought a book, we left, and she said she had a headache. Then she confessed that she was married. I didn't see her after that."

"Did you break it off, or did she?"

Miguel sighed. Ran his hand down his face. "She was married. I stopped calling. She stopped coming to the restaurant. I haven't seen her since."

"Until last Friday," York corrected.

Miguel gave a single nod.

York cocked an eyebrow. "You live in the same town. She was a prominent member of the community. School board member for years, and current board president. You're a member of the Chamber of Commerce. A businessman in Santa Sofia. You never put it together that Vanessa Arnold was also Nessa Renchrik?"

"I'd been on leave. I left Santa Sofia and didn't come back until recently. I don't have any kids. I have no reason to be involved or even aware of Santa Sofia school politics. There's a Cliff Renchrik in the Chamber. Maybe that's her husband, I don't know. He's in property management, or something, but since I knew her as Vanessa Arnold, no, I didn't put it together."

Miguel's voice had grown terse. He did not like the line of questioning York had taken.

"And you haven't looked at any news reports since the murder Saturday? Haven't seen Nessa Renchrik's photo plastered all over the media?"

Again, Miguel shook his head. "I went into the city yesterday—"

"San Francisco?"

"Right. I went on a bike ride with a friend."

"Ah, an athlete." York didn't sound impressed.

"I cycle."

"And you didn't read any updates on the murder yesterday when you got back. And today?"

"The restaurant is closed on Mondays." He gestured to the kitchen. "I've been testing out new recipes and waiting on a repairman. Hot-water heater."

Miguel was not the type of person to be glued to his phone, especially when he had other things going on that kept him occupied. He preferred a print book to an e-reader. Real newsprint rather than an online version. It wasn't that he was a late adopter. But he liked the feel of a book in his hand and the rustle of newsprint as he turned the pages.

The lift of York's eyebrows showed just how skeptical he was about Miguel's story. He wrote something else in his notebook. "Tell me about your encounter with Mrs. Renchrik on Friday evening."

Miguel ran his hand over his face again and sighed. "It was brief. We'd just opened when she showed up. She'd placed the order earlier in the day."

"Were you surprised to see her?"

"Yeah. Absolutely. I didn't recognize her at first. Her hair is lighter now."

Once again, he spoke of Nessa Renchrik in the present. He'd said "is," not "was." I hoped York took note of it this time around, if he hadn't the first time.

York didn't blink. "Did you talk?"

"Not really. I ran her credit card. Went to check the kitchen for her order. It wasn't ready yet, so I got her a Diet Coke while she waited and I went back to my work."

Once again, York wore his doubt on his face. "No conversation? After ten years, you had nothing to say to each other?"

"Captain," Miguel said tersely, "we dated a long time ago. Briefly. She ordered food for pickup. There was nothing to say."

York stayed silent for a moment, as if he was debating whether or not to let this line of questioning go. After an awkward silence, he said, "And was it Mrs. Renchrik who contacted you about sponsoring the Spring Fling?"

Instead of answering, Miguel stood and walked into the little sunroom in the back of the house. The windows looked out to the backyard. The house was built on a hill. He'd built a tiered garden system to make the hill usable. He didn't do anything halfway. He'd already planted, and come summer the boxes would be bursting with tomatoes, artichokes, cucumbers, and whatever else he decided to grow.

He returned carrying a satchel. Setting it down on the table, he rifled through it, then submerged both hands into the case to remove a stack of paperwork. He flipped through it, finally landing on a slip of paper. "Someone called Baptista's about a week ago. One of the hosts took the call and passed the message on to me." He handed it to York.

"No name," the captain commented.

"So you don't know who called?" I asked Miguel. Miguel said, "No idea. I never called back."

"The message just says: 'The Santa Sofia school board. Please call regarding sponsoring the Spring Fling.' " Captain York slid the message back too Miguel. "There's a phone number."

I peered over at the piece of paper. It wasn't that I didn't believe York, but it seemed so strange that I wanted to confirm it for myself.

York put his notepad and pen down, then looked pointedly at Miguel. "Why don't you make that call."

"Right now?"

"No time like the present," he said. Cliché, but I happened to agree with York. I wanted to know who had left that message for my boyfriend.

Miguel's cell phone was on the table under a different stack of papers. I uncovered it for him and handed it over. He took it, meeting my eyes with a less than enthusiastic expression. He sighed, dialed by tapping the numbers onto the keypad, then pressed the Speaker button before setting the phone, face up, on the table. The moment he pressed the Enter button, the numbers vanished. My stomach plunged.

Vanessa Arnold's name scrolled across the top of the screen.

Chapter 6

We all stared at the name on the phone. I resisted the urge to grab it and slam my finger against the Off button to silence the ring. After another two seconds, there was a click and a woman's voice came at us from the phone's tiny speaker, like a ghost speaking from the great beyond. "You've reached Vanessa. Leave me a message."

I looked at Miguel. Miguel looked at me, then at York. York looked at Miguel. "Wait," I said. "She calls herself Vanessa there. Does that mean she has two phones—one for her regular life as Nessa, and the other for her clandestine activities?"

Captain York's cheeks had bloomed with a faint shade of pink. Excitement from the clue, or him thinking he'd found a prime suspect in Miguel? He looked at Miguel's phone, comparing the number on the screen to the one he had in his notes. "Apparently," he said as he picked up his notepad again and jotted something down.

Maybe she was a serial cheater, I thought. Why else use two different names and have two different phones? "Where is her phone?" I asked.

York lifted his eyebrows. "We haven't found it. Yet." He turned to look at Miguel. "But we will." The veiled threat was evident. When they found it, they'd be looking for conversations between Vanessa and Miguel.

Miguel's jaw pulsed and I knew his blood was simmering, but he remained silent.

"Mr. Baptista," Captain York continued. "I may have additional questions. I suggest you refrain from further cycling trips out of the area for the time being."

Miguel's nostrils flared—with agitation? Anger? Fear? Maybe all three—and he opened his mouth but stopped himself from saying anything. His mouth was tight, but he nodded.

With nothing more to glean, Captain York finally left. Behind him, though, lingered the very clear, yet unspoken, idea that Miguel was somehow involved in Nessa Renchrik's murder, or that he knew more than he was saying.

The instant the door closed behind York, Miguel swung around to face me. "I had nothing to do with her death."

I'd left the table and headed out to the veranda. I had my hair up in a topknot, but the late afternoon breeze loosened strands around my temples. I brushed them away from my eyes as I turned to lean my back against the railing, the Pacific behind me. "Of course you didn't. I know that."

He leaned his side against the railing, facing me, his left forearm lying across the top of the wrought iron. "I didn't know she was married when we started seeing each other."

I turned to face him, laying my hand over his. "Miguel, you had a life before I came back here, just like I did. You don't have to explain."

He dipped his chin, looking at me. "But I want you to know, I would never have knowingly dated a married woman."

I believed that one hundred percent. "What was she like?" I asked. Candy's account of Nessa likened her to Machiavelli. Lulu Sanchez-Patrick had made it clear that she wasn't mourning Nessa Renchrik. I was curious what Miguel's experience with the dead woman had been like.

He turned so his back leaned against the railing. "It was a long time ago."

I told him what Candy and Lulu had said about her. "Did you see any of that?"

He shook his head. "Like I said, it was a long time ago. She was friendly. Pretty flirtatious. I've never gone out with a customer, and I wouldn't have gone out with her unless she'd initiated it."

I gave him a cockeyed grin. "She just couldn't resist you, huh?"

"Until she could. After that encounter she had in the bookstore, she turned cold. Honestly, it was pretty weird."

"No idea who she'd been talking to?"

"I didn't then. Some random guy. I wondered if it was someone else she'd been dating, but now . . ."

He trailed off, but I knew what he was thinking. I finished the sentence for him. "You wonder if it was her husband."

"Right. Like maybe she'd said she'd be somewhere else, but then he ran into her at the bookstore."

My Spidey senses tingled. "Or maybe he suspected something was up and followed her. Confronted her."

"Anything's possible."

With nothing else to go on, and a lingering suspicion that Captain York wasn't done with Miguel, I decided that paying a visit to Nessa Renchrik's husband was on my list of things to do.

I spent Tuesday morning at Yeast of Eden baking bread and staffing the front counter. Maggie worked the afternoon shift after she finished school, and Olaya was down a morning helper. I was filling in until she hired someone new. Olaya and Felix Macron, her right-hand baker, always arrived by 4:30 AM, but often earlier than that. The life of a bakery owner was not an easy one, although Olaya thrived on the crack of dawn hours. She was in bed and asleep by eight o'clock on most nights.

I'd filled in for her recently when she'd been sick, which was a rarity. All I can say is that I was glad when she was well again. I liked working at the bread shop and I wanted to learn everything Olaya had to teach me, but waking before the sun rose and going to sleep before Miguel's restaurant even closed was not my preferred schedule.

Once Maggie arrived, I retreated to the kitchen to help Olaya with preparations for the next day. She was in her office, a browser open on her computer showing a produce delivery order. The office was tiny, with barely room for the desk and her chair. I scooted by her and sat in the one other chair she'd managed to squeeze into the space. She looked up, giving me a smile. "The Vincent van Dough bread," she started. "We will be making it early Saturday morning."

With all the prewedding preparations and events, I hadn't been able to help her with the batches she'd made for Billy and Emmaline. Another chance? I was in! "Are you going to start carrying it in the shop?" I asked.

Olaya hailed from Mexico, where her love of traditional long-rise bread had begun. She'd been in the States a long time, but she still had a slight accent and Spanish words often peppered her language. She tilted her head, considering. "I have thought about it, *pero* only for special occasions, I think."

"Why are we making more on Saturday?"

"And Sunday," she said. "The Spring Fling for the elementary school. I was asked to be a sponsor."

I sat up straighter. "You were?" My thoughts immediately went to how she was asked. "Did someone call you to ask?"

"A woman from the school," she said.

From the school, not the district. So, Nessa Renchrik had called Miguel on behalf of the school.

I leaned forward, propping my elbows on her desk, wondering if it had been Nessa. "Could it have been the school board president?"

"The woman who was killed?" She considered, tapping her index finger against her lips, then held up a finger telling me to wait. She typed something on her keypad. "I wrote notes. Ah, here it is." She read silently before saying, "Misty Jackson."

Huh. Nessa had limited her involvement to Miguel.

My phone beeped and a text appeared on my screen: *The medical examiner has concluded her report.*

Em was working, even from afar. Another text followed before I had a chance to respond to the first one.

York has his eye on Miguel. Did he really date the woman?

I replied with a quick: *Yes.* Then I added: *But he didn't kill her.*

Oh, God, of course not. Three dots flashed on the screen before a follow-up message popped up: *I'm not sure I trust York.*

Bad hire? I typed, wondering if York would be myopic in his investigation now that he had Miguel in his line of sight. Would he follow the evidence he found, or would he find evidence to fit his theory?

I don't know yet. Keep your eyes and ears open, okay?

She didn't have to tell me twice. *Already looking into it.* I shifted gears: *How's Costa Rica?*

Dreamy.

Olaya gave me a little wiggle of her fingers and pushed back from her desk and headed to the kitchen. *I have to go,* I typed to Emmaline.

Keep me in the loop, she messaged.

I started to tuck my phone in the back pocket of my jeans, then remembered what her first text had said. With my phone turned sideways, my thumbs flew over the keyboard. *What about the medical examiner's report?*

The three little dots appeared. I waited. And waited. Finally, the message came through. *Blunt trauma resulting in internal hemorrhaging. No defensive wounds. She didn't see it coming.*

That meant she'd had her back turned or she didn't suspect that whoever she was with would do such a thing, I thought.

With one of the chairs?

Yes. No fingerprints. It was wiped clean.

I started to type. To ask if one blow from the chair would kill her. As if she'd read my mind from her tropical paradise, a new text came in. *She fell and was hit a second time. The leg of the chair made impact with the back of the head.*

Without thinking, I reached back and touched the nape of my neck with my fingertips. I couldn't imagine. If I was attacked by surprise, I was sure adrenaline would kick in, but it seemed Nessa hadn't seen the attack coming and had had no chance to fend off her assailant.

I wondered if she'd been able to fight, would she have been able to save herself? From what I'd gathered about her so far, though, she used her Machiavellian mind to manipulate people. She probably didn't have a clue how to defend herself from a physical attack. If her assailant caught her unawares, she'd never had a chance.

"Why didn't she run?" I wondered aloud.

"Cómo?" Olaya poked her head into the office as she tied a white apron on. "Are you talking to me?"

I told her what Emmaline had conveyed about the medical examiner's findings. I played the scenario in my head. "Let's say Nessa was in the board meeting room. It was a Saturday. Not open to the public. It wasn't like a surprise assailant could have happened upon her, but she couldn't have been surprised. Could she?"

"The building, it was locked?"

One hundred percent. Mrs. Branford and I had had to jump through hoops to get through during regular business hours. The school district was a government office. Open eight to four Monday through Friday, and closed on the weekends. "Unless she left it unlocked when she went in, but I don't see why she would do that." I remembered the side door Candy and I had gone through leading to the parking lot. It was possible Nessa had left it unlocked, but why would she?

"Let us assume it was locked, then." Olaya leaned against the doorjamb. "How would someone have gotten in?"

I snapped my fingers. There was only one reasonable answer. "Because she *let* that person in."

"Maybe she was meeting someone there," Olaya said.

"A prearranged appointment." She hadn't run from her assailant because she hadn't suspected whoever she was meeting was going to attack her.

I went back to my phone, my fingers once again flying over the screen. *Was her purse at the scene? Was anything taken?*

I pressed Send and the message fluttered away to the nearest cell tower before it was delivered to Emmaline.

Em's reply came moments later: *Her tote bag with her phone, wallet, keys, and the board agenda was there. Nothing appears to have been taken. Her husband confirmed that.*

She knew her attacker, I texted.

Again, Em's response was almost instantaneous: *Seems likely.*

Her main phone was found, I thought. *What about the other one? Vanessa's phone? Had the killer taken it?*

I looked up at Olaya and related what Em had texted. "Nothing was taken, so it wasn't robbery." Not that I, or anyone else, had thought it had been, but eliminating the possibility helped me focus. I continued my thought process aloud by asking, "Who knew she was going to be there?" Then I answered my own question just as quickly. "The other board members?" Would she have told them she'd be stopping by the district office? "Her husband, of course."

"Not of course," Olaya said, "but probably."

She was right. Who knew what Nessa Renchrik's relationship with her husband was like? Had the almost-affair with Miguel been a one-off, or had she strayed regularly in her marriage? Did her husband know?

I'd spent enough time on the district website over the past few days to know that the meeting agenda was posted, although I hadn't read the entire thing. What was on that agenda, and could it have anything to do with the murder? Did someone want to stop a vote from happening? It seemed ridiculous to think that anyone would kill over stopping a vote on adding crosswalks or approving a new employee, but it wasn't outside the realm of possibility. Murderers, by definition, were not rational thinkers. "There could be any number of people who knew her routine."

Olaya lifted her shoulders in a noncommittal shrug. "You, Ivy Culpepper, will find out."

I wasn't as optimistic as she was. Nessa had been murdered, and if that murder had anything to do with her position as a school board member the fact that the meeting agenda was posted well before the actual meeting meant that the suspect pool could be well beyond what we originally thought. It left the door wide open for the killer to be . . . anyone.

I felt my expression grow stony. "They had a closed-door session planned before the meeting."

"Closed session? What does that mean?"

"When the school board has things to discuss that are personnel related or are not part of the public meeting, like trainings and things like that, they hold closed session meetings before the public meeting. At least I think that's what it means," I said. I'd looked it up, but my explanation was my interpretation of what I'd read.

Olaya made a sound acknowledging my explanation.

"I have an old friend on the school board," I said, referring to Candace Coffey. "She told me that Nessa was in the habit of going in on the weekend to review the board packet. Anyone who knew her well enough to want to kill her probably knew her habits. They'd have known where she'd be."

"*Entonces*, that is motive, no?" Olaya said as she walked to her baking station. She picked up a foamy concoction that I knew was a preferment. She'd mixed flour, cool water, and yeast together the day before so it would be ready to use today. I'd seen her use this process before. Olaya was a firm believer in the long rise and a long fermentation process. It evoked a deep nutty sweetness in the grain and enhanced the texture. "You can allow this to ferment for three or four hours, but overnight is better," she'd told me when she had first explained the process.

She poured the goop into a bowl, added warm water and a tablespoon of yeast, then dipped one hand into the mixture, letting her fingers break apart the preferment. Next, she added cup after cup—six in total—of her special bread flour and whole wheat flour blend, some of it ground right here in the kitchen in her grain mill, plus salt, and olive oil. She attached the dough hook, set the mixer to low, and turned back to me. "I am making another sample before we do the bake for the Spring Fling."

"Do we get to decorate it today?"

"Oh yes, in a few hours. It must rise first, of course," she said. "Now, back to the problem."

We shifted gears to the school board. "The posted agenda is possibly a motive, but it seems farfetched, doesn't it?"

"What do you mean?

I searched the school district on my phone, navigated through the site until I found the agenda, and scanned it. It seemed like basic stuff. Presentations from a few schools about their programs, a discussion regarding one of the high school graduations, the hiring of a new central office employee. "Nothing here seems really volatile. Nothing worth murdering someone over." Not that there was ever a good reason to kill someone, but on a sliding scale, this seemed to fall on the low end.

"But the closed meeting you mentioned. What is to be discussed during that time?"

I didn't have the answer to that question. It was a behind closed doors meeting for a reason. The subjects to be addressed were private or sensitive in some way. Did Nessa's death mean a postponement of one of the agenda topics? I doubted it. It seemed to me that school district business was still school district business. The show had to go on, even in the aftermath of tragedy.

I tucked my phone back in my pocket as Olaya checked her dough. She stopped the mixer, removed the dough hook, and covered the bowl with a clean cloth. The dough had to rest before she did a stretch and roll process with it, allowing it to rest in between the three actions.

"I have another theory," I said.

Olaya looked at me expectantly and I relayed what Candy had said about Nessa's husband possibly not being the father of their son.

Olaya's eyebrows lifted, her forehead crinkling. "She does not sound like a good woman."

"You're not the only one who thinks that," I said.

"Nessa Renchrik seemed to have a bit of an entitled personality. She wasn't very nice to the people who worked
for her or who provided services to her—"

"Like the hairdresser you mentioned?"

"Like the hairdresser. It seems like there are a lot of
people with possible motives." I wondered if Nessa had
gotten her hair done on Friday before the charity event
she'd gone to. I added that to my list of questions to find
answers to. I hadn't mentioned Lulu Sanchez-Patrick.
And it had crossed my mind that there could be others
like her. "Four school board members, who knows how
many disgruntled community members, her husband, the
hairdresser. That could add up to a lot of people."

Olaya moved to the industrial-sized stainless-steel
sink and wetted her hands. Back at her station, she began
working the dough while it was still in the bowl. She
stretched it, then folded it over itself, turning the bowl
and repeating the process. I kept my eyes on the angled
mirror above the workstation, watching her work the
dough in this way, stretching and folding, until it became
a smooth ball. I caught her looking at me and I knew she
was trying to figure out what was going through my
mind.

I couldn't tell her because I wasn't entirely sure. My
mind felt like the preferment she'd just used in the focaccia dough—a goopy mess. "I'll be back in a few hours," I
told her. "Don't do the van Dough art without me!"

"I will wait for you," she said. "And, Ivy."

I turned.

"Be careful."

Chapter 7

As of Monday night, after the visit from Captain York, I no longer cared that I hadn't known Nessa or that I wasn't a police detective. Miguel was a suspect in Nessa's murder. Emmaline wasn't here to be a buffer between York and his theory. I couldn't fill Em's shoes, but I could do everything I could to prove Miguel's innocence.

My handy notebook—thank you, Mrs. Branford—was in my purse. I left Yeast of Eden and headed straight for the district office. I had no legitimate reason for visiting Dr. Sharma and I was afraid that if I called ahead of time she wouldn't take a meeting with me. My solution to that was to show up unannounced and hope for the best.

The same not-so-chipper receptionist from my first visit with Mrs. Branford manned the front counter, but I knew the routine now. I withdrew my driver's license from my wallet and scanned myself into the kiosk system. A name tag printed out, which I affixed to my Yeast of Eden T-shirt before stepping up to the counter. The re-

ceptionist's hair was in the same style as before—pulled
back into a ponytail. Her Angelina Jolie lips were
adorned with the same rosy pink lipstick.

"Hi!" I smiled big, hoping she'd recognize me and let
me in without issue. "I'm here to speak to Dr. Sharma.
Ivy Culpepper."

She glanced at my name tag and frowned. "Do you
have an appointment?"

My heart sank. This wasn't going to be easy. "No,
but I—"

"Dr. Sharma isn't available for drop-in visits."

"Yes, but I—

She cut me off again, speaking more slowly this time
and with a pointed stare. "Dr. Sharma is not available for
drop-in visits."

"Ivy?"

I looked past the receptionist to a woman in the hallway beyond. It took me a second to place her, but with a
final blink, I did. "Mei?"

Mei Masaki came up next to the receptionist and
smiled at me. "What are you doing here?" she asked.

My mind pivoted. I'd seen Mei at Billy's wedding.
She was married to Terry, Billy's best friend. She and
Terry had met in college, gotten married, and moved back
to Santa Sofia to raise their family. I didn't know her
well, but there was no time like the present. "I didn't
know you worked here!"

I was maybe a wee bit over-enthusiastic, but I went
with it.

She came around and opened the door leading to the
offices. "I work in HR."

The receptionist sat up straighter and pointed at me.
"She can't—"

"It's okay, Tonya. She's with me." She glanced at my name tag. "And she's already signed in. Perfect."

Tonya exhaled her objection, but Mei ignored her and led me to her office. Mei was petite. She wore chunky heels under her slacks, but even so and even with my sneakers, I was a good head taller than her. I looked at each door we walked by, noting the names. No Dr. Sharma, so we hadn't passed the superintendent's office.

The placard hanging outside the door where we stopped said: Mei Masaki, Assistant Director of Human Resources. The phone rang as we entered her office. "Excuse me a second," she said, hurrying to her desk and reaching for the handset.

"Of course. No problem." I took the opportunity to look around. The lowest section of a dark wood bookshelf held a slew of binders marked with labels about district and HR procedures and information. More resource books lined the other shelves, as well as a few photographs of Hana as a baby and through her toddler years. A family shot of Mei, Terry, and Hana on the beach under a large colorful umbrella sat on Mei's desk. Her desktop computer monitor screensaver was the Santa Sofia Unified School District logo.

Mei hung up the receiver of her office phone and sat at her desk, pointing to another chair for me to sit in. "What are you doing here?" she asked.

I hadn't spent much time with Mei at the wedding. Then she'd been wearing a spring dress that hit at the knees, and a coral lightweight cardigan. Today she was in her professional clothing—a pair of black slacks and a button-up white blouse with black polka dots. Her black hair had been down and wavy at the wedding. Now it was pulled back into a slick low bun at the nape of her neck.

Her oval eyes angled up, a fold of skin over the upper lids. Mei was nothing short of beautiful. Next to her, I felt a little frumpy and unkempt.

I hadn't thought of how to explain my mission, so I pivoted again by saying, "How long have you worked here?"

"I took this job when Terry and I first moved to Santa Sofia, so seven years or so now."

A contact from within the system. Maybe Mei could give me a little insight. Help narrow down the suspects. "So, you knew Nessa Renchrik?"

But that idea was shot down. "Not really. I've had to do a few presentations for the board over the years, but my boss is the main point of contact for them."

"Hard to believe someone was killed right here."

She grimaced. "Yesterday it was a madhouse. Reporters and investigators. It's been quiet for a little while now, thankfully. I could hardly hear myself think with all the commotion."

"I bet."

"Why are you here?" she asked me again.

"Oh, well, um . . ."

Mei tilted her head to one side, waiting while I hedged.

With no other story to explain my visit, I went with the truth. Maybe the connection between Mei's husband and my brother would be enough for her to want to help me. "I'll be straight with you, Mei."

She waited, her hands clasped on the desk in front of her.

"Em asked me to help her out a little bit. You know, with the murder investigation?"

"Oh really? Like a deputy or something?"

I'd already learned that Mei didn't give too much

away with her facial expressions. She was a closed book. I pressed on.

"Kind of. Since she's on her honeymoon, I'm kind of like her boots on the ground."

"Doesn't she have people in the sheriff's department for that?"

I shrugged noncommittally. "I'm just helping out."

She tilted her head slightly, her brow furrowing. "Terry said you'd done a little sleuthing."

It seemed I was earning a little bit of a reputation. I wasn't sure whether to sink into my chair or sit up straighter. "A little bit, I guess."

"What does the superintendent have to do with this, though?" she asked.

"Oh, nothing!" I really didn't know Mei. The last thing I wanted was for a rumor to start that Dr. Sharma was involved in Nessa Renchrik's murder. "I was hoping to talk to her, but Tonya said she's not available."

At this, Mei's porcelain expression faltered. "Dr. Sharma is here, but . . ."

"I'm sure she is busy."

Mei studied me for a moment. "If she isn't involved in the murder, then why do you need to see her?"

I gave a small shrug of my shoulders. "Emmaline and I went to school with one of the school board members—" She raised her eyebrows in a question. "With Candace Coffey."

Mei kept pushing. "But why the superintendent?"

I didn't want to tell Mei any more than I already had. The fact that there was a murder meant there was a murderer. No one was in the clear. "It's nothing. Just a question I have," I said, pretty sure Mei was done with my cryptic answers to her questions. But she stood suddenly and gestured for me to do the same, then led me down the hallway in the opposite direction from which we'd come. We turned a corner and passed a break room. Two women sat at an old fifties-style table. One of them hunched over a cup of coffee, gripping it between her hands. The other sat back, one leg crossed over the other. She was angled in her seat and rested one forearm on the table. "Hi, ladies," Mei said, stopping in the doorway. "Lori, are you okay?"

The woman hanging on to her coffee cup for dear life looked up at Mei but remained silent. The other woman spoke up. "She's scared. There's a murderer on the loose."

I met Lori's shaken gaze and gave her what I hoped was a reassuring smile. I was on it, I wanted to say, but of course I couldn't.

"They'll find him, whoever did this," Mei said. "They'll find him."

I nodded my own reassurance and followed Mei on down the hall. She slowed as we came to an office, the door cracked open. Voices drifted out and I heard someone say, "Because she was putting in a bid for state senate, and she had a good chance of winning."

I drew in a sharp breath. What timing! They were talking about Nessa Renchrik. Mei held up her hand, fingers rounded, knuckles exposed. Her wrist faced up as she moved her hand forward to knock on the door.

My hand shot out and I touched her arm, stopping her. *Wait*, I mouthed.

We peeked in. A person stood at the door, but I honestly couldn't say if it was a man or a woman. My gut said woman—but I wasn't sure at all that that would be how she identified. She, if she was a she, was about five feet five, a bit on the lumpy side, and had short blond hair combed to the side. The slacks and blazer were gender neutral—navy and a loose cut—and she wore heavy Doc Martens. A second later, the other person in the room came into view. She was roughly the same height as the first, but thinner with darker skin, dark hair, and shimmering brown eyes. She wore a straight skirt and a sleeveless patterned blouse. I caught a glimpse of a blazer hanging on the back of a chair. "Ms. McLaine," the second woman said. "While I appreciate your interest in the story, I am afraid I cannot help you. I have no comment."

So the first person *was* a she—and she was apparently a reporter. If she had a pair of dark sunglasses, she totally could have been one of the Men in Black, and this a call to investigate rogue aliens rather than a dead school board member, which was, I assumed, why she was here.

"Just McLaine, thanks," she said as she sat down.

The other woman, then, had to be the superintendent. She looked nonplussed. And less than pleased. "McLaine," she said, a touch of warning in her tone. "As I just said, I have no comment."

McLaine looked at her. No smile. No disdain, either. It was a noncommittal look, as if she was withholding judgment until there was something to judge on. "I understand that, Dr. Sharma, but there are rumors—"

"What rumors?" Dr. Sharma demanded.

McLaine was not fazed. "Rumors that you and Nessa Ronchrik didn't, shall we say, see eye to eye on things."

Dr. Sharma's brown skin took on an odd pallor, but she threw her shoulders back and rallied. "In any organization you'll find that people disagree. Those professional differences certainly do not lead to murder."

"In most cases," McLaine said.

Dr. Sharma drew her lips into a thin line. She nodded,

conceding the point, but added a caveat. "You assume Nessa's death has something to do with her role as a school board member."

McLaine sat quietly for a moment, then said, "Given her political aspirations and her overall commitment to the position, it's a logical place to start." Dr. Sharma's arms hung by her sides and her chin lifted, but McLaine continued before the superintendent could say anything. "The Communities in Schools fundraiser Friday night. It's my understanding that you and Mrs. Renchrik had a bit of a run-in."

Dr. Sharma sighed. Dark circles framed her eyes. She suddenly looked very tired. "As I said, people in any organization disagree. Mrs. Renchrik and I had differing opinions on how to allocate resources. That's all. Here is my official statement, Ms. McLaine. The school district is saddened by the death of its school board president. It is a tragedy beyond measure, I'm sure you'll agree. Mrs. Renchrik was an advocate for students and learning in Santa Sofia and she will be missed. Now, if there's nothing else . . ."

She moved toward the door. McLaine followed.

Mei's eyes went wide. She turned on her chunky heels and gave me a shove. For such a thin-framed, petite woman, she was surprisingly strong. "Let's go," she hissed, dragging me back toward her office. I managed a furtive glance over my shoulder just as Dr. Sharma shut the door to her office, leaving McLaine in the hallway alone. The reporter jotted something down in her notebook before slinging a satchel over one shoulder and heading down the hallway the way Mei and I had just come. I watched, but McLaine kept her head straight, never even glancing our way.

Mei and I gave synchronized jagged sighs. She pressed an open palm to her chest, her calm composure clearly shaken. "My heart is pounding."

Mine was, too, although it wasn't as if we'd heard anything incriminating. Or even very interesting, for that matter.

But Mei was done. "Ivy, if you want to talk to Dr. Sharma, you should make an appointment. Now is definitely not a good time."

I agreed, in part because getting in to see Dr. Sharma right now seemed impossible, but mostly because I suddenly had other fish to fry. "I'll do that. Thanks, Mei. It was good seeing you."

She gave me a hug and I could feel her heartbeat in her chest. Or maybe it was mine. Anticipation. I rushed out without a backward glance or wave. Into the lobby. Out the door to the parking lot. I scanned the cars, hoping I hadn't missed my opportunity, but then I saw her. McLaine leaned against a shiny white-and-black Jeep, her arms folded across her chest. I exhaled with relief. I hadn't missed her.

She raised her arm straight up. She looked right at me.

I turned around, thinking there was someone behind me. Someone she was signaling to.

There wasn't.

Facing her again, I put my palm to my chest. *Me?* I mouthed.

McLaine smiled and nodded, then beckoned me toward her.

My heart beat ratcheted up a notch. This was unexpected. I walked over, stopping in front of her.

"Hello," she said.

"Hi."

"I noticed you inside a minute ago."

Oh, wow. I didn't think she'd seen me. "Oh, right. I was visiting a friend who, uh, works for the district."

McLaine dipped her chin. "And listening at doors. Is that something you and your friend are in the habit of doing?"

I swallowed, my nerves tangling, though for no good reason. Eavesdropping wasn't a crime, after all. "I'm not sure what you mean," I said, feigning innocence.

But McLaine was having none of it. "Oh, but I'm sure you do."

I raised one eyebrow at her as the breeze blew wayward strands of my hair into my eyes. "Did you want to talk to me?" I asked.

She cut right to the chase. "I want to know why you were standing at the superintendent's door listening to our conversation." Somehow I managed not to sputter. "No point in denying it," she continued. "What are you playing at?"

In a split second, I evaluated my possible responses. 1. Despite her telling me there was no point in it, I could deny; 2. I could say that I'd overheard her in with the superintendent as I was walking past and had been drawn to their voices, like a moth to a flame; or 3. I could flip the tables on her by answering her question with a question of my own.

Obviously, I went for option 3. "Do you think Dr. Sharma has something to do with Nessa Renchrik's death?"

McLaine's eyes became mere slits. "Now why would you ask me that?"

Because Nessa Renchrik and Dr. Sharma had been at the Friday night event together and had had a run-in, to use McLaine's words. That was enough to make me suspicious. Then there was the fact that McLaine was here at all. Why would she be, unless she suspected there was a connection? "Just curious." The instant the words left my mouth, I mentally kicked myself, but I quickly regrouped with a question of my own. "Why wouldn't I?"

"What do you have to do with Nessa Renchrik?" she asked me.

I answered with another question. "Do you work for the newspaper?"

Instead of answering, she closed her eyes for a second. When she opened them, she said, "Look, Ms.—"

I saw no reason not to give her my name. She could easily go bug Mei to give it up, or the not-so-friendly Tonya at the front desk. "Culpepper."

"Ms. Culpepper. I'm an investigative reporter. A school board member died mysteriously. I have reason to believe her death may be related to school board business. Now. I've told you my story. Why don't you tell me yours."

She was still leaning nonchalantly against the Jeep, arms still folded. Her hair was too short to be ruffled by the breeze, but the loose strands of mine stuck to my lips and eyes. Once again I considered my options before I responded. "I went to school with one of the school board members," I said, going with a slimmed-down version of my interest in the case. "She's upset. I've had a little luck looking into some nefariousness in the past, so I thought I'd ask a few questions."

McLaine cocked her head at me. "Nefariousness?"

It was an SAT word. Mrs. Branford would be so proud. "Never mind. Let's just say I'm curious."

"But you didn't know Nessa Renchrik?"

I told her I didn't, which didn't appease her interest in me. "Curiosity killed the cat, Ms. Culpepper."

The way she said my name sent a shiver down my spine. "The same could be said for you, McLaine," I said, using her name with the same even tone she had. Two could play this game.

She gave a little shake of her head. "It could, except my interest comes from my role as a reporter. I'm doing my job."

"And what have you discovered? Suspects?"

"I'm afraid I can't divulge that. You?"

"That would be a question for the sheriff's department," I said.

"Ah yes, I spoke with Captain York. He said he has a 'person of interest'"—she used air quotes—"he's looking at closely. He's chomping at the bit to solve the murder of a local politician with a promising legislative career."

Now my jaw tensed. Miguel's face floated before my eyes, but I blinked it away. "I heard she had plans to run for office."

"Apparently she spoke with a potential donor the day she died."

This was news to me. Excitement bloomed inside my chest. But I tempered it just as quickly. Why would McLaine let slip this little tidbit? She didn't blink. Didn't clamp her mouth shut, wishing she could pull those words right back in. Had it been intentional?

"At the district office?" I asked, wondering if she'd give me any more.

She pushed herself off the Jeep and started to walk around to the driver's side. "Alas, Ms. Culpepper, I believe I've already said too much."

Chapter 8

"**I**'m being followed."

California is a hands-free state, so I turned up the volume on my car's stereo and spoke aloud in my car thinking maybe I'd heard wrong. "What did you say?"

Miguel's voice boomed through the Fiat's speaker system. "York is having me watched. I'm being followed."

I reacted without thinking; my right foot moved from the gas pedal to the brake pedal. The car jerked. A horn blared behind me.

"Ivy?" Miguel's voice again. "Are you okay?"

He was being targeted for murder, but he was worried about me. I hit the gas and straightened out the car, glancing in the rearview mirror and throwing up my hand in apology to the driver behind me. "I'm fine," I said. "How do you know?"

"A guy was parked across the street from my house all night. Now same car is in the parking lot at the restaurant.

They're not being very stealthy. It's like they want me to know they're there. York really thinks I did this."

An icy hand squeezed my heart. "I'm going to call Emmaline."

"I already did," he said. "I left her a message."

She and Billy were probably out snorkeling or traipsing through a rain forest, which was exactly what they *should* be doing. Still, I wanted to hear her reassurance that York could be reined in.

I told Miguel about Nessa's potential donor visitor. "I'm going to look into it," I said.

"You think you can figure out who it was?"

"I'm going to try." I'd made up my mind that a visit to Nessa's husband was in order. "I'm going to go see her husband, Cliff."

"I'm going with you, Ivy."

"But the restaur—"

"I'll put Mateo in charge. I can't sit back while York tries to condemn me for a murder I didn't commit."

I'd have felt the same way. "I'm going to help Olaya for a while. Meet me at the bread shop at three?"

"Yep. I'll get things squared away here and I'll find out where Vanessa's husband works."

Not that it meant anything, but I noted that he'd called her Vanessa rather than Nessa. "Sounds good," I said.

My knuckles turned white as I clenched my fists around the steering wheel. I tried not to think about the tail York had on Miguel as I drove to Yeast of Eden. It didn't really work. Em wasn't here to keep him in line. That meant it was up to Miguel and me to figure out what had happened to Nessa. Failure wasn't an option.

I mulled over McLaine's big reveal that Nessa Renchrik had met with a potential donor the day she'd died.

Cliff Renchrik might be able to answer the question of who that donor was. I thought through the list of suspects I had so far, murmuring them to myself as I parked the car in the lot behind the bread shop. I walked to the back entrance. Not even the flower beds Olaya kept with vibrant hydrangea blooms, bursts of lavender, or the array of columbine, coral bells, bellflowers, and daisies could distract me. Any one of the people I'd written in my notebook was a more realistic suspect than Miguel Baptista.

And if it was true and Nessa met with a donor, that was yet another person to add to the potential suspect list— and someone else to pull Captain York's attention away from Miguel.

By the afternoon, all the day's normal baking was finished. These were the hours Olaya devoted to her other baking projects. She was contracted to make rolls for Sofia's Steakhouse, the newest restaurant in town. She baked for Baptista's three times a week. And she had several other regular customers. None of this included special activities. Catering, funerals, the annual Art Car show and ball. The list went on and on.

When I walked in the back door, Olaya stood at her baking station with a melamine cutting board, a chef's knife, and a mound of vegetables. This was not an everyday sight at the bread shop. It was all for the van Dough focaccias. I looked around the kitchen. Not a single loaf of bread remained on any of the bakery racks, I noted. Olaya's bread was known for its healing properties. I'd have taken almost anything in hopes that a bite might relieve some of the worry clawing its way through my insides.

She glanced up at the mirror above her station, smiled,

and started to say, "You are just in time," but her smile faded and the words froze on her lips. She dropped her knife and turned to face me. "What is it?"

I hadn't realized I wore every single emotion I was currently experiencing on my face to be read by her. "It's Miguel."

She wiped her hands on her apron, then swept her arm wide, gesturing to a stool. "Sit. Tell me. Miguel, is he all right?"

I perched on the stool, trying to school my expression. "For now," I said. I filled her in on the tail Captain York had on him, ending with, "I'm worried. What if York doesn't consider anyone else for the murder? What if he's got Miguel in his sights and that's that?"

"Then you will find the truth. There is nothing else to be done. You will find the truth."

I drew in a deep inhalation. "I'll find the truth," I said, as if saying it aloud would make it so.

"Help me, Ivy," she said, pointing to the stack of aprons.

Baking had become a soothing activity for me. I washed my hands and donned an apron with the Yeast of Eden logo. The logo was a simple oval. "Yeast of Eden" was written in a typed font with "Artisan Bread Shop" just below in an easy cursive. Clean and classic.

At the baking station next to Olaya, I shaped two focaccias while Olaya finished preparing the vegetables for the van Dough art. We each worked on one. Piece by piece, we pressed the greens from scallions into the dough to create flower stems. Basil leaves and thin bell pepper rounds with slices of olives in the center created the rest of the flowers. Slices of cherry tomatoes looked like bunches of berries. We used thin strands of red onion, slices of garlic cloves, and Kalamata olives to round out the design. For a while there, while I was designing, my mind stilled. The dilemma was still present, but things didn't look quite so dire.

"*Perfecto*," Olaya proclaimed. Before she slid the trays of focaccias into one of the preheated ovens, she spritzed them each with clean water from a spray bottle she kept in the kitchen.

Just as the oven door closed, a knock came on the back door. It opened and Miguel poked his head in before stepping inside. Olaya made a beeline for him. Miguel was six feet tall. Next to him, she looked tiny. She wrapped her arms around his shoulders and he bent to accept her embrace. Finally, she patted his back and let him go. "*M'ijo*. It will all be okay."

I smiled at her use of the word *m'ijo*, the endearment meaning "my son." She hadn't known Miguel well before I returned to Santa Sofia. Now, though, she thought of him as family.

I untied my apron and lifted it over my head, then washed my hands. "Go," Olaya said, shooing us out of the bread shop's kitchen and back into the parking lot. "Go find the truth."

Chapter 9

Living in a coastal town had its perks—incredible sunrises and sunsets, walks on the beach, the ocean breeze. It also had drawbacks, though. Tourists topped the list. They were good for the local economy, pumping money into lodging, restaurants, and other businesses—like Yeast of Eden. The bread shop was a tourist destination in and of itself. But if it was peak season and if you needed to find quick and easy parking, had visiting friends who needed an Airbnb, or just wanted to go out to dinner without waiting an hour for your table, you were out of luck.

It seemed that Cliff and Nessa Renchrik made their living off of the tourists who came to Santa Sofia. Miguel had found out that the power couple owned and operated a high-end property management company for people who visited our little seaside oasis. Seaside Property Management offered both condo and private home rentals, most on the shuttle route to the public beaches in Santa Sofia. "They have a full-service business model," Miguel said.

He drove and I sat in the passenger side of his truck, Seaside Property Management's address in the GPS. "What does 'full-service' mean?"

"They meet you to let you in or have keyless entry pads, there's a cleaning service, but get this. You can also elect to have someone cook for you or do your grocery shopping."

"That's full service, all right." I guess if you were on vacation, you might want and be willing to pay for those perks. How could they afford to keep staff on to take care of all that? Surely it was hit or miss for people who would want those premium benefits.

I looked up Seaside Property Management on my phone. "Should we call? Make sure he's there?"

Miguel shrugged, which I took to be agreement. I pressed the Call button. It rang three times before a woman answered with a peppy, "Seaside Property Management. How can I help you find the perfect Santa Sofia lodging today?"

I improvised. "Hi. Hello. I've been working with Cliff. I'm wondering, is he available?"

"Oh, I'm so sorry. Cliff had a family emergency. He's working from home for a few days. I'd be happy to help you, or I can connect you to his voicemail."

"Oh, right, of course. Voicemail would be great," I said. "Thanks so much."

"No problem. Have a great day." The line clicked and a recorded voice came on telling me I'd reached the voice mailbox of Cliff Renchrik and directing me to leave a message.

I hung up instead. "He's working from home," I told Miguel.

He hit his palm against the steering wheel. "Of course he is." He pulled the truck over to the side of the road while I searched up the Renchriks's address. I'd been afraid it would be private, but it came up on the White Pages. There weren't many Renchriks in Santa Sofia. Only one address, actually. Miguel entered it into his phone's GPS and stuck the phone back in its holder.

Fifteen minutes later, we arrived at an understated home in Laguna Heights. The area was upscale. A cool million and a half was the low-end price for a starter home. The Renchriks were *not* in a starter home. Their house was also not the fanciest on the block. Real estate agents would be quick to say you never want to be the white elephant in a neighborhood. The highest price point did not allow good negotiating leverage. Being on the low end gave you room to grow. Being somewhere in between was the sweet spot. The Renchriks' house was solidly in the middle.

Miguel parked right in front of the house with its white stucco walls, red Spanish tiled roof, and the courtyard walls topped with smooth red brick. The landscaping was immaculate. Not a tree limb was out of place, not a weed to be seen. Whoever did their yard maintenance was a keeper.

The house was symmetrical, with a short flight of brick steps bisecting it. Miguel and I walked up them side by side. As we stood in front of the arched dark wood door with iron grating over a beveled window, I had a moment of guilt. We were about to barge in on a grieving husband.

Miguel leaned over and bumped my arm with his. "Remember what Olaya said. We're finding the truth."

And exonerating him, I wanted to add, but I kept that part to myself.

I raised my hand to knock . . .

. . . and as if someone had been just on the other side of the door waiting, it flew open.

A teenage girl with muddy-blond hair, a lightweight turtleneck, and a pallor that was not conducive to beach life scurried backward with a yelp.

"Oh!" I jumped back, just as startled as the girl was. My feet twisted under me, but Miguel grabbed my arm, righting me before I could fall.

The girl came forward again, eyeing us. "Please tell me you don't have another casserole or mixed green salad. If you do, I'm gonna puke."

The words were forceful, but her voice was not. She sounded tired. Exhausted, really. Her eyes were red rimmed, her cheeks hollow. With that, combined with her sallow skin, she looked more like a zombie than a thriving teenager. I assumed this was Nessa Renchrik's daughter, Rachel.

I held up my empty hands. "No casseroles or salads."

She waited, one hand on the door, the other on the doorframe. Her body blocked the entrance to the house, but the little bit I could see was beautiful. I caught a glimpse of a framed oil painting of a woman, her skirt billowing in the breeze, her back to the viewer as she looked out over a meadow. A movement behind her caught my eye. Just over her shoulder, a woman came into view.

The girl followed my gaze, turning around. "I'm fine, Fernanda." Under her breath she added, "Jesus, just leave me alone."

The woman nodded but let her dark-eyed gaze linger on the girl's back for a moment before melting away.

I lifted my eyebrows in a question.

"Nanny," she said with a roll of her eyes. "Like we needed another one."

"You're Rachel?" I asked.

She nodded.

"I'm an old friend of Candy's. Candace Coffey? I saw her yesterday. She's worried about you."

Like a faucet had been turned on, tears pooled in Rachel's eyes. Her lips parted as if she was going to say something, but then she changed her mind and they closed again.

Her grief seemed to exude from her pores. I wanted to reach out and touch her hand. To comfort her. I settled for saying, "Are you okay?"

She gave a slow blink, squeezing her eyes for a beat before asking, "Do you want to see my dad?"

Miguel answered. "Is he home?"

She responded by swinging her body so she faced the inside of the house and hollering, "Dad! Someone's at the door for you."

She didn't wait for a reply—or even acknowledgment—but skirted by Miguel and me. "See ya," she said as she hurried down the stairs, turned left at the sidewalk, and disappeared.

At the same time, a man appeared. He had an oval face. The bridge of his nose was wide. I blinked. Rachel was the spitting image of him, from her pale complexion, made sallow through grief, to her green eyes, to her light hair, face shape, and nose. I'd only seen photos of Nessa, but even so, Rachel clearly favored her father.

"Mr. Renchrik?" I put my open palm against my chest. "I'm Ivy Culpepper." I looked at Miguel. "And this is Miguel Baptista."

"I'm not talking to reporters," he said. He had a cell phone clutched in one hand and started to close the door with his other.

I stepped halfway in, placing my foot to block the door. "We're not reporters," I said, wondering if McLaine had been here.

He looked down at my foot, then slowly lifted his gaze. "Then who are you?" he demanded, his voice gruff.

Miguel and I both hesitated. I realized that we hadn't thought this through well enough. It wasn't like Miguel could say, *I went out with your wife when she was married to you and now I'm a suspect in her murder. Can we come in?*

Cliff Renchrik narrowed his eyes and peered at Miguel. For a second, I thought maybe he knew who Miguel was. Had he been the one in the bookstore Nessa had had a run-in with that night? Had he seen Miguel?

But then his lids lowered to half-mast and he sighed. "What do you want?"

"We just want to offer our condolences," I said. "We're so sorry for your loss."

"You knew Nessa?"

Miguel remained motionless, but I said, "I'm old friends with Candace Coffey. . . ." I trailed off, hoping he'd fill in the blank. If I knew Candy, I must therefore have known his wife.

He exhaled a shaky breath. "Candy's been helpful. She organized a food tree. We have casseroles coming out of our ears." He swallowed. Ran his palm down over his face. "But we appreciate it. Candy's been real helpful."

"Do you mind if we come in?"

He stepped back and held the door open for us, his

concern over us being reporters gone. Still, he didn't look happy about the intrusion. We'd have to make it quick.

We went from standing outside on the porch to standing inside in the foyer. The painting I'd glimpsed on the wall was accompanied by several other pieces, as well as a curio cabinet filled with collectibles. The marble floor was polished to a gleam. If it had been me, I'd have an area rug to soften the stark feel of the entry room. As it was, it felt cold and unwelcoming. From the corner of my eye, I saw Fernanda wiping a frame in the hallway that led to the kitchen. From where I stood, I could see the refrigerator and a corner of a dining table.

Cliff did not lead us deeper into the house. We stood awkwardly and I tried to figure out how to approach this man.

Miguel beat me to it. "Vanessa did a lot of good in the community. She'll be missed."

Those two little sentences woke Cliff Renchrik up. "No one called her Vanessa."

Miguel didn't miss a beat. "When I first met her, that's how she introduced herself. That was years ago—"

His eyes narrowed. "When—"

Cliff's cell phone rang, cutting off the question he'd been about to ask. He kept fierce attention on Miguel as he answered with a clipped, "This is Cliff."

Whoever was on the other end spoke. Slowly, Cliff's eyes narrowed even more. "They're here now. Thanks." He hung up and closed his eyes for the briefest moment, as if he was gathering strength. "You're interested in a rental so you came to my house? But you knew Nessa?" He shook his head, his expression a mix of anger, frustration, and bafflement. "Who the hell are you?"

"We called your office first," I said, "but we're not looking for a rental. We live in Santa Sofia."

"You're clearly not here to offer condolences, so what do you want?" he asked again.

"We're just as stunned by Nessa's murder as you are—"

"Who said I'm stunned?"

This was not the response I'd expected. "You're not?"

"Look. Nessa was a strong woman with strong opinions. Not everyone liked those opinions. That's politics."

"But people don't usually kill someone because they don't agree with their politics or opinions," Miguel said.

Cliff's expression hadn't softened, nor had his voice, but he answered all the same. "All I'm saying is that she pissed plenty of people off. One of them took their anger too far."

I had no idea if he'd keep talking, but I wanted to try. "What did she do that made people so upset?" I asked.

"She made me upset every damn day!" he snapped. The second the words were spoken, his eyes opened wide and he sucked in a breath, as if he were trying to suck the words right back in.

I had no expectation that he'd elaborate, but I said, "Oh?"

His phone rang again. *Damn.* He held up one finger to us and pressed the device to his ear. "This is Cliff."

He listened for a few seconds, then replied to the caller in halting Spanish. My high school Spanish was rudimentary at best. I glanced at Miguel, who was listening intently.

Abruptly, Cliff hung up. He turned and bellowed, "Carmen! I'm going out. Make sure Tate gets dinner."

The woman in the hallway nodded solemnly. I peered at her. Why did Rachel call her Fernanda, but Cliff called her Carmen?

It was a question for another time, because Cliff moved to the front door. "I have to go." He looked back over his shoulder and hollered, "Tate! I'm going out for a while."

Just like Rachel had earlier, Cliff didn't wait for a response. He picked up his wallet from the glass-topped table next to the door, waited for Miguel and me to leave, then followed us out.

The front door opened behind us and a little boy stood there. He was skinny, dark haired, and had a heart-shaped face that ended with a pointy chin. Like his mother, I thought. "Where are you going, Dad?"

"To one of the rentals. I'll be back soon." Cliff's voice was gruff.

The boy closed the door. Cliff didn't say anything else to Miguel or me. He gave us a final look before heading to the black BMW sitting in the driveway.

"That was really strange," I said, getting back into the passenger side of the truck. "What was the phone call about?"

"One of the landscapers at a rental property didn't show up today," he said, translating what he'd heard.

I tapped my finger against my chin. "So he's going to go pull weeds himself?"

Miguel had started the truck but hadn't moved. Cliff backed out of the driveway, and drove off. When we could barely see the taillights of the Beamer, Miguel finally pulled away from the curb. I turned to look at him. "Are you going to follow him?"

"Something's off about him."

"What do you mean?"

He slowed, keeping a good distance from Cliff's car. "I can't put my finger on it, but I don't like him."

"Is he the man Nessa argued with in the bookstore?"

He made a face as if he was searching his memory banks, trying to remember. "I don't think so, but I don't know. It was a long time ago, and I didn't see him well."

I went back to Miguel's belief that something was off about Cliff Renchrik. "You think he could have killed Nessa?" If Tate wasn't Cliff's son and he'd recently figured that fact out, could it have pushed him over the edge?

Miguel glanced at me. "Don't they say it's usually the spouse? York should be looking into this guy. If we can give him a reason to—"

He broke off, but the rest of the sentence hung in the air between us—it would take the heat off Miguel as a suspect.

Cliff drove through town with Miguel keeping a good distance behind him. Cliff ended up at a cliffside house overlooking the Pacific. Miguel pulled off the road as Cliff pressed a code into the keypad. A gate opened and the BMW rolled through. After a solid minute—enough time to make sure Cliff was well out of sight—Miguel put the truck in drive and drove at a snail's pace past the house.

I stared down the long drive, catching only a glimpse of the house itself. Or rather, the mansion. "That is a rental?"

"Looks like their management company is for the rich and famous."

"Maybe the rich and not famous," I said. Celebrities tended to vacation in Malibu, Santa Barbara, or Laguna Beach rather than Santa Sofia, but the wealthy went wherever they wanted.

There was no chance of us getting out and surveilling the house. The gate kept the property secure, and if Cliff left while we were out prowling he might very well spot us.

Miguel parked down the street far enough that we could see but not be seen. We stayed put, watching an old work truck pull up to the drive. A man drove and someone else sat in the passenger seat. The driver entered the gate code, the gate opened, and the truck disappeared onto the property. The landscaper, at last?

A solid ten minutes later, the gate opened and Cliff's Beamer rolled out and hung a left. He was heading right for us. Miguel and I ducked out of sight as Cliff drove past. There was no way to know if he'd seen us or not, but we decided it was too risky to follow him, and to what end? Other than the fact that the spouse often did it, we had no reason to suspect that Cliff Renchrik had actually killed his wife.

Chapter 10

The next morning started out with a coffee date with school board member Katherine Candelli at The Coffee House across from Santa Sofia's main pier. As I sipped on a caramel latte, Katherine dropped a bomb. She had had coffee with Nessa Renchrik the morning of the day she'd died. "Two school board members can get together," she said, her words coming with a hyperquickness. She had energy to spare. "No problem. But three or more. Nope. Then it constitutes a meeting. Makes things tricky sometimes, especially when you're friends, you know? Of course, we weren't really friends. Just co—board members."

That was an odd thing to say. Katherine, like everyone else I'd spoken with, except Nessa's daughter, did not seem particularly fazed by Nessa's death. "Did Nessa ask you to meet her?"

Katherine cupped her hands around her mug of herbal tea. It was a good choice. Coffee would exacerbate her high energy. "Yeah. Saw her the night before. There was a fundraiser. She asked me to meet her the next morning. I had a bike ride scheduled for ten, so we met at eight thirty."

"What did she want to meet about?" I asked, excited to learn that Katherine had met with Nessa in the hours before her death.

"We had a vote coming up. Allocating funds," Katherine said. "We didn't agree."

Ah. Another person Nessa was at odds with. "And she was trying to sway you?"

I wondered if she'd asked to meet with the other board members privately, too. From what I could tell, she seemed to be a true politician, lobbying to get what she wanted.

Katherine continued to speak in staccato sentences, punctuating her vigor. She shrugged, as if whatever Nessa was trying to do during their meeting, it didn't make a bit of difference. "We have passions. Hers was different than mine."

"What was her passion?" I'd asked.

Katherine let out a short laugh. Almost a scoff. "Surfing."

"She liked to surf?" She'd looked fit in the photos I'd seen, but surfing? That was a tough sport that required a lot of upper body strength and great balance.

"Yep. She competed."

My jaw dropped. "Like, actively competed?"

Katherine wagged her hand. It was more aggressive than a flutter. Quick, tight movements swept my question away. "No. When she was in college. She thinks— thought—every kid should surf. Builds character. That's what she liked to say."

My latte was gone and Katherine was taking the last sip of her tea. "Do you have any idea who would have wanted to do this to her?" I asked before she could end our meeting.

"Who wouldn't?" she said. "I did."

We both froze and she seemed to realize what she'd said. Her eyes opened wide and she chuckled. "Kidding. Of course I'm kidding. I didn't. Do it. Kill her, I mean."

I forced a smile. "Of course not."

"I don't know who did. She had enemies."

"So I've heard."

Katherine shoved her chair back and stood. "Gotta run. Biking twenty miles today."

I thanked her for taking the time and watched as she left. She got into the driver's side of a dark green minivan that had seen better days. She pulled out and leaned forward as she zoomed down the road, two hands on the steering wheel, looking one hundred percent focused on what was ahead of her. My spine crackled. She was off in a hurry.

The biggest takeaway from the meeting was that, as Candace had said, Nessa had had a cadre of people lined up ready to do her in.

I hurried into my car, threw it into drive, and eased into the road. I was no expert at surveillance, despite Miguel and me following Cliff Renchrik the day before. To save Miguel from York's scrutiny, I would give it a go on my own. Once the road was clear, I slammed my foot down on the gas pedal and caught up to the green jalopy. Once I had Katherine in view, I eased off the gas and hung back.

She drove, never altering her posture or hand position on the steering wheel. I stayed a few car lengths behind her. We drove for just under ten minutes until, finally, Katherine pulled into the parking lot of Santa Sofia's outdoor mall. Twenty-mile bike race. Hah.

Why had she lied?

The parking lot was moderately full. I didn't know if there were enough people milling around the mall for me to melt in and not be seen, but I'd give it a try.

By the time I parked, Katherine was out of her car and heading toward the cobbled walkways. I left my car and tiptoe-ran, darting amid the cars, until I was close enough to see—but not be seen. Her arm was extended in front of her and she held something. A small mirror? A compact?

I got a little bit closer. Ah, it was a cell phone.

My first impression of Katherine Candelli was that she had lived her first forty-eight years outside and under the full force of the sun's UV rays. She was unnaturally tanned and prematurely leathery. Her ordinary brown hair was pulled back into a ponytail, strands falling loose around her face. But extreme sun exposure hadn't slowed her down. The woman was quick. She speed-walked through the outdoor mall, weaving through the casual shoppers, chatting on the phone the entire time.

She suddenly stopped and turned. To look in a shop window? Or had she sensed that she was being followed? I darted into a storefront, turning my back to her. A moment later, I sneaked a peek. She'd continued on her way, completely absorbed in her conversation, oblivious to everyone and everything around her. She held her phone out in front of her face, talking animatedly to whoever was on the other end of the line. She had it on speakerphone! If only I could get close enough, I'd be able to hear both sides of the conversation.

She kept walking. I darted to the next store, falling in

beside a group of young adults who cruised along at a casual pace. We approached the mall's fountain.

Someone screamed in the distance behind me.

Everything slowed to slow motion.

Katherine's head slowly turned toward the sound. I reacted without thinking and dove behind the fountain. My body hit the hard ground with a bruising thud. I tucked. I rolled. I was sure she'd seen me. I held my breath, waiting for her to barge through the shoppers and confront me.

But nothing happened. Nothing besides a gaggle of mall-goers who *did* see my nose dive staring slack-jawed at me. I ignored them and army crawled to the corner, peering around it. Katherine was a good hundred and fifty yards away and still walking away from me. In one incredibly smooth move that I hadn't known I had in me, I hopped up and took off after her. A straight line was the quickest route between two points, so that's what I took. I leapt over an abandoned fast-food bag, dodged shoppers and small children, and swerved around the occasional bench, keeping Katherine in my sights the entire time. I slowed as I came up behind her, still leaving some space between us. She still had her cell phone out in front of her, the tinny voice coming from it loud and clear.

"I need a black dress for the funeral," Katherine said. "The dog got to the one I had. Tore out the hem."

"You and that damn dog," the female voice on the other end of the line said.

"Yeah. He's out of control—"

"I know, but you love him." There was a pause before the voice said, "She didn't deserve it."

I came up short as Katherine stopped walking.

"Maybe," Katherine said as she started up again and made an abrupt turn into a public restroom.

I caught the voice's gasp and her saying, "Are you saying she *did* deserve it?" before Katherine disappeared.

I weighed my options. I could fall back and hide, waiting for her to come out, then keep following her. Or I could sneak into the restroom to eavesdrop on her conversation. The smart thing to do was fall back and wait. After all, she might not still be on the phone. And if she caught me, there was no way to explain how I ended up at the same outdoor mall she did after just meeting with her at The Coffee House.

In the end, there was no way I couldn't try to hear more. I pressed my back against the wall as I moved into the bathroom, creeping along to stay as hidden as possible. I could hear Katherine's voice. I peered around the corner, holding my breath and hoping the coast was clear. I was in luck. No one was in sight. Two of the three toilet stall doors were ajar. The third was closed. The conversation between Katherine and whoever she was on the phone with echoed in the small space. Apparently, Katherine had no problem doing her business while chatting with her friend. Gossip waits for no one and nothing.

With stealth I didn't know I possessed, I slipped into one of the empty stalls, staying close to the opposite wall so Katherine wouldn't see my feet. I quietly closed the door. As I reached for the latch, though, it swung back open. The lock was broken.

The talking in the stall next to me suddenly stopped. Had Katherine heard? Did she know she was no longer alone in the bathroom?

I held my breath. Five seconds. Ten seconds. Fifteen seconds. Was I busted—?

And then Katherine started talking again. "Sorry about that. I had to respond to a text."

I silently exhaled, relief washing over me. I extended my arm, pushing the door closed again, holding it with my fingertips.

"No problem," the voice said. "But seriously, what do you think happened?"

"What, to Nessa?"

"Yes, to Nessa. She was *killed*!" The voice grew shrill on that last word.

Katherine gave a harsh chuckle with not a trace of mirth. "A million people wanted her dead. Not a single one of them is crying over it."

The voice gave a sharp inhale. "I can't believe you're saying that."

"Marge," she chastised. "You know it's true."

Marge. Marge. Marge. I repeated the name in my head, finally landing on who it was. It had to be Margaret Jenkins-Roe. She was one of the board members. I had high hopes for a conversation with her since Katherine had definitely been holding out on me. It wasn't a new theme, but I did want to know who she thought had it in for Nessa. Maybe Marge would give up that information.

"Kath, you're speaking ill of the dead. It's not right."

Katherine sighed; then the toilet flushed. "You're right, but if I'm being honest, I'm not going to miss her. And the vote went our way last night. You know you're happy about that."

"I still don't understand why she was so against the funding for technology in schools."

The stall door next to me swung open with a creak and Katherine moved to the sink. I peered through the crack at my stall door, listening intently. She set her cell phone on the counter as she washed up. "Because it was for Chavez Elementary."

There was a moment of silence before Marge said, "Really? Is that why?"

Katherine turned and leaned against the counter, holding her phone out in front of her again. Her eyes swept the stall doors, landing on mine. "That Cabrera woman, don't you remember?"

Marge sucked in a breath. "Oh my God. I remember her."

I willed them to continue so I could get the lowdown on the Cabrera woman, whoever she was. Instead Katherine gave an ambiguous grunt. Her eyes were still on the stall door I was hiding behind, but now they had narrowed. "I have to go, Marge. I'll call you later."

She hung up before Marge could reply. Katherine gripped her phone and took a step toward the stalls, her arm outstretched. I backed up, trying to melt into the stall. I braced myself, knowing I'd be found out in a split second, but just as her fingertips would have reached the door, her cell phone rang. I slammed my hand over my mouth, stifling the yelp that had climbed up my throat. Katherine let out her own startled squeak and jumped back. At the same time, a group of chattering teenage girls blew into the bathroom. They completely ignored Katherine.

Since I'd moved back to get out of Katherine's line of sight, I was no longer holding the stall door. I held my breath as it started to swing toward me. I could barely see the girls, but the stall was small. There was nowhere to hide. Any second, they'd see me and the jig would be up.

But luck was on my side. I could see Katherine now and she was no longer looking in my direction. She had her phone pressed to her ear again. "Someone's poking their nose into Nessa's—"

She broke off and shot a glance at the teenagers who all crowded in front of the mirror. Luckily, my position wasn't revealed in the mirror.

"Hang on, Jerry," she said, and just like that, she left the bathroom and was gone.

I stayed put and leaned against the side of the stall, finally letting out the breath I hadn't known I'd been holding. My heart pounded in my throat. That had been too close a call. What would I have said if she'd caught me?

"Doesn't matter," I whispered, trying to calm myself.

I waited till the chatty girls left the bathroom before I came out into the open, my mind processing what I'd heard. The second phone call Katherine had taken had to have been Jerry Zenmark, the only male school board member. A chill wound through me like a swirling ribbon cinching my insides. It was Katherine's words, as much as the harsh tone her voice had taken when she'd said someone was nosing around, that had me on edge. She cut off, but I knew she'd been about to say *into Nessa's death*.

And I knew she'd been referring to me.

Chapter 11

After the near bathroom stall collision with Katherine Candelli, I hightailed it home. "It was a close call, Agatha," I said, scratching the pug's smooshed head.

She looked up at me with her bulbous eyes and gave me a slow blink.

"No sympathy, huh?" I said. "I get it. If I stayed in my lane, I wouldn't have had a close call. But, Agatha, I don't have a choice. York has his sights set on Miguel."

Agatha opened her mouth in a big, lazy yawn. "Fine," I said, opening the French door to let her outside. "Go on."

She didn't budge.

I bent down to give her a little nudge. "I'll be right out. Just let me get my computer."

Agatha snorted, then trotted outside, disappearing into the blossoming flower garden.

Tracking down @MarisasMama, aka Lulu Sanchez-Patrick, turned out to be easier than I thought it would be. I simply searched her name and Google came up with the answer. She worked for a law office as a paralegal. I called to schedule an appointment. Her first available was Friday morning at eleven o'clock. "I'll take it," I said. Agatha reappeared and found a sliver of sunlight, lying down in it. I gave her a thumbs-up. Success!

"What's the consultation about?" the receptionist asked me.

"I'd rather not say. It's personal."

"Got it." I heard the *click click click* of her finger pads hitting the keys of a keyboard. Making notes in the calendar app.

With that appointment made, I turned my sights back to the school board.

It had taken a while and a lot of skimming through Google's findings to figure out what Cabrera woman Katherine Candelli and Margaret Jenkins-Roe had been talking about, but eventually I found her. Sylvia Cabrera. Her name came up in a random mention in connection to Seaside Property Management, but from the conversation between Katherine and Margaret, there had been some negative issue with Sylvia and Nessa and whatever happened at Chavez Elementary.

No matter how many times and ways I searched, I couldn't turn up anything specific. The only address I could find for a Sylvia Cabrera was on the outskirts of town. There was no time like the present. I texted Miguel my plan—someone had to know where I was—brought Agatha back in, and headed out with the address plugged into my maps app on my phone. It took a good twenty-five minutes to get there. There turned out to be a trailer park. It had neat shrubs on either side of the driveway entrance and the abodes were well kept, with flowerpots in front of some and window boxes on others.

I drove slowly through the neighborhood. Here and there, a curtain pulled back as if someone was watching, or miniblinds fell back into place as if someone *had* been watching before retreating to some place away from the window.

I found Sylvia's address toward the back, threw my car into park, and got out. I was nowhere near catching a killer, but something in my gut told me Sylvia was going to help me get to the truth.

Just as I caught a glimpse of the back end of a blue pickup truck parked behind the home, the sound of a car driving through the center street caught my attention. It slid into the space next to my Fiat, nearly taking me out in the process. I jumped out of the way and blinked. Then blinked again. What in the world . . . ? It was Mrs. Branford's old Volvo.

The passenger door flew open and there she was in her lavender velour lounge suit and her spiffy white sneakers.

"Mrs. Branford? What are you—" I broke off. If she was in the passenger seat, who had driven? I bent to peer through the open door. If someone had come up to me and brushed me with a feather, I would have fallen right over. Olaya Solis sat in the driver's seat.

"What are *you* doing here?" I asked her, followed by an amended, "What are you *doing* here?" Then I looked from Olaya to Mrs. Branford and said, "What are you *both* doing here?"

"We're here to help you, of course," Mrs. Branford said. She swung her body sideways, placing her cane on the ground to support her as she stood.

Olaya circled around and joined us. "Penelope, she does not take no for an answer."

Right. For Mrs. Branford, no often meant yes. "But how did you know I was here—"

"Miguel," they said in unison.

Of course. He'd raised the alarm, calling on two people he knew would drop everything in a heartbeat to be my backup. My face must have revealed my uncertainty at exactly what they could do to help me, though.

Mrs. Branford sighed patiently, as if she was being tolerant of my thickheadedness. "Olaya speaks Spanish, and I had Sylvia Cabrera, née Garcia, in my class—"

My mouth gaped open. "You did—?" I stopped and closed my mouth. Of course she did.

"A million years ago," Olaya said.

Mrs. Branford smiled with satisfaction. She loved the fact that she knew practically everyone in Santa Sofia from her decades of teaching. "She was a smart girl with a bright future."

I hoped Mrs. Branford's assessment was correct and that Sylvia Garcia had gone on to do great things.

The three of us walked up the to the small but tidy home.

The front door was open, covered only by a screen door. The sun was setting behind us as I knocked on the screen door's frame and called, "Hallo?"

A man appeared. He was short and stocky with what was once dark hair, now graying, and five o'clock white stubble on his face. "Yes?"

"Hi. My name is Ivy." I gestured to my companions. "This is Penelope Branford and Olaya Solis—"

His mouth opened and he stared at Olaya. "Olaya? *De la panadería* Yeast of Eden, *verdad*?"

I understood enough to know he'd asked if she was from the bread shop.

"*Sí*," she said with a smile, and then she spoke to him in Spanish. She ended by saying Sylvia Cabrera's name, so I knew she'd asked him if he knew her, or maybe if she was home.

"*No está aquí*," he said. My rudimentary Spanish kicked in and my hope faded. She wasn't here.

"*Dónde está ella?*" Olaya asked.

Yes, where was she? At the market? At work? Would she be back soon?

"*En Colombia*," the man said. I didn't have to know any Spanish to understand that Sylvia was, apparently, out of the country.

"Colombia?" I asked, trying hard to keep the shrillness from my voice. "Why is she in Colombia?"

The man looked at me with a grimace. He spoke in halting English. "She was deported."

Oh no.

Mrs. Branford had been silent, but now she muttered something harsh under her breath and stomped her cane against the wooden floor of the porch. "She cannot have been deported."

But the man nodded. "It is true."

"But Sylvia grew up here. I remember her. I remember her saying she'd been in Santa Sofia her whole life. How could she be sent away?"

No one had an answer for her.

"What happened?" I asked.

He understood what I'd asked, because he responded in Spanish to Olaya. She translated a moment later. "He says it was a surprise raid. ICE came and rounded people up. Sylvia had gotten caught in the middle."

"She should not have been there," he said in heavily

accented English. "It should have been me." His chin quivered with emotion. He said something else in Spanish, which Olaya translated. "She came here as a baby, but I come here later. I did not go to school here. It should have been me."

"When did it happen?" I asked him.

Olaya repeated the question in Spanish and he answered in English. "February 23."

I looked at Mrs. Branford. She looked at Olaya. Olaya looked at me. They hadn't heard about the raid, but I had. Thanks to @MarisasMama.

Suddenly my hopes of getting inside information about the Renchriks' business were dashed. With Sylvia Cabrera gone, it was a dead end. More than anything, though, I felt for Sylvia. She'd been ripped from her home and sent to a country she didn't know. It was unfathomable.

Olaya gave a heavy sigh. "*Y tú?*" she asked. "*Quién eres tú?*"

Good question. Who was this man?

He pointed to his chest. "*Yo? Me llamo Roberto García.*"

I touched Olaya's hand. "Ask him if he's related to Sylvia—"

"I am her brother," he said slowly. "*Quién eres tú?*"

At this Olaya looked at me. "He wants to know who we are."

"Sylvia's name came up in connection with a woman named Nessa Renchrik," I said.

Olaya translated and he nodded.

"Did she work for her?"

He didn't wait for the translation before nodding.

"For Seaside Property Management?" I clarified.

"*Sí.*"

"Did anything happen between the Renchriks and Sylvia?" I asked.

Olaya translated. Mr. Garcia shrugged. "*No se*," he said. "I do not know."

"*Gracias por tu ayuda*," Olaya said after another few minutes. There didn't seem to be anything more Mr. Garcia could offer.

"Yes, thank you," I echoed.

As the three of us turned to leave, his voice stopped us. "*Necesitas hablar con el esposo de Sylvia?*"

We all turned back around. "What did he say?" I asked Olaya.

"He wants to know if we want to talk to Sylvia's husband."

My jaw dropped open. Sylvia had a husband! "Yes, please," I said at the same time Olaya replied, "*Sí. Por favor.*"

I drew in a breath. Maybe all hope wasn't lost.

Mr. Garcia called back into the house. "Guillermo, *ven aquí.*"

A few seconds later, a man came up next to Mr. Garcia. Even through the screen door, I could see how handsome he was. He wore dark khakis, a white button-down shirt, open at the collar, and was a few inches taller than his brother-in-law. The older man said something to Olaya, who translated for us. "This is Guillermo Cabrera," she said. "Sylvia's husband."

Guillermo shot Mr. Garcia a look, but I couldn't decipher its meaning. He said something to Roberto in Spanish. Mr. Garcia pushed the door open and he and Guillermo stepped out onto the porch. "Hello," he said.

"It's so nice to meet you," I said, one hundred percent sincere.

Guillermo's piercing brown eyes were the first things I noticed. He looked at us with an intensity that made my skin prickle. "Can I help you?" he asked. His English was perfect. Unlike Mr. Garcia, if I had to guess, I'd say he was born and raised here.

"We were looking for Sylvia," I said. I left it open-ended, hoping he'd pick up some thread of a narrative, but all he did was nod. "Is she doing okay?" I asked, because deportation had to be so hard on so many different levels.

"Depends what you mean by 'okay.'" Now he sounded angry. With good reason, I thought. His wife had been ripped from her home. From him. We waited in silence for him to continue. "She's been in the U.S. since she was a baby. Now she's in a country she doesn't even know. Before the raid, she had never even been to Colombia. Now she's stuck there. She's alone."

His jawline tightened and his chin quivered, but he controlled the emotions bubbling inside him.

Saying I was sorry didn't even begin to cut it. I said it anyway. "I'm so sorry."

Mrs. Branford leaned heavily on her cane.

Mr. Garcia took the cue. He blustered as he held the screen door open. "*Lo siento. Con permiso.* Como in. Come in."

As we followed him in, Mrs. Branford threw a glance my way. Pure calculation. I stifled a smile.

The door opened straight into the living area. A nubby cream-colored couch made with heavy fabric and with wooden legs and trim on the arms and a black faux leather recliner angled to face a small television. A stack of mail sat on one end of an oval wood coffee table, a plate with half a sandwich and chips, as well as an open can of beer on the opposite end. We'd interrupted Mr. Garcia's dinner.

Guillermo led Mrs. Branford to the recliner. She perched on the edge, holding tight to her cane braced in front of her. She looked up at him. "I taught your wife, you know. English at Santa Sofia High School."

Guillermo's thick black eyebrows rose. "Wait. You're Mrs. Brandon. No, Bradshaw." He shook his head. "No, that's not right."

"Penelope Branford," she said.

He snapped his fingers. "Right! That's right. You taught her about Gabriel García Márquez, no?"

Mrs. Branford nodded sagely. She took her literature very seriously. "Oh yes. I remember it well. Sylvia—your wife—wanted to connect more with her Colombian heritage because she'd never been there. *One Hundred Years of Solitude*. Sylvia adored him."

Guillermo pointed to a small upright bookshelf. Along with a few family photographs, a cross, and a few other knickknacks, the shelves held an array of books. Even from where I stood, I could see a collection grouped together of Márquez's work.

When I looked back, Mrs. Branford's eyes had turned glassy. "Thank you for sharing that, Guillermo. For a teacher, there is nothing more powerful than knowing you have had a significant impact on a person's life. To bring literature to someone . . ." She sighed. "My heart is happy about that for Sylvia, at least."

"We won't take more of your time, Guillermo. I was just hoping to talk to your wife about the Renchriks," I said.

He blinked, a slight pause before he responded. "What about them?"

"She worked for them?"

He nodded but grimaced. "We both did. I still do."

My spine cracked. "You do?"

"I manage the maintenance crew for Seaside Properties."

"The yard maintenance?" I asked.

"That. Food services. Transportation. All of it."

"And your wife?" Olaya asked.

"We met there. She was in Housekeeping. Then she became Nessa's personal assistant."

Mr. Garcia muttered something under his breath in Spanish.

"He says they ran her ragged," Olaya translated for us.

Guillermo nodded. "It's true. Just like in the movies. They had her running errands. Taking the dry cleaning. Picking up fruit from the farms for their special guests. Picking up and delivering fancy coffee. It was a tough job. A thankless job. But it was a job."

"How long have you been married?" I asked.

Guillermo's gaze dropped to the ground. "My brother-in-law likes to say me and Sylvia were married, but we weren't in the eyes of the law. We married each other on the beach. She is my wife."

"But not with a license," I said, filling in the blanks. They had had their own ceremony, but it wasn't recognized.

"Right. We met ten years ago and fell in love, but she—" The tension returned to his face. "I don't know what we could have done differently. She was . . . a victim of her circumstances."

What an incredibly sad story. They'd found love with each other late, but they'd found it. And then it had been taken from them.

"You're a citizen, then," Mrs. Branford said.

Guillermo dipped his head in acknowledgment. "Born and raised in Los Angeles."

"If you were engaged to Sylvia," I started, but Guillermo seemed to know where I was going with my question and he shook his head. "She was undocumented—"

"As a baby," Mrs. Branford said.

"You know her story," Guillermo said, "but it doesn't matter. She came unlawfully. That's what the lawyer said. We are trying for a provisional waiver. And we are praying."

"Mr. Renchrik didn't care that she was undocumented?"

Guillermo shrugged. "Most of his people are undocumented. Cheap labor."

An idea came to mind. Nessa Renchrik had a dream of running for state senate. She'd met with a potential donor. Could the fact that her family paid workers under the table have come to the surface? Surely that would ruin her chance of running. Could Nessa and the donor have argued about it? Could the donor have killed Nessa and could the whole thing stem from the undocumented workers the Renchriks employed?

It was possible. I needed to find out who Nessa had met with the day she died.

A little girl appeared behind Guillermo. He reached behind him and cupped his hand around her shoulder. She looked to be about eight, or so. Giant brown eyes. Soft brown hair. Sylvia's child. Another child without a mother.

We left with that sobering fact hanging in the air. Guillermo probably felt guilty for not being able to protect the woman he loved. And Mr. Garcia clearly felt guilt. He'd said he'd come here later than his sister. Her whole life was here, whereas he'd had a life in Colombia. Not that that made the idea of being ripped from your home any easier. Ripped from your child.

I thought about the article @MarisasMama had sent me the link to and the ICE raid. Maybe it wasn't Nessa who was involved. I pivoted my attention to the decidedly un-grieving widower. Cliff Renchrik. Could he have been behind the ICE raid?

I dismissed the idea as soon as it fully formed in my head. That made no sense. He employed undocumented people, so why would he do anything to send them away? All that did was deplete his workforce.

My head pounded with contradicting information. I came back around to Sylvia and Guillermo, and their little girl. I felt for this little family and the hole that was there without Sylvia.

Chapter 12

"The ICE raid was in the news," I said to Miguel. We stood side by side in my kitchen. He used tongs to place grilled chicken on two plates, followed by a spoonful of rice, while I tossed the salad I'd made. I thought about the link @MarisasMama had sent me. "I mean it's definitely there, but it was pretty buried."

"Sounds like they kept it on the down low." He carried the plates to the table.

I sliced half a loaf of a baguette I'd picked up from Yeast of Eden on my way home from my visit with Guillermo Cabrera, and brought it, and the salad, to the table. We sat down, but I wasn't very hungry.

The article @MarisasMama sent me had been from Santa Lucia, a neighboring town. "Why wouldn't our paper report it?" I mused, referring to the *Santa Sofia Daily*.

"Maybe it did, Ivy. Maybe we just missed it."

Or maybe it was because the *Daily* was notoriously

un-journalistic. They didn't really investigate things; they just reported feel-good pieces that supported the community. There was a place for that, but not at the expense of the actual truth.

Miguel had a forkful of chicken and rice halfway to his mouth when I asked, "How about a scandal at Chavez Elementary School a few years ago? Does that ring a bell?"

He stopped, grains of rice falling back onto his plate. "Oh yeah. That was crazy."

I tore off a piece of bread and dipped it in a dish of olive oil. God, it was good. A baguette didn't have a lot of ingredients, but getting the bread right so that it was soft and luscious on the inside and crunchy on the outside could be tricky. Olaya did it perfectly every time. "Tell me," I said.

"There was a new teacher. Young. Latina. Freshly minted teaching credential. Her first year, I think. It didn't come out till the spring of that school year, but she'd been bullied for more than half the school year."

How horrible. "Students bullied the teacher?"

He popped a chunk of bread in his mouth. "No, that's not what happened. She wasn't bullied by students. It was teachers."

I almost poked a finger in my ear. Had I heard him right? "Wait. What?"

"Some of the teachers at the school bullied this new teacher. I don't remember what they did, exactly, but I remember it was pretty bad."

"So not the students."

He shook his head as he tore off another hunk of bread. "Nope. Other teachers."

I couldn't even imagine. What if something like that

had happened to my mother when she'd taught at Santa Sofia High School? Or to Mrs. Branford. I shook away the very idea. No one would mess with Penelope Branford. "So what happened?"

"It was a few years ago. I think the teachers lost their jobs—"

I couldn't stomach any more food, but I sipped the Sangiovese red Miguel had poured. "I would hope so."

"What would that have to do with Sylvia Cabrera or Nessa Renchrik?"

Being a person of interest in a murder hadn't diminished Miguel's appetite. He shrugged as he finished up his meal. "Maybe nothing."

But it wasn't nothing. Katherine Candelli and Margaret Jenkins-Roe had talked about it. It had to mean something.

Miguel and I finished our dinner, then went for a walk on the beach. A little salt air to clear the mind. At least that's what I'd hoped for, but my mind was beyond clearing. I kept coming back to the bullied elementary school teacher. Could Sylvia Cabrera and Nessa Renchrik have been involved in some way? And how had Sylvia ended up working for the Renchriks?

Something about the situation and the lack of information about the scandal felt very fishy. I wanted to know more.

Like all schools these days, the entrance to Chavez Elementary was firmly locked and armed with a buzzer. No one was getting in without being explicitly buzzed in. I pressed my finger against the button, and a moment later the door clicked and I was able to pull it open and enter the vestibule. Glass doors straight ahead led to the interior of the school, but they also were locked. From where I stood, I could see through the glass doors into the school. The walls were covered with student work, and cool bulletin boards celebrating learning.

To the left was the front office. A posted sign read: *All visitors must check in at the front office.*

I entered, my eyes instantly drawn to the patchwork quilt hanging on one wall. Each block represented a character trait like thoughtfulness, honesty, and honor. At first glance, this was not a place I would have associated with adult bullies masquerading as teachers.

The woman sitting at the front desk looked at me. She had beautiful black skin, long braids with a few pulled back and clasped behind her head, and large hoop earrings. She wore a wraparound cobalt-blue dress that, even from her seated position behind the counter, accentuated her curves. She was the perfect face for the school with her warm smile that extended up to her eyes. The placard on her desk said: Miss Jackson.

"What can I do for you today?" she asked.

I'd come up with a story on the drive over and now I launched into it. "My name's Ivy Culpepper. I work at Yeast of Eden, the bread shop downtown? We're one of the sponsors for the Spring Fling this weekend."

Miss Jackson brought her hands together and her smile, unbelievably, grew bigger. "Of course! We're so excited you all are sponsoring one of the booths this weekend."

I did a mental head slap. Of course! The Miss Jackson before me had to be the same woman who'd tapped Olaya to sponsor a booth at the Spring Fling.

"I adore Yeast of Eden!" she continued. "When you

have challah? And with the poppy seeds? Oh man, that stuff is dangerous."

"I know exactly what you mean," I said with a smile. "Dangerously good, though."

She laughed. "You got that right."

The door from the school's hallway opened and a young woman came in. She was petite, with a short pixie haircut, olive skin, and a tentative smile. Her body was stick straight with no hint of a waist or curves. From the back, she looked like she could be one of the sixth-grade students. "Miss Jackson?" she said, her voice as tentative as her demeanor.

The receptionist turned her full-wattage smile to the young woman. "Whatcha need, Miss Betancourt?"

At Miss Jackson's warmth, the woman, Miss Betancourt, visibly relaxed. "Julian Krazinski's mother is coming to pick up some work for him."

"Is that boy out sick again?" Miss Jackson rolled her eyes heavenward.

Miss Betancourt answered by stepping closer to the counter Miss Jackson sat behind. She held out a thick goldenrod envelope. "There's enough work in there for today and tomorrow. If she asks."

Miss Jackson took it and set it next to her keyboard. "You got it."

Miss Betancourt thanked the receptionist and scurried back out into the hallways of the school.

Miss Jackson looked back at me with arched pencil-thin brows. "I had to be on my deathbed for my mama to excuse me from school. Nowadays, all it takes is a fake cough or a tiny little sniffle. Good lord, kids today."

"Parents today," I added, because it was the permissive parents who let the kids get away with their shenanigans.

Miss Jackson chuckled and grinned at me. "Snap! You are right about that."

I looked toward the hallway Miss Betancourt had disappeared into, as if she'd left a trail of stardust and I could trace it with my eyes. "She seemed very nervous. . . ."

"Who?" She followed my gaze to the empty hallway. "Oh, you mean Miss Betancourt?"

"Yes. A little bit scared of her own shadow."

Miss Jackson frowned. "There was an incident a few years back. It, um, really affected her."

Oh wow. Was she referring to the bullying scandal? Was Miss Betancourt the victim?

"You mean the bullying scandal?" I asked, my eyes wide and innocent. "That was horrible."

"That doesn't even begin to describe it. Poor thing's still as skittish as can be."

"So that was the teacher that was bullied by other teachers? That is such a crazy story. I think about it sometimes and I still can't get over how bizarre it was."

Miss Jackson picked up a thick-walled stainless-steel tumbler and sipped from the rubber straw sticking out of the top. "You got that right. Those teachers were something else." She leaned toward me a little bit, though the raised level of the desk was still between us. "You never woulda suspected that group of the horrible things they did, either. Low-down and dirty."

I laid my forearms on the top level of the desk and clasped my hands together. "How did they get away with it?" I asked.

Miss Jackson lowered her voice to a whisper. "There

was a group of 'em, and they convinced her that they were just a snapshot of the rest of the staff. Poor thing was so scared, she didn't know if she was comin' or goin'. She almost quit teaching for good. That woulda been sad, too, 'cause she's a good teacher. In the classroom with those kids, she comes alive. I wouldn't believe it, but I've seen it with my own eyes."

"What about the teachers who did the bullying? What happened to them?"

"That lot? They lost their jobs and their teaching credentials. Miss Betancourt didn't press charges, although personally, I think she should've."

I did, too, but maybe she just wanted to put it all behind her. Couldn't fault her for that. Now that I had Miss Jackson talking, I hoped she'd keep going. "Sylvia Cabrera was here around then, wasn't she?"

The receptionist drummed her fingers against the envelope Miss Betancourt had given her. Her voice returned to full volume. "Sylvia Cabrera. Sylvia Cabrera. Sylvi—" She slapped her open palm down on the envelope. "Of course! I remember her! She's the one that got Miss Betancourt to finally say something about what was going on."

"Oh, that's right," I said, playing it off as if that little tidbit had been buried in my mind somewhere.

"If I'm remembering right, her daughter was in Miss Betancourt's class? I think? Anyway, she heard about the bullying through the grapevine, or, I don't know, maybe she saw it firsthand. I really don't know about that. But when it didn't stop, she marched right on in here, met with Miss Betancourt, and reported what was happening to the principal and to one of the school board members." She raised her pencil-thin eyebrows again. "The one that just died. Nessa Renchrik. Now *that's* another sad situation. She was just here last week." She lowered her voice. "The day before she died, if you can believe it. She stood right where you are."

My eyes popped wide. A second connection between Sylvia and Nessa, and another person who'd seen Nessa the day before she'd died. "That's crazy. Why was she here?"

At this question, Miss Jackson rolled her eyes. "Trying to make it look like she cared about this school. Playing the part, you know?"

"She didn't? Care, I mean?"

Miss Jackson shook her head. "Not the constituency she cared about, if you get my meaning."

I wasn't sure I did.

"A lot of the parents here can't vote."

Ah. I understood. Nessa Renchrik didn't care about Chavez Elementary School because it didn't benefit her career. "Have you heard anything about the murder?" I asked.

"Only what the news is saying, and I think they're trying to keep it on the down low. She was a piece of work, though. That, uh, situation with Miss Betancourt? Ms. Renchrik tried to control it. She somehow did manage to keep it out of the papers. I still don't know how she did that, you know? The district, too. They managed to hush it up."

Nessa must have called in some favors to keep it quiet. "So, Sylvia was kind of like the whistle-blower?"

"That's exactly what she was. Ms. Renchrik, she was not a happy camper, let me tell you. If she could have unblown that whistle, she would have."

"Guess it didn't look good for her, since the school's in

her district?" I asked, but really, I didn't understand. It wasn't like Nessa had been one of the bullies. If the school district and the board dealt with the situation, I'd think that would make them all look good in the end. And Sylvia was gone, so she couldn't have killed Nessa, even if she'd had a motive. Which, if she had, I couldn't see it.

I kept spreading the gossip to see what other information Miss Jackson would cough up. "Ms. Renchrik must have got over it. I heard Sylvia worked for her."

From the way she reacted, though, Miss Jackson hadn't heard *that*. "No, really?!"

An explanation suddenly popped into my head. What if Sylvia had asked for a better job—one other than the labor-intensive housekeeping—and Nessa gave her one . . . in return for her silence? To keep the story about the bullying from spreading too far and wide? "I think she became her personal assistant. That's what I heard anyway."

A buzzer sounded. Miss Jackson looked past me to the entrance of the school, then pressed a button. A moment later, a delivery driver wheeling a stack of boxes on a dolly came in.

Miss Jackson flipped a braid behind her shoulder and batted her long eyelashes. "How you doing, Kyron?"

"Doing great, Misty. How you?"

Before she could answer, a door to one of the interior offices opened and a man dressed in a suit, his tie snug around his neck and his ash-blond hair brushed to one side, came up to the reception desk.

Kyron, the delivery guy, deposited the boxes against one wall. He gave Misty Jackson a smile, then turned to leave. "See ya next time."

She wiggled her fingers at him. "You sure will, baby."

"Misty," the man in the suit said. "Would you give me a hand? We've got to get the Spring Fling notices out to teachers before two thirty. They need to be counted and distributed."

"Sure thing, Mr. Davies." She stood to follow him but stopped suddenly and turned back to me. "You needed somethin'. About the Spring Fling?"

I waved her off. "Oh no. It's okay. I'm good."

She tilted her head and this time, instead of going up, her eyebrows pulled together as her brow furrowed. "You sure?"

"Nah. I'm good. I'll see you there, though?"

"You better believe it! My little boy? He'll be the one zipping around like a banshee. Don't say I didn't warn you."

I laughed. "I'll be on the lookout for him."

"Okay, Miss . . . Ivy, was it?"

I nodded.

"Okay then, Miss Ivy. See you Saturday."

I hoped so, because I liked Misty Jackson. And she'd given me food for thought.

Chapter 13

After my visit to Chavez Elementary School, I went home, made a batch of popovers, and sat at the kitchen table with my laptop open. Agatha lay stretched out on the floor by my feet.

I'd decided my next step was to figure out who the political donor was that Nessa Renchrik had met with the morning she died. I tore a popover in half and slathered it with plum jam from a local farm. Bread, coupled with something sweet, had a way of soothing the soul.

It only took a few minutes to track down the Renchriks' home number. I was only slightly surprised they had one. Nessa had been a public figure, so it made sense she'd have a landline with a number separate from her cell and her husband's business. I dialed, it rang once, and a boy picked up with a tentative, "Hello?"

"Oh, hi," I said, surprised at hearing a real voice. I'd half-expected to get an answering machine. I immediately regrouped, placing the young voice with a name. "Is this Tate?"

"Yeah. Who's this?"

"My name is Ivy. I spoke to your dad a few days ago at your house."

"Oh."

"I was there with my friends. You came to the door as your dad was leaving?"

"Oh yeah."

He wasn't a chatterbox, that was clear. He'd probably been ingrained with the idea that you don't talk to strangers. "Your dad, he was going to work when we left, I think?"

"Maybe. To one of his properties."

"Right, right. Something about Sylvia, I think." I was fishing, and part of me felt guilty for trying to get information from a child, but I had no choice.

"Syl—?"

There was a scuffle and a female voice came on the line. "Who's this?"

I recognized the voice right away. "Rachel?"

"I said, who is this?"

"Ivy Culpepper. I met you the other day at your house? I was talking to your dad with my friend—"

"The hot guy. I remember."

My eyebrows shot up. "Right."

"My dad's not here."

"I'm sure he's dealing with a lot right now."

Silence.

I tried again. "I just have a quick question for you. Do you know Sylvia Cabrera?"

Again, silence.

"Rachel?"

Crickets.

I tried again. "Did she work for your mom?"

"Yeah. Why?"

"I just learned that she was deported. I, um, I didn't know if you knew that."

Rachel gasped. I could picture her putting one hand over her mouth. "Deported? You mean sent back to Mexico?"

"Colombia, actually. And yeah. Sent back."

"That can't be right."

"I spoke to her husband. It's right."

"But my mom and dad, they would have told us."

Her reaction raised a red flag. Why would her parents have told her about Sylvia? "Did you know her pretty well?"

"She babysat Tate sometimes when Carmen was off duty, and she was kind of like our cook. Plus, she worked for my parents' company."

"I thought she was your mom's assistant."

"Yeah. Household assistant."

So a glorified gofer? I slathered more plum jam on my popover and took a little bite before answering. "I mean I know she worked for the business. I just didn't know she worked at your home, too. When did you last see her?" I asked.

She fell silent for a beat before answering with, "It's been a couple of months. End of February, I think? My dad said she went on a vacation."

The timeline according to Rachel fit with the February 23 raid.

Her voice cracked. "I guess. . . . After Carmen, I should have. . . ."

She trailed off, ready to beat herself up for not knowing. "You couldn't have known," I said. "Did you ever meet Sylvia's husband?"

"No," she said. "Why?"

Good question, but I couldn't explain that Guillermo Cabrera and his daughter with Sylvia were shouldering a huge loss. That little girl could use a friend, I thought.

"Who are you?" Rachel asked. "I mean why do you care about Sylvia?"

I'd been waiting for this question. "I work at Yeast of Eden, the bread shop in town? We are one of the sponsors for the Spring Fling. We want to do a small memorial for your mom at our booth—"

"What does that have to do with Sylvia?"

"We just have a mutual friend and I just found out Sylvia worked for your parents, that's all."

"Okay. So? You're doing something for my m-mom?"

Once again, her voice faltered as her emotions took over. Candace Coffey's comment about Rachel missing important time with her mother came back to me. Rachel might be a senior and close to graduation, but she was still just a girl—and now a girl who'd lost her mother. "We are. I'd like to invite you to be there."

"Saturday?"

"Right. The Spring Fling starts at noon on Saturday and Sunday. We thought we'd have a few people speak in a little tribute to your mom starting at one o'clock on Saturday."

"Tate should come?"

"Absolutely. And your dad."

She made a guttural sound. "I don't know if he will."

"Oh?"

"He and my mom weren't getting along very well when she died," Rachel said.

"I'm sorry to hear that," I said, though in truth, I was glad to have a little inside information. "Is there anything I can do? I can invite him myself?"

"No," she said quickly. "I'll do it."

"Rachel, can I ask for your help with something?" There was a pause before she answered. "Okay."

"I heard your mom met with a political donor. I'm wondering if you know who it was. I'd like to extend an invitation to the memorial."

"You mean Joseph Patrick?"

An alarm bell in my head went off. Any connection to Lulu Sanchez-Patrick? "That's it. Thank you." I wanted to find out one more thing before I ended my call with Rachel. "What did your mom do the morning she died?" I asked her.

She hesitated. "Why?"

"Your mom and I have a mutual friend. We're just trying to work out what happened, you know? It's been really upsetting."

"Mmm." I could picture her staring out a window, zoning out.

"Rachel?"

She snapped back to attention. "Yeah. Um, I don't know. Whatever her and my dad always do. They fight. I spent the night at my friend Ronnie's house. When I got home, she was already—"

She broke off, but I knew what she'd been about to say. By the time she got home from her sleepover, her mom was already dead.

"Why weren't your mom and dad getting along?" I asked, hoping I'd built enough of a rapport with Rachel that she'd keep talking.

She gave a heavy sigh. "Me going to college. Something with Tate. Their business. Her politics. You name it. They fought about everything, all the time."

Not the makings of a happy marriage, I thought, and like a game of Whac-A-Mole, Guillermo slipped back into his hole and once again Cliff Renchrik popped out, rising back to the top of my list of suspects.

"Thanks, Rachel. I'll see you Saturday?"

"Sure," she said, and we hung up.

I considered the information I'd come away with. Strife between Mr. and Mrs. Renchrik. Silence about what had happened to Sylvia Cabrera. And the name Joseph Patrick. I had to wonder if he was related to @Marissas Mama. If so, it would certainly put her animosity toward Nessa Renchrik in a new light. Maybe Cliff Renchrik would slip back into his hole and someone else would pop up as the most likely suspect

Chapter 14

Nessa Renchrik's funeral took place on Friday. The Lutheran church, St. Anne's, was two streets down from Yeast of Eden. I'd driven around the block, thinking I'd find a spot in the church parking lot, but it was overflowing. I circled around, left my car in the back lot of the bread shop, and walked back to the church. I spent most days in jeans, leggings, or some other easily laundered pants and an equally casual top, and had sneakers or flats or some other comfortable shoes on. Today, however, I'd donned a black skirt that hit at the knees, a gray blouse, and two-and-a-half-inch heels. They put my feet in an unfamiliar position to begin with, but walking a few blocks while wearing them made them scream. By the time I got to the entrance of the church, I was already counting the minutes till I could get back home and kick off the heels.

Based on the lack of parking available, I'd expected the sanctuary to be full. Full to bursting was more like it. Nessa Renchrik's funeral was a star-studded event—if you counted the muckety-mucks in Santa Sofia as stars. From where I stood at one of the doors between the vestibule and the sanctuary, I could see the entire school board was there, members of the city council, a local representative, people on the board of the Chamber of Commerce, and so many others who, from their nicely appointed suits and tailored dresses, looked to be important people.

The front pews were reserved for family and the rest of the seats looked to be taken. It was standing room only. I moved to the right side of the church, working myself into a spot between two people. I looked over to see whose space I'd invaded and stared. "Dad?"

My dad stared right back at me. "Ivy?"

We spoke at the same time: "What are you doing here?"

My dad had been through the wringer since my mother died. Only recently had he begun to smile again. His sallow skin had started to absorb the sun and he had color in his cheeks. He'd even gained back some of the weight he'd lost, due, in no small part, to his frequent visits to the bread shop. Like I had, he was making his way through every one of Olaya's offerings. His grief was still there, inside him, but he had decided it was time for him to live again. The only lasting outward effect of his loss was the graying of his hair. He'd gone from dark hair to silver fox. There was no going back, but it suited him well.

My dad didn't like the fact that I seemed to have a propensity for crime solving. My telling him that I was digging into Nessa Renchrik's death wouldn't sit well with him. Here, at the victim's funeral, seemed like the wrong setting for such a discussion. "An old high school friend is on the school board. I thought I'd support her," I said. "How about you?"

My dad lowered his voice. "Comes with the job."

My dad was City Manager, so I guess it made sense that he might have interactions with the school board. "Did you know her?"

He paused for a beat before saying, "Let's just say we had a few interactions."

What I heard was code for: "Any interaction we had was not pleasant."

The service was distinguished, with accolades for Nessa being spouted by everyone who spoke.

"She was a leader in our community."

"A prominent voice has been silenced."

"She had a vibrant career."

As I listened to each person who spoke at the funeral, and afterward at the reception, what stuck with me was the fact that not a single comment was about her as a person. No one said she was well loved, or that she had been a friend to the students in the school district, or even that she'd be missed. I thought again of Candace and her telling me that there was a line of people who might have wanted to do Nessa in. I'd come to believe that one hundred percent.

Santa Sofia didn't have a convention center, but it did have a lovely historic grange hall. The Renchrik family held the reception after the funeral there, catered by a local business. My dad and I stood side by side, each of us holding a glass goblet of iced tea—unsweet—and a napkin. I was saving my appetite for the bread I'd have at Yeast of Eden when I went to retrieve my car, and my dad said he had dinner plans. When I was growing up, his business dinners once a week, or so, were common occurrences. I was glad to know he was getting out and completely back in the swing of things at his job.

"So, tell me," I said to him.

He glanced around to make sure no one was close enough to eavesdrop. Satisfied that the coast was clear, he said, "She made my life miserable, truth be told. Always calling or emailing about this or that or the other thing. 'There needs to be a park on the south side of town.' 'Why can't this area be zoned commercially?' You name it, she wanted to be part of it. It's in poor taste to say it, but she was a thorn in my side."

Selfishly, all I could think was that I was so glad Captain York didn't know how much Nessa Renchrik irked my dad or he might be right up there at the top of the person of interest list next to Miguel. We talked for a few more minutes before my dad said, "Time to go. Coming?"

I debated, not sure if I'd be able to learn anything useful from a room full of politicians, but at that moment, I saw Candace across the room, goblet in hand. She was talking, rather animatedly, I thought, to a man and a woman. She swung her free arm out and her head moved around making her look a touch like a bobblehead.

"No," I said to my dad. "I'm going to go talk to Candy. My school board friend," I added when he raised his eyebrows in a question.

He leaned in to kiss my cheek but ended up whispering in my ear. "I know what you're doing. Be careful, Ivy."

I never could fool him. I squeezed his hand and gave him a smile. "Always, Dad."

He slipped out and I started across the hall. As I got closer to Candy, I recognized her companions from seeing them at the district office—and from their photos on the district's website. They were the two of the four school board members I hadn't actually spoken with yet: Jerry Zenmark and Margaret Jenkins-Roe. Margaret was short like Candace, but where Candy was in the Mrs. Claus school of plump, Margaret looked like a strong wind could snap her in half, and that her bones would break with a brittle crack. Skin hung from her arms revealing the shape of the bones underneath. Her hair was blond, but unlike Candy's, which was curled and fluffed, Margaret's hung in strands that looked like they might never be completely clean. Sunken cheeks, bulging eyes, and thin lips. Poor Margaret did not look healthy. She also didn't look particularly grief stricken.

She looked to be in her early sixties, but I thought it was possible that she was actually younger than that. Jerry, on the other hand, looked younger than he probably was. I put him in his early forties, but he looked more like late thirties. He was tall and lanky, and he wore black slacks, a gray button-down, and a dark gray blazer. He and I were twinning. His thinness, compared to Margaret's, looked completely healthy. He had an oval face with deep-set brown eyes, skin that had been sun drenched— probably from running or cycling—and brown hair shorn close to the scalp. I wondered if he and Nessa had been allies.

"Candace," I said as I came up to their small group.

Candy started, clearly surprised to see me. "Ivy? What are you . . . I didn't know you'd be here."

I just smiled and she held her hand out to the board members, palm up. "Jerry. Marge. This is an old friend from high school. Ivy Culpepper, these are two of our school board members. Jerry Zenmark and Margaret Jenkins-Roe."

"So nice to meet you both. You do such great things

for our community." They both smiled. Jerry dipped his head in a nod. "I'm so sorry for your loss," I said, holding my breath as I waited to see if Marge showed any sign of recognition. I thought my identity had remained hidden after my near miss with Katherine Candelli in the restroom, but I couldn't be one hundred percent sure. Maybe Katherine had hidden somewhere and waited to see who came out of the restroom. She'd definitely been suspicious. Or maybe she'd somehow caught a glimpse of me when I'd been following her. Had she mentioned my name to Marge?

I exhaled. Apparently not, because all Marge said was, "Thank you," while Jerry Zenmark said, "I'm still getting my head around it. Quite a shock. Really, quite a shock. She was a powerhouse. Hard to imagine a person like Nessa suddenly not being here."

"I'm sure she was a huge asset to the school board."

Jerry muttered under his breath, but not quietly enough that we didn't all hear. "Yeah. I lost my vote because of it."

"Your vote?" I asked just as Candy dipped her chin and glowered at him. "Jerry."

He held up a hand and bit his lower lip. "Sorry. My bad. Poor taste."

I waved away the apology. "It's okay. I didn't know Nessa. I'm just here for moral support. I'm sure there is huge gap on the board now. What happens to her seat?"

"I'll become president," Candy said. "We'll appoint someone to fill her seat until the next election." Jerry opened his mouth and started to speak, but Candy interrupted him with a hand in the air. "No, Jerry. The technology funding passed. Your surfing program is tabled. We voted. It's over."

I looked from Candy to Marge to Jerry. "Technology for Chavez Elementary?" I asked.

Jerry turned his full attention to me. "You are up on school board business?"

I gave him what I hoped was a fetching smile. "Just a bit."

"We had an important item on the agenda at the school board meeting Tuesday. Kids spend far too much time on devices and in front of screens. We don't need more of that in schools. We need them out doing things. Being active. It was Nessa's passion project."

"The vote didn't go Jerry's way," Candace said with a grimace. "It's all in the public record."

"You-all didn't understand the issues," Jerry said. "There are grants you can get for more computers. Tech companies want their products in schools. Tap foundations. That's what they're for. But our after-school activities need district support. District funding. Nessa understood that. She fought for this."

Candy held up her hand to him. "We're not debating this again. The vote was three to one. Even if Nessa was here, it wouldn't have passed. It's over."

Jerry's nostrils flared as he exhaled. It didn't look like it was over for him. He directed his gaze at Marge. "Is that right, Margaret? Would Nessa have lost?"

Marge swallowed and her eyes bugged more than they did naturally, but she didn't answer.

Jerry kept at it. "She had your ear at the Communities in Schools dinner."

"Jerry!" Candace snapped. "Enough."

Jerry snapped his mouth shut, but not before I filed away the information that Nessa had been working over

Marge the evening before she'd died. The Whac-A-Mole game continued. Here was yet another person who'd had a sketchy interaction with the woman just before her death.

Across the room, someone waving their arms caught my attention. It was Mei Masaki. Terry stood next to her. I waved back, then held up one finger. I wasn't quite done with Candy, Marge, and Jerry.

They, it seemed, however, were done with one another. When I turned back to them, Jerry was walking away, Marge was near tears, and Candy looked like she could throttle someone. I decided to leave them be. "I'll see you later, Candy. Nice to meet you, Marge," I said. As I glanced at Jerry's back, he turned his head and caught my eye. He dipped his chin in a single nod. I nodded back before weaving my way through the mourners to Mei and Terry.

Mei wore a simple black wrap dress. Her hair looked like a shimmering sheet of black satin. Terry wore a dark gray suit. Just as it had been at the wedding, his hair was parted in the middle and had a gentle wave in it.

"Didn't expect to see you here, Ivy," Terry said after a hug. "Did you know Nessa?"

I felt like a broken record as I said, "No, just here for moral support."

Mei arched one brow but didn't remark. She knew I had something else on my mind. Maybe she hadn't told her husband about my visit to the district office and our eavesdropping on the superintendent and the intrepid reporter who'd come to visit.

"How are the honeymooners?" Terry asked. "Have you heard from them?"

I scanned the room as I answered. "I got a few texts from Emmaline, but otherwise no. I'm sure they're having a great time."

"Have you heard anything more about Nessa?" Mei asked. "Did you talk to that reporter?"

Terry looked from his wife to me. "What?"

"Ivy stopped by the office the other day to see the superintendent."

"She was wrapped up with a journalist, so I never got the chance." I left out the fact that I'd talked with McLaine in the parking lot and she'd clued me in about the donor. I turned and searched the crowd again, wondering if he was here.

"Are you looking for someone?" Mei asked.

"Joseph Patrick. Do you know him?"

It wasn't Mei but Terry who answered my question. "I know who he is. He's in finance. Involved in state politics. He's a pretty big player, in fact. Backs politicians who will fight for education issues."

"Why do you ask?" Mei asked.

"I was hoping to talk to him. He met with Nessa the day she died."

Once again, Mei arched a brow, and looked at her husband. "How do you know that?"

I shrugged. "Just through the grapevine, you know?"

"He was going to back her senate bid," Terry said. He scanned the room. "I saw him earlier."

"There he is!" Mei pointed to the door leading out of the Grange Hall. A tall man with graying hair and a receding hairline stood in front of the exit talking with someone. I realized a second later that it was Candace. Perfect! She'd introduce me.

"Thanks. Good to see you both," I said, giving both

Terry and Mei quick hugs before I hurried away from them and toward the exit.

My feet ached in my heels, but I gritted my teeth and pushed through the crowd. Once I got close enough for her to hear me, I raised my hand and called out. "Candy!"

Both Joseph Patrick and Candy turned toward me. "Ivy," she said. "You're everywhere, aren't you?"

She sounded a little irked. I smiled and shrugged. "Running in the same circles lately." I looked up at her companion expectantly.

Candy seemed to realize she had to introduce us. "Ivy, this is Joseph Patrick. Mr. Patrick, this is an old friend of mine. Ivy Culpepper."

With some people, you get an immediate impression of who they are and what they're about. Joseph Patrick came across as a high-powered *don't mess with me* type. His dark eyes bore into me and made me want to take a step back. I held my ground.

"A pleasure," he said. "How did you know Nessa, if I may ask?"

"I didn't actually. Friend of a friend."

"Ah."

I plunged ahead. Why not? "I understand you were going to donate to her campaign? I hear she had the potential for a great political career ahead of her."

I wasn't sure what response I expected from Joseph Patrick, given the animosity of Lulu Sanchez-Patrick, aka @MarissasMama, but all he said was, "I was. She had potential. It's the skeletons that do you in." He turned to Candy, said an abrupt good-bye, and gave me a nod before walking away.

How very cryptic. We stared after him as he walked out the door. "What did he mean by that?" I asked.

Before she answered, Candy surveilled our surroundings. No one was within earshot, so she said, "He was going to donate to Nessa's campaign till he found out she and her husband have had undocumented workers work for them over the years. She might have been able to overcome it, but he didn't think so. He withdrew his support."

I thought of Sylvia being deported, again wondering if Nessa could have somehow had a hand in it. But getting rid of their workers didn't change the fact that they'd used them in the past, so why would she bother? "Why did he come today if he withdrew his backing?"

"He's a decent guy, and very much a humanitarian. He didn't support her, but he can still pay his respects to the dead, right? Plus, he's a board member of Communities in Schools. People like him have to make an appearance."

It all boiled down to the PR. I had a sudden thought. Maybe Nessa hadn't known some of their people were in the United States illegally. Was the crew that took care of their management properties paid under the table? I thought about the tension I'd heard about between Cliff and Nessa. Cliff seemed to be in charge of Seaside Properties. Maybe he'd found the workers and Nessa had been in the dark. Maybe he'd thought it would never come to light—until his wife decided to run for public office.

I thought about the woman I'd seen at the Renchriks' home. Rachel had called the housekeeper Fernanda, but Cliff had called her Carmen. Had that been an automatic response, calling out the name of a person so ingrained in the mind? An idea hit me. What if Carmen had been the housekeeper before Fernanda? Could she have suffered the same fate as Sylvia?

Another thought came to me. What if Nessa had only found out about the undocumented workers recently? Maybe getting rid of them was payback to her husband for ruining her career? If that was the case and he'd found out, could he have simply snapped? Miguel had said it, and I knew it was true. Always look at the spouse. Cliff popped back up as prime suspect.

As I drove home, I thought about this new scenario, but my thoughts drifted to my conversation with Jerry Zenmark and Margaret Jenkins-Roe. If Nessa had been at the school board meeting, would the funding for the technology upgrades have passed, or would the vote have gone to her and Jerry's pet project? Margaret was the swing vote, and Nessa controlled her. If Nessa hadn't died, would she have pressured Margaret into voting her way? Jerry certainly seemed to think so. That led me to another question. Why was Nessa against technology in the schools in the first place? It only helped to better prepare students for a future in a society filled with technology. By not being offered that pathway, those students were put at a disadvantage.

And surfing? Sure, it got kids out in the sun, but it was hardly going to give them an edge in their future careers. Marge seemed completely incapable of handling any object that could kill a person, and she was so brittle looking, I doubted she had the strength to do the deed.

There were just too many potential suspects.

I almost slammed on the brakes when another idea hit me. Candy said she would now become the school board president. Was that enough of a motive to kill Nessa Renchrik?

Chapter 15

The afternoon sun was setting as I walked along the beach, Agatha trotting by my side. I'd ditched my heels from the funeral the second I'd gotten home and changed into sweats, a hoodie, and sneakers. So much better.

Pinks and oranges and streaks of blue painted the sky like an airy watercolor. The temperature had dropped and the breeze had picked up, pushing locals and visitors away. They'd left the beach just for me. I walked down to my favorite rock formation near the pier where Baptista's Cantina and Grill was already busy with the dinner crowd. This part of the beach had been my mother's favorite spot, and it's where I still came when I wanted to feel close to her. Now, as I struggled to make sense of what had happened to Nessa Renchrik, I could hear my mother's voice in my head. *You'll find the answer, Ivy. Don't give up.*

But there was a big problem with that advice. The

issue wasn't that there was no clear path leading to Nessa Renchrik's killer. The problem was that there were too many paths. And so far, I had not been able to shut down any trail leading to Miguel. Candace had been right when she'd said there was a line of potential suspects. She was now one of them . . . and I hadn't even gotten to the hairdresser yet. The suspects were coming out of the woodwork. I wondered about the strife between Nessa and Cliff. Candace had all but said that Tate might not be Cliff's son. Had that fact come to light? Could Cliff have killed his wife over her infidelities and the betrayal of bearing another man's child?

I just didn't know.

The ocean breeze kicked up a notch and the sunset did not bring me any clarity, so I headed home. Miguel was working at Baptista's tonight, so I was on my own with my thoughts. With Agatha laid out at my feet, I perched on the stool at the bar in my kitchen. When I'd first seen the old Tudor house, I'd fallen in love with the kitchen. A brick arch over the stove highlighted the professional range and the window there overlooked the front yard. The island, where I now perched on a barstool, had a reclaimed oak countertop. It was hard to pick my favorite thing about the space, but the wood counter might just be it. Pale yellow cupboards were distressed by time, but they were functional and complemented the rustic wood floors.

This was my comfort room where I baked, cooked, worked, and lived. At the moment, I had the back end of the Yeast of Eden website open. Sometimes, I'd found, distraction was the best solution. If I let my mind process on its own, a solution might just surface. I was hoping my brain would solve the problem of who killed Nessa Renchrik while I thought about bread.

The first thing I did after coming in from my walk was call the Renchrik house again. I didn't care if Rachel or Tate answered. I just hoped it wasn't Cliff who picked up the phone. I was in luck. After three rings, a voice I now recognized as that of Nessa's daughter said, "Hello?"

"Hey, Rachel. It's Ivy Culpepper. From Yeast of Eden? I just wanted to remind you about the Spring Fling tomorrow and the memorial."

"Oh. Yeah. Hi." Rachel didn't sound pleasant exactly, but also not unpleasant. "One o'clock, right?"

"Right."

She gave a tired sigh, like she was exhausted by life right now, but she said, "Okay."

"Rachel, before I go, I was wondering about your nanny."

"What about her?"

"It's just, your dad called to someone named Carmen the other day when I stopped by. But I only saw Fernanda. . . ."

I trailed off, hoping she'd pick up the story. After another pause, she did. "Carmen was our nanny. For a long time."

"Oh. That makes sense, then. He was just used to saying 'Carmen' and it slipped out."

"Probably."

"When did she leave?" I asked, raising my mug to take a sip of the hot tea I'd made.

She heaved another sigh, but this one was a little shaky. Emotions seeping in, I thought. "February."

I spat out the tea from my mouth, sputtering.

"Are you okay?" Rachel asked.

I recovered, setting my mug down and wiping my

mouth with the back of my hand. "Yeah. Fine. My tea was too hot. You said February?"

"Yeah."

"Where did she go?" I asked.

Rachel was difficult to talk with. Heavy pauses dotted the entire conversation. There was no easy back-and-forth. Whatever rapport I thought I might have developed during our last conversation had dissipated. Finally, she said, "I don't know." Pause. "And then Fernanda came. She heats up the casseroles."

I laughed. "Yeah, that's handy."

There was another awkward pause. "You've been through so much, Rachel. I'm so sorry."

She sniffed and drew in a ragged breath. "Yeah."

"I'll see you Saturday, okay?"

"Yeah," she said again; then the line went dead.

Alone with my thoughts, I wondered about Carmen. February 23 was the date Guillermo had said his wife had been picked up for deportation. Was it a coincidence that both Carmen and Sylvia had gone away in February? They were both connected to the Renchriks. Could they both have been picked up in the same sweep? I had a hard time believing it was happenstance. It pointed a solid finger at Nessa's being part of it.

As I pondered this, I added a new blog post to the Yeast of Eden site, inviting families with schoolchildren in Santa Sofia Unified to come to the Spring Fling on Saturday and Sunday, where we'd be showcasing a brand-new focaccia Olaya had created. Next, I went to the bread shop's Instagram feed and uploaded the artistic photos I'd recently taken of slices of layered babka and one of a bread case, the camera focused on the corner of a skull cookie peeking out from amid a blurred pile of dinner rolls. I pressed Share just as my doorbell rang. Agatha's head instantly popped up.

"It's okay," I said, bending to scratch her behind the ears before heading to the entryway, my cell phone in hand. My front door was wood and iron with a window cutout at the top. I rose to my tiptoes and my stomach dropped as I caught a glimpse of Captain York's feathery hair practically glowing under the porch light. Oh boy. A visit at home could not be good. Before I answered, I quickly texted Mrs. Branford: *Call me in five minutes.*

I cracked the door open. "Captain."

"Ivy."

Again with the informality. It irked me.

He glanced over my shoulder. "Mind if I come in?"

"What's this about?" I asked.

"I have a few questions for you."

My heart beat heavily in my chest. I didn't know this man from Adam. Wasn't it irregular for the police to pay an unexpected visit to someone at night? I wondered if my text to Mrs. Branford was enough. If something went wrong, an eighty-six-year-old woman was not going to be able to save me.

But, I reasoned, Emmaline had hired Craig York and put him in charge of criminal investigations. She must have seen something in him that had earned her trust and confidence, despite her concerns when she left for her honeymoon.

"Ivy?"

Making up my mind, I stepped back and held open the door, closing it again after he came in. He wore the same cowboy boots he'd had on at the wedding and when he'd popped in unexpectedly at Miguel's house. Same khaki pants with crisply pressed lines down the centers of the legs. Same button-down shirt. Same navy windbreaker with "Santa Sofia Sheriff's Department" printed on the back. "What can I do for you?" I asked, sneaking a quick glance at my phone. No response from Mrs. Branford.

The smile he'd had for me when standing on my porch faded to a thin line. "I'll cut to the chase," he said. The exact words he'd used when he'd dropped by to talk to Miguel Monday night. "I hear through the grapevine that you've been asking around about Nessa Renchrik."

From the kitchen, Agatha barked. Any male voice alerted her to trouble. Evidence of the abuse she'd suffered in her early years.

"What grapevine is that?" I asked, standing across from him in the entryway. I folded my arms over my chest like a barrier to his bad juju.

"You mean besides seeing you at the district office the other day?"

"I have a friend on the school board."

"Mmm-hmm."

"What grapevine?" I repeated.

He seemed disinclined to answer any of my questions. Instead, he posed one of his own. "What are you doing?"

I looked through the archway that led to the kitchen. "Right now. Besides talking to you? I was working on the bread shop's website and social media." I knew perfectly well that was not what he'd been referring to, but I wasn't going to make this easy for him.

He grimaced. "Your boyfriend is a person of interest in this murder. You need to butt out of this investigation."

My breath caught in my throat. This was the first time I'd heard him say it aloud. If York thought that would get me to stop looking into what happened to Nessa Renchrik, he was absolutely insane. If anything, hearing that

Miguel was in his crosshairs made me want to dig deeper. Faster. Harder.

"Is that what you came to tell me? Because I can think of a lot of other people who should be of more interest to you than Miguel—"

"I'm not interested in your thoughts," he interrupted.

My chest rose as I inhaled. "They're solid, though. I'm following the clues, not trying to find clues to fit a stupid theory."

A purple vein suddenly popped in his temple, pulsing with his anger. "Butt. Out."

I feigned innocence. "I don't know what you're talking about."

He ignored the fact that I'd just said I was following clues. "The hell you don't. You've been making the rounds. Stopping in to grill Mr. Renchrik is not acceptable, nor is showing up uninvited to a funeral."

"Both times I was paying my respects," I said, but my heart was suddenly pounding and climbing from my chest to my throat. I couldn't tell him Emmaline *asked* me to butt in. And how did he know all my comings and goings?

"Butt. Out," York repeated.

Agatha heard the terseness in his voice. She started barking again. I could see that she'd stood up. She lifted her head as she barked, sounding hoarse and agitated at the same time. "It's okay, Agatha," I said. I looked up at York. "I think you should hear what I have to say."

"I am not interested. You are a civilian."

"But the sheriff—"

"The sheriff is not here at the moment. I am in charge of this investigation. Just because you don't want your boyfriend to be involved doesn't mean he's not. You'd be wise to be cautious."

My hackles rose. "Miguel doesn't have anything to do with Nessa's death! Look at the husband! They were not on good ter—"

He held up his palm to me. "Stop." The single word shot out like a bullet before I could suggest Candy or Joseph Patrick or any of the hundred other people who seemed to hate Nessa Renchrik.

The front door opened behind York, and Mrs. Branford's snowy head appeared, along with her cane. So, she *had* gotten my text. "Ivy?" Her voice was strong, with nary a flutter about. "Are you all ri—"

York spun around, cutting her off. "Who are you?"

Mrs. Branford had to tilt her head back to look up at him with a steely gaze. "Who I am is not important. What is important is that I am invited here. I think a better question is why are *you* here?"

York narrowed his eyes. "Wait a second. I remember you. From the wedding."

"Indeed. And I remember you. The sheriff's new hire."

A sound came from his throat. This guy was not happy being second fiddle to Emmaline. That message was coming through loud and clear.

"Captain York, if I'm not mistaken," she said, Mrs. Branford stepped all the way into the house but kept the door open. "And I see you're leaving."

York looked from me to Mrs. Branford, a scowl on his face. "I am, actually," he said to her; then to me he said, "This is not a request."

I got his meaning. It was an order.

An order I would not be listening to.

Chapter 16

I tossed and turned all night. Ten or eleven years. That's how long ago Miguel had dated Nessa Renchrik. I would have been twenty-six or so and living in Austin, married to Luke Holden. I had my own past, so why was Miguel's past bothering me so much?

And more than that, why would York think he was involved in her death after so many years? It didn't make any sense to me. I rolled over, sleep still eluding me, wishing Em and Billy were back from their honeymoon.

I was not single-minded like Captain York. Or at least my single-mindedness was only in proving Miguel's innocence. I was still convinced of it. We'd only reunited recently, but still, it was like no time had passed. We were connected from our past, and had forged a new path together into our future. I trusted him, so yes, I knew he was not involved with Nessa Renchrik's death in any way.

The only way to prove it was to find the actual guilty party. The next day and a half would be spent on the

Spring Fling. That left just the morning to visit Nessa Renchrik's hairdresser. I texted Candy to get the woman's full name, but all she could provide was the place she worked. Soho Salon. I debated making a phone call to see if I could finagle who had styled Nessa's hair from the receptionist, but in the end, I decided it was smarter to go in and ask in person. Nobody could hang up the phone on me that way.

Soho Salon was located just outside the historic district, so not too far from my house. Close enough to walk. I harnessed Agatha, locked the house, and headed off. Ten minutes later, I walked up the wooden ramp of the converted house and stood just inside the doorway. The reception area was the former living room of the home and was now a large open area. The reception station sat toward the latter half of the room. A table with a printer, lamp, and filing trays was against the back wall, turning the L-shaped desk into a U. Three ladder bookcases created a wall of shelving, which housed collections of hair products. The left side of the room had armchairs, a rack of handmade clothing made by a local designer, and a table adorned with handmade cards and jewelry.

The woman at the reception desk had long gray hair pulled into a side ponytail. She looked like she'd been beamed right out of the 1960s. "Can I help you, honey?"

"I hope so," I said. I'd spent the short walk over planning my approach. "Nessa Renchrik is a client here—you might have heard what happened?"

The woman nodded solemnly. "Yes. Quite a surprise."

Again with the odd response. "It is." I moved in, Agatha trotting right along with me.

"Oh, would you look at him!"

"She's a her, actually. Agatha."

"As in Christie?"

I nodded.

"Oh, what a sweet face."

I bent down and scratched Agatha's head and said, "You *are* a sweet girl, aren't you?" I looked back at the receptionist. "Is it okay . . . ?"

She stood and circled around the desk, coming over to me. "Absolutely. She's precious." She crouched down in front of Agatha but looked up at me. "May I?"

"Oh yeah, she's friendly." Except to the odd captain from the sheriff's department.

A woman in a black apron came into the front area from the hallway to the right. "I'm going to grab some coffee, Sunny. If my nine o'clock arrives, tell her I'll be right back."

The receptionist nodded to the woman. "Will do, honey." She cradled Agatha's head, rubbing the sides of it with her thumbs. To me she said, "Now, what were you saying?"

"I've always loved Nessa's hair. I need a cut, so I thought now would be a great time to finally use her hairdresser," I said to Sunny.

She gave Agatha a final pet and stood back up. "Sure thing," she said as she circled back around the big desk that served as reception and pulled up a calendar on the computer. "Oh. She came in early today for an appointment, but it was canceled," Sunny said. "Depending on what you need done, she can probably fit you in."

My brain whirled. A hair appointment was personal. I patted my mop of ginger curls. Did I need it styled? Highlighted? Chopped off? It *was* kind of a mess. I couldn't remember the last time I'd been to a real hairdresser. Since I'd left Austin, I hadn't taken the time to find one. I kept it pulled back in ponytail or up in a top-knot if it got too unruly. Which, I admit, was a lot lately.

"I think I need a consult."

"Sure thing, honey. Lemme go talk to her." Sunny disappeared down the hallway the other stylist had come from. Agatha lay down by the front desk as if she were the salon mascot. I left her to her slumber and went to look at the cards featuring photographs of places in Santa Sofia created by a local artist, then moved on to the hand-made candles. Patchouli was one of the most heavily used scents, but there was also lavender, papyrus, and evergreen.

"Hi," someone said behind me. "Sunny said you need a consult?"

I spun around. The woman before me had short blond hair and a headband with a little bow. She looked like a pixie. My gaze traveled down. A very pregnant pixie. She wore overalls embroidered with flowers that stretched over her round belly. Goodness, she was adorable.

And young. I placed her in her early twenties.

Once again, I patted my hair. "I think I do?"

"I had a cancellation, so if you want, we can talk about it."

Sounds great," I said. "I'm Ivy."

"Oh my God, I love your name! I'm Gretchen." She clapped her hands together. "So nice to meet you."

I immediately recognized that Gretchen was the type of person to speak in exclamation points. I'd never met Nessa Renchrik in person, but I suspected she was *not* an exclamation point kind of woman. The two women seemed like they'd be complete opposites. It made me wonder why Nessa wouldn't have just found someone else. "Nice to meet you, too. Can I bring my dog back?" I nodded to Agatha, still asleep.

"Leave her with me," Sunny said. "I'll take good care of her."

I hesitated, but Agatha was completely comfortable, and I hated to rouse her. "If you're sure . . . ?"

Sunny fluttered her hand in front of her. "You go on. Me and Agatha, we'll be just fine."

Gretchen waddled as she led me down the hallway, past a washing station on the right, a bathroom and cutting stations of the left, and through an open area with chairs fixed with helmet hair dryers. Her station was in the very back of the salon. A window overlooked a grassy area, the sidewalk, and the street beyond. Sheer panels fluttered from the fresh air. I removed the hairband that kept my hair in a topknot as I sat in the salon chair. Gretchen stood behind me and ran her hands through my hair, tugging gently on the knots my curls tended to form. She looked at my reflection in the mirror in front of us, which served as a divider separating her space from the hairdresser behind it, her smile stretching across her face. Her hands were clasped and resting on her bulging stomach. "You have *beautiful* hair. Absolutely gorgeous!"

"Oh." I felt myself blush. "Thanks."

She bent her head to examine the ends. "Tell me what you're thinking, Ivy."

"Well, I've always debated cutting it short, but I think it might just stick straight out to the sides if—"

Her hands fisted around locks of my hair. "You cannot cut it! You can't. People would kill for hair like yours."

Not that that was a good reason to keep it long if I didn't want to, but I smiled, flattered. No one had ever been so enthusiastic about my untamed mop. "Oh. Well. It was just a thought. I haven't had it short in a long time—"

"With good reason! It's perfect as it is."

I pressed my lips together for a moment processing the compliment. "A trim, then?"

Gretchen grabbed a white towel from a stack on the shelf behind her. She wrapped it around my shoulders and secured it with a metal clip. "Perfect. You don't need anything more than that." She pointed to the low shelf on the table in front of me. "You can leave your purse there. Let's go wash and condition; then we'll clean up the ends."

Okay, so it was happening now. I felt nervous but followed her. At the washing station, I sat in one of the black reclining chairs. Gretchen used a lever to raise the footrest and I leaned back, my neck supported by the horseshoe cutout of the sink behind me.

"I'm so glad I came in," I said.

"Me, too!" She sprayed warm water over my head, taking care not to spatter it on my face. "Are you a local?"

I closed my eyes as she guided the water to moisten every strand of my hair. "I am. Born and raised, although I was living in Texas for a long time. I came back here pretty recently."

"Well, I'm glad you came in! I love meeting new people. I'm kinda new here, too. I came to Santa Sofia about three years go."

"What brought you here?"

She smiled, a little dreamily. "We lived in Kalamazoo. Long way from here, but my dad brought me a few times when I was really little. I fell in love with this town then and always knew I'd come back."

That I understood. "I couldn't wait to get away when I

was younger. Sometimes you can't appreciate what you have until you leave it behind."

"Isn't that the truth?! That is a great piece of wisdom, Ivy! I'm going to remember that."

"I never knew this salon was here. I live in the historic district. I walked here this morning, in fact. I don't know how I missed this place."

"You discovered it now, that's what matters, right?" Gretchen pumped a dollop of shampoo into one hand, rubbed it together with her other hand, and began sudsing my head.

The head massage during a shampoo was, in my opinion, the best part of a salon appointment. I was after information about Nessa Renchrik, but Gretchen's magic fingers almost made me forget.

Almost, but not quite.

"That's right. I'm here now." I sighed, contentedly. Gretchen was a master shampooer, her fingertips, then her fingernails, moving along my scalp. I enjoyed it for a few minutes before I said, "Nessa Renchrik came to you, didn't she?"

Her fingers slowed for a beat, the pressure lessening before she caught herself and amped up again. "Yes. She did. Did you know her?"

Her voice had lost the built-in enthusiasm it had held a moment ago. No exclamation points. I needed to reassure her, so I didn't lose her. "No. No. We have a mutual friend, that's all. I told her I was looking for someone to do my hair. She mentioned you."

Gretchen's hands relaxed back into their movements, but she didn't say anything more about Nessa. I tried again. "Really tragic about her death."

"Mmm. Yeah," she said as she finished the shampoo,

rinsing it out with warm water before working in conditioner. "We'll let it sit for a few minutes," she said.

"How did you meet Nessa?" I asked, trying again.

Gretchen leaned her back against the wall and folded her arms over her baby bulge. "I remember that day like it was yesterday!"

I exhaled. The exclamation points were back. "Oh really. Why?"

"Rachel—that's her daughter—called to schedule the appointment. She wanted an updo for homecoming. The nanny brought her. Carmen. But she couldn't stay, so Mrs. Renchrik picked her up. She was not happy about it, either, let me tell you. I felt bad for Rachel. Mrs. Renchrik wasn't the type to yell, but she always had a way of making you feel pretty bad."

"Mmm."

"Carmen was a saint. And now Fernanda." She shook her head. "I couldn't do it."

"But Nessa started coming to you, so she liked you?"

Gretchen pushed off the wall and came back to the washbasin. She ran the water until it was warm, then rinsed the conditioner from my hair. "I wouldn't say that. Honestly, I don't think she really liked anyone. Definitely not me!"

"But my friend Candy, she said Nessa came to you for a couple of years. Why would she keep coming to you if she didn't like you?"

She hesitated before saying, "To be honest, I don't really know. She never seemed to like what I did to her hair and she always left me the crappiest tips."

I looked up at her from my reclined position. Was she holding something back? "Why did you keep taking her appointments?"

Gretchen patted her swollen belly. "I can't be choosy right now, you know?" She squeezed the excess water from my hair, wound it up in a towel, and led me back to her cutting station. "Look, she didn't like her own family. That first homecoming updo I did for Rachel, it looked good. I mean, it looked *gooood*! But Mrs. Renchrik hated it. She said it make Rachel look like fifteen going on twenty-three." She laughed. "Twenty-three like me! And Carmen. Poor thing. I got to know her pretty well. She always brought Rachel. Mrs. Renchrik never did. She only picked her up that once. Carmen did everything for Mrs. Renchrik, only to be deported. Mrs. Renchrik didn't lift a finger to help Carmen. Oh man, Rachel was so upset when Carmen left. So sad."

I thought about this as Gretchen finished towel drying my hair, then combed through it until it was tangle-free. I hadn't thought it was possible, but my estimation of Nessa lowered even more than it had already been. Estranged from her own family. More enemies than friends. Even if she'd had a part in it, she hadn't even pretended to help her children's nanny when she'd been picked up for deportation. I knew for a fact that Nessa Renchrik and I would never have been friends.

Gretchen got to work, talking all the while. She'd completely warmed up to the subject and didn't need any other prompting from me. "Sometimes I wonder if Carmen is better off now. I mean she didn't want to go back to Mexico, I'm sure. She was here for a long time. You know, she practically raised Rachel and her little brother. That's what Rachel told me, anyway. And then she was just gone. Can you imagine? She was just ripped from the life she'd made here. At least she didn't have to deal with

Mrs. Renchrik anymore. That's the silver lining, I guess, if there is one."

"How long had she worked for the Renchriks?" I asked.

"Oh wow. Since before Tate was born, I think. A long time."

Candy had said Tate was in fifth grade. That made him around ten years old. If Carmen had been with the family since before the boy was born, that was a long, long time. Gretchen was right. To be ripped from the family you'd worked for for so long would be heartbreaking. My thoughts drifted to Sylvia. She'd been torn from her own family, her job, the country she'd been raised in and called home. I sighed. There had to be a better way.

The hairdresser with the station beyond the mirror appeared out of nowhere with a client. Her chipper voice carried over to us.

"Hey, Ali!" Gretchen called.

Ali poked her head around the mirror and waved. She was tall and rail thin. Half her hair was shorn close to her scalp, but the other half, which started at a side part, was dyed pink and hung artfully down one side of her face, falling loosely over one eye. "Heya, Gretchen. How's little G doing?"

Gretchen laughed, glanced at me, and pointed to her belly. "That's what we call the baby. I don't know if it's a boy or a girl."

"Little G. That's for 'the Gymnast,' not for 'Gretchen,'" Ali said to me with a wink. "That baby does somersaults like you wouldn't believe."

Gretchen patted her belly. "Needless to say, I don't sleep much. But I don't mind!" She looked at Ali. "Full day for you?"

"Nope. Leaving at three today. Rendezvous with my baby daddy."

In the mirror's reflection, Gretchen's eyebrows arched. "Really? I thought he was out of the picture."

"He wants to be, but I'm not going to let him off the hook that easy. I got in touch with him." To me, she said, "He didn't want to have anything to do with us, but it's his kid, too, right?"

"Right," I said, loving the camaraderie here.

Gretchen clapped, bouncing on her tiptoes. "You go, Ali. You got this."

Ali winked at us both before ducking back behind the mirror and returning to her client.

Gretchen leaned down, her voice low. "No secrets in a hair salon."

"I guess not," I said with a laugh, hoping that would work in my favor.

A moment later, Gretchen began cutting my hair, combing through long strands, pulling the curls straight, then using her sharp scissors to trim the ends. Next, she angled her scissors down to thin each section.

Gretchen was very train-of-thought, talking about whatever came to mind. I sat back and listened, waiting for an opportunity to ask another question about Nessa. The pregnant hairdresser was the furthest thing from a murderer I could imagine, but it was possible she could shed some light on Nessa's life. Anything that could help direct me to the truth. She started talking about children, her pregnancy, and her boyfriend, who wasn't very interested in the baby they were having, then moved on to her apartment and the obnoxiously loud neighbors they had living over them. "They don't walk. They clomp." She dropped the strand of my hair she'd been ready to slide her scissors through and proceeded to stomp in a circle around me. "I mean, I don't sleep as it is, but how am I supposed to get any with them pounding on my ceiling like that all the time?"

That would be tough. I felt for her. "Have you talked to them about it?"

"Yes! I've tried. Hasn't done one bit of good. I have to say, I ask every one of my clients about this dilemma thinking that maybe someone will have a brilliant idea." She frowned.

"No?" I asked.

"No."

She went back to my hair, finishing up the last of the trim. "Ivy! It's done. I'm going to use a diffuser to keep your curls —"

"Ivy?" a voice called. "Ivy, is that you?"

I knew that voice. "Mrs. Branford?" I said, raising my voice above Ali's from the next station and the din of hair dryers, chatter, and other salon noises that permeated the air.

"Let me help you," a woman said with a slight accent, but Mrs. Branford's voice said, "I'm perfectly fine, Yasamin, but thank you." I could picture Mrs. Branford waving Yasamin, who I assumed was her hairdresser, away. A moment later, Mrs. Branford appeared from around the corner. Her thin white hair was wound around small curlers lined up in neat rows on her head. Her lime-green velour lounge suit was half-hidden under a navy styling cape. Her pristine white shoes practically glowed. "Ivy Culpepper. Speak of the devil."

My smile faltered. Mrs. Branford did not speak randomly. "Speak of the devil" meant she'd been discussing something related to me, presumably with Yasamin.

Gretchen had just said there were no secrets in a salon. I hoped Mrs. Branford wasn't spilling any of mine. "Oh?"

Mrs. Branford smiled, her lips thin but amused. "Yasamin is a former student."

"Who isn't?" I said with a laugh. To Yasamin, I said, "Nice to meet you."

Yasamin pulled a chair forward for Mrs. Branford and guided her into it. "You are at the bread shop," she said. "And a little detective, too, right?"

Her accent, heavy with stressed vowels, was from somewhere in the Middle Eastern region. Persian would be my guess. Iranian. The skin of her forehead was pulled taut and had a sheen to it. I couldn't detect a single smile line at her eyes. Botox, I thought. Her dark hair had a burgundy wash over it. I placed her somewhere in her fifties, but I couldn't pinpoint early, middle, or late. She came across as hip and younger than she was.

"That's mostly right," I said.

"And important to the sheriff, this lady says." She grinned at Mrs. Branford "This one is your biggest fan. I have heard so much about you. So much."

I shot Mrs. Branford a look, but she just bent her head forward slightly and patted her curlers. "Yasamin, how you do go on," she said, but to me, she added, "You are too modest, my dear."

Gretchen's eyes popped wide. She stood back, her hands once again clasped over her round belly. "You're a detective?"

I fluttered my hands. "No, no, I'm not. I'm a photographer and I work at the bread shop. That's it."

"Pshaw," Mrs. Branford said, a proud grin on her face. "You have helped the sheriff time and time again."

"Only because she's my friend," I said slowly, hoping Mrs. Branford would get the hint to stop.

I hoped in vain. Gretchen picked up the conversation. She was no fool and put two and two together in no time flat. "Oh wow! You're trying to figure out who killed Nessa Renchrik, aren't you?" Her voice seemed to bellow throughout the salon.

Ali poked her head around the mirror wall again and looked at her friend. "That crazy bit—" She stopped herself just in time. "I mean, that woman was horrible to you. And you, of all people—"

Ali broke off when she looked at Gretchen and saw her eyes turning glassy.

It was true. You should be kind to your hairdresser. They kind of hold your life in their hands—at least until a bad haircut grows out.

"How was she horrible to you, dear?" Mrs. Branford asked. Her voice was sweet, but I knew she was gathering information. She knew I was worried about Captain York's laser focus on Miguel and she was on a mission to help me get to the truth.

Gretchen blinked away her tears and gave a little shrug. "It doesn't matter."

"Tell them," Ali urged.

Gretchen just shook her head. "It doesn't matter what she was like to me. She thought she was a good mother, but she wasn't. I thought she wanted me to help her understand Rachel. She'd talk a lot about her, you know? Like she was trying to prove she knew her daughter. That she loved her. How can you just ignore your own child?" She swallowed and swiped at her eyes. "Some people aren't meant to be mothers," she said, gently circling her hand over her belly, "but I'll be there for Rachel."

Chapter 17

Gretchen wrapped up my hair, giving me just enough time to speed walk home with Agatha, then race across town to the law offices of Brendall and Choken. They were a small outfit situated in a business park that also housed a physical therapy practice, a medical supply company, and a printing company.

Before I'd raced out of my house, I'd changed from the jeans and T-shirt I'd worn to the salon. Now, with my hair full of product, the curls controlled and in place, and wearing a pair of black skinny pants and a sheer floral-patterned blouse with a cami underneath, I felt ready to face Lulu Sanchez-Patrick.

The receptionist greeted me with a pleasant smile. "How can I help you?"

"I have an eleven o'clock appointment with Ms. Sanchez-Patrick," I said, matching her smile and raising her by exposing my teeth. "Ivy Culpepper."

She checked her computer. "I'll let her know you're

here. If you'd like to have a seat," she said, indicating the armchairs in the waiting area.

I thanked her and picked up a magazine before sitting. It was a current copy of *Newsweek*, the label addressed to the firm at this address. Impressive. Often, the address labels were either cut out or blacked out because the magazines went to a person rather than the company that later displayed them. Good to know that Brendall and Choken spent some of their clients' money to keep them entertained while they waited.

I flipped through the pages, stopping here and there to read a story or sidebar that caught my eye, but eventually replaced the magazine on the table and pulled out my phone. I called up my texting app and sent a message to Olaya. She was probably busy finishing up the daily baking and getting ready to start the prep for the Spring Fling. She might not see the text right away —or at all— but I sent it anyway: *At an appointment. I'll be in to help soon.*

To my surprise, three dots appeared, followed by a single-word response: *Bueno.*

I tucked my phone away just as the door between the waiting area and the offices opened up. A woman stepped out, her eyes zeroing in on me. She was curvy in all the right ways. She wore a slim navy skirt, pale pink blouse, and fitted navy blazer, along with high-heeled pumps. Highlighted streaks artfully flowed through her auburn locks. Frankly, she was gorgeous, and even with my newly trimmed and styled hair and the dressy clothes I'd changed into, I felt dowdy in comparison.

"Ms. Culpepper?"

I nodded and stood.

Her lipsticked mouth curved into a welcoming smile.

"I'm Lulu Sanchez-Patrick. You can call me Lulu. Come on back."

I tried to picture her together with her husband, Joseph Patrick. He was tall and graying, with piercing eyes. She was Eva Mendes in a suit. They were a power couple, through and through.

"And I'm Ivy," I said as I followed her back and into a small conference room with a rectangular table and chairs all around. A small table along one of the side walls held a telephone set up with more buttons than an airplane cockpit, two rows of unopened plastic water bottles, and a basket with snack goodies like granola bars, boxes of raisins, and fruit snack packs.

"Help yourself," Lulu said as she sat down and folded her hands over the yellow legal pad on the table in front of her.

I kind of wanted a pack of gummies, but I resisted and sat across from her empty-handed.

Lulu cleared her throat. "I have just fifteen minutes for a free consultation. From there, we can make an appointment with one of the firm's lawyers. Sound good?"

Fifteen minutes. I didn't have a minute to waste. I also didn't have a story concocted that would fool this woman. What I did have was the element of surprise. I would ask whatever I could before she figured out that I was on a fishing expedition. "Nessa Renchrik," I said. "She was a client here."

Lulu raised her chin. I'd been hoping for nonplussed, but she was cool as a cucumber. Her only tell was that her hands clasped tighter. "I am not at liberty to discuss our clients' cases."

"Oh, of course not," I said, but I took her non-answer

as an answer confirming my suspicion. "It's just that I'm wondering why you'd be happy she's dead."

Again, I'd expected a reaction of some sort, but Lulu Sanchez-Patrick was married to a politician and she worked for a law office. She was a pro. When she spoke, it was slowly and clearly, each word enunciated, every consonant pronounced, an emphasis on each and every word. "I am certainly not happy that Mrs. Renchrik is dead."

I smiled sweetly and cocked my head to one side. "But you are @MarisasMama on Twitter?"

Her lips parted and her eyes opened wider. I'd shocked her, but her physical reaction was a blip that she corrected almost instantly. Eyes back to normal. Mouth drawn into a tight line. She pressed her hands against the table and stood, the movement shoving her chair backward. "I think you should leave, Ms. Culpepper."

I kept my gaze steady on her and said, "Ding dong, the witch is dead."

She stared at me, and this time her composure did break. Her breathing grew audible and her nostrils flared. She was rattled. "What?"

"A few nights ago, you tweeted: 'Ding dong, the witch is dead'—"

"I would never—"

I channeled Mrs. Branford and tsked, wagging my finger at the same time. "Ah, Lulu, but you did. You told me she was just another politician and that she didn't really care about the kids in Santa Sofia. You said she had people in her pocket."

She pulled her chair under her and sat back down. Her voice dropped to a hiss. "Who are you?"

I answered her question with one of my own. "Do you know who killed Nessa Renchrik?"

Her beautiful olive skin paled, making her brick-red lips look stark and unnatural. "Are you with the police?"

"No," I said.

Her eyes narrowed. "I don't believe you."

The first thing that came to mind was that she had something to hide. And didn't police officers have to answer honestly when asked directly? Otherwise it would be coercion. "I'm not a police officer." I didn't add that Captain York would be beyond furious if he found out I was still digging around. "Do you know who killed Nessa Renchrik?" I asked again.

"Of course not."

I rested my forearms on the table, clasping my hands together. "Did you kill her?"

She leaned in, mirroring my posture. "Of course not."

"Okay then."

Realization hit her. "You're Ivy Baker."

It took her longer than it should have to figure that out. I nodded. "I am."

She looked me up and down, as much as she could given I was sitting. "You don't look like you bake."

"I do. I swear. At Yeast of Eden."

Her eyes opened wide again, but this time it was because I'd said the magic words. Yeast of Eden had that effect on everyone. "The sourdough loaves there are dangerous."

I smiled. "I hear that a lot."

"You must not eat what you bake."

"I do. How could I not? Olaya is amazing."

"I've heard about her."

"She's taught me everything I know."

Lulu leaned back and folded her arms over her blouse and blazer. "What do you want?"

"Someone killed Nessa. I want to find out who."

"You're not the police, and you're not related to her?"

"No, and no."

She still looked skeptical. "So why do you care?"

I had no idea if she or her husband was involved, but at this point, I needed her to trust me. To know that I was telling the truth. "Because the police think someone I know is involved."

This time she cocked her head at me, and her smile turned into a small smirk. "They think someone you *know* killed Nessa Renchrik? Friends with murderers?"

"My friend is not a murderer and I'd rather not get into it," I said, "but I *am* trying to figure out what happened to her."

"Well, I don't know anything about her death," she said. "When I saw her at the Communities in Schools dinner, she was perfectly fine."

I inhaled and braced myself before asking the next question. "But your husband met with her the morning she died?"

The words hit her like a sucker punch to the gut. Her voice dropped to an accusatory whisper—as if I'd been the one to meet with the woman hours before she died. "How do you know that?"

Of course, I answered her question with my own. "Has he been questioned?"

"Joseph had nothing to do with that woman's death. She was vile. It's true, neither one of us are grieving a loss here, but he was not involved."

"And you?"

She met my gaze head-on and scoffed. "I was not involved, either."

"What was their meeting about that morning, Nessa and your husband?"

She was silent for a moment, debating how to answer that question. She sighed and lowered her arms, her hands in her lap. A breaking down of the barrier she'd erected. Was she going to tell me the truth? "He had planned to back her senate bid. He was going to endorse her and be a campaign donor."

So far this was nothing I didn't already know. "And?"

"And then he found out that she and her husband were operating some part of their business, mmm, outside the law. Nessa would not have passed the vetting process. She had skeletons."

"Meaning what?" I asked, but I thought I knew the answer. Joseph had used the same word and had implied that the old bones in Nessa's closet had done her in.

"Like I said, she would have been called out during vetting. A state senator should be above reproach." I opened my mouth to offer myriad examples of elected officials who were the exact opposite of above reproach, but she held up a hand to stop me. "Don't bother. I know the scum exists. But Joseph won't put his name behind someone he doesn't respect and who doesn't have integrity."

"And because Seaside Properties uses undocumented—"

"Look. He believes in immigration reform. And he believes in human rights. What he doesn't believe in is someone in a position of authority, especially in politics, subverting the law for their own benefit. Joseph wants to back someone who will tackle immigration reform with compassion and fairness, not someone who speaks out of both sides of her mouth."

"Okay, so your husband withdrew his support for

Nessa. Did he tell her that morning? The morning she died?"

Lulu shook her head. Emphatically. "No! He'd already told her. Then she called and said she wanted to see him. When I told him, he said he had nothing more to say to her, but he changed his mind. He agreed to meet with her out of courtesy."

Once again, the situation seemed to warrant the victim having a motive to kill the suspect rather than the other way around. If Joseph withdrew his support because of some failing on Nessa's part, that would give Nessa a motive to retaliate against Joseph. Joseph, on the other hand, would have no reason for killing Nessa. He was the one in the power position.

Unless, I thought, she'd reacted badly and launched herself at him, forcing him to react—killing her to stop her attack.

I drummed my fingers against the table. It was possible.

Lulu Sanchez-Patrick sat with her spine straight and her neck tight, veins popping along either side. Where was this tenseness coming from? Something she'd said a moment ago slid to the front of my brain. "You said you talked to Nessa?"

Her shoulders rose like a defensive move. "I didn't say that."

"Yes. You did. Just a minute ago you said Nessa called and wanted to meet with your husband again. You said you told him, but he said no."

She swallowed. "He was in the shower. I answered his cell phone."

"When was that?" I asked.

"Saturday morning. We were getting ready for a brunch event. Joseph ended up missing it to go see her."

"How did she sound when you talked to her?" I asked.

Her eyes flicked up to me. "What, do you mean did she sound like she was going to be murdered that afternoon? She sounded fine. As snippy as ever. When Nessa wasn't *on*, you know, playing the part of the caring politician, she was horrible."

"But she was trying to get your husband to back her. She wasn't polite to you?"

She gave a scornful laugh. "No. It's like she had a certain amount of niceness. She wasn't about to waste any of it on me when I wasn't the one she was trying to woo."

That seemed odd to me. As Joseph's wife, it seemed to me, Lulu wielded a lot of power that Nessa would have wanted to harness rather than alienate.

"Don't think too hard on it. Nessa Renchrik was a model of contradictions," Lulu said, seeming to read my mind. "School board member who supposedly cared for the kids in the district but didn't lift a finger to help out the kids in her own sphere—"

"What do you mean?"

"Look. Her daughter and my daughter were in the same grade. They were friends, but Nessa put a stop to that back when they were in third grade. At that point, Joseph wasn't in a position to help her. He was a public defender with no donor capacity or political presence. She dismissed us, and so she dismissed our daughter."

A vibe was coming off of Lulu—that of a woman scorned. A chill swept up my spine. Another player in the Whac-A-Mole game. Was I sitting across the table from a killer?

Chapter 18

Back at Yeast of Eden, Felix Macron and his crew were still buzzing around the kitchen. As always, he wore a white chef's shirt. It had three-quarter sleeves and buttons running up the right side of it. His belly was looking even rounder then it had been a week ago. Felix was an amazing baker and he liked to partake of all he baked. I couldn't blame him. It was all so good.

His hair was shorn close to the scalp and his light eyes were a glorious contrast to his black skin. A dimple etched into his cheek as his face lit up with a smile when he saw me. "Ivy!"

We did an elbow bump in greeting. "You're here late, Felix," I said. Normally he was gone by late morning. It was almost one thirty.

"The Spring Fling waits for no one."

"Indeed, it does not," I said. I looked around the busy kitchen. Olaya had extra bakers working to get the regular Friday restaurant orders complete while we also worked on the Spring Fling offerings.

"How are we doing?" Olaya called from her office off the side of the kitchen.

Felix and I moved to the doorway. She sat at her desk, pen in hand, making notes on a pad of paper. She had her apron on, legs crossed. A wide black-and-white scarf was wound around her head, the ends tied into a knot under one ear. She wore wide-legged black pants and a gray short-sleeved T-shirt. How she managed to wear black and not have it covered with flour dust was a mystery to me. She always looked fresh and clean and as if she'd just arrived for the day, but I knew she'd already spent hours in her commercial kitchen working alongside Felix before I'd arrived.

"I've got the steak rolls for Sofia's Steakhouse rising," Felix said. "Working on the star bread next. Five full stars, and twenty-five star points to wrap and sell separately."

Olaya nodded her approval. "Fillings?"

"Keeping it simple. Strawberry jam."

"Perfect," she said with an approving nod.

"And we're doing the van Dough focaccia, right?" I asked.

"And the hot cross buns," she said. "We will need an early start tomorrow to finish the baking first thing and set up at the festival."

As if we'd synchronized our next movements, the three of us scattered to our prep stations. I started rolling out the focaccia rounds from the already-prepared dough.

Three hours later, the rest of the crew was gone, but the three of us were still hard at work. Usually the bread shop was prepped for the next day and locked up by four o'clock. Not today. The van Dough focaccias took time. I printed out several pictures to use as models for the vegetable placement. Piece by piece, the focaccias became stunning representations of the Dutch postimpressionist painter's work. Olaya and I even got creative enough to make a rendition of his field of irises.

While Felix worked to finish up the star bread, we covered each and every tray of focaccias—and there were many—with plastic wrap, moving them all onto racks in the walk-in refrigerator. I stopped to stare at the baking that lay ahead of us in the morning. It didn't even include the overnight hot cross buns. "Will we be able to get it all done in time?" I asked.

"I'm coming in at three thirty," Felix said, a grin on his face.

He might be the only person on the face of the earth who'd feel excited about starting work at that ungodly hour. I couldn't deny it, though. He was definitely happy. Or even giddy.

Olaya patted his back. "He is a good boy." She looked up at him. "You are a good boy."

I laughed. Felix was a twenty-six-year-old man and I was beginning to realize that Olaya loved him as a son.

"We'll get it done," Felix said, answering my question more directly.

Looking at him, I knew we would. I only wish I felt as confident about exonerating Miguel and finding Nessa Renchrik's killer. I wondered if her death would cast a pall over the Spring Fling. We'd see tomorrow.

"We will make the dough for the hot cross buns. It will rise overnight; then we will bake on in the morning before the event," Olaya said to me. She looked at Felix. "Go home. Get some rest."

He covered the star bread trays, slid them onto the rack in the refrigerator, and checked to make sure he'd cleaned up his station before heading out.

Alone in the kitchen, Olaya and I set to work on the hot cross buns. Just hearing the words sent me back to my childhood. I hadn't had one since my mother had made them when I was probably thirteen or fourteen years old. There were a lot of stories regarding the history of the buns and the marking of the cross on top. From spring festivals in pagan Britain where the cross was said to represent the four seasons, to a twelfth-century Anglican monk who marked the buns with crosses to represent Good Friday, to the story of a widow in England who hung a marked bun on her door every Good Friday until her son returned home from a sea journey, the spiced sweet rolls had become a symbol of spring and were said to bring good luck to any baker who made them, and to everyone who ate the buns that baker prepared.

Olaya believed in the long-rise method of bread making. Apparently, the same method was used with her hot cross buns. The dough would slowly rise in the refrigerator overnight and they'd be ready to bake first thing in the morning.

"I haven't photographed either the hot cross buns or the star bread. I'll do that tomorrow and add the pictures to the website."

"*Bueno*," she said. She retreated to her office and returned, handing me an envelope.

My paycheck. I smiled, grateful for it. My hours at Yeast of Eden helped fulfill my desire to bake bread, but they also helped me make ends meet while I built up my photography clientele. "Thank you."

She smiled, her eyes sparkling as she silently communicated what we both felt. We were the family we'd chosen for each other.

I folded the envelope and tucked it into my back pocket. Leaning against the stainless-steel workstation, I gathered up the front of my apron in my hands. "I've been thinking a lot about Sylvia Cabrera."

"*Pobrecita*. And her daughter, left here without her mother. It is a shame."

I knew firsthand what it meant to lose a parent. Guillermo and Sylvia's child, as well as Rachel and Tate, would feel the effects of their loss for the rest of their lives. I tried to swallow down the lump that rose from my gut to my throat, but it remained firmly in place. I didn't know if I could trust it, and I didn't know how, but my gut was telling me that Sylvia Cabrera's story was intertwined with Nessa's in a way I didn't yet understand.

I put my thoughts to the side and set to work, following Olaya's lead. She was all about small-batch preparation whenever possible. We worked at our respective stations, starting by making the sponge by warming milk in the microwave, then adding sugar, yeast, and whole wheat flour. We let our sponges sit until they became bubbly, meanwhile whisking the butter until it was fluffy, then adding the rest of the milk, brown sugar, cinnamon, nutmeg, and eggs. After mixing the sponge into our respective bowls, we added the rest of the flour, stirring until we each had a stiff ball of dough.

Next came my favorite part the kneading. Something about curling my fingers into the soft dough, folding and turning, folding and turning, was meditative. As I worked, I realized the logical next step in my secret investigation.

We let our doughs rise as we started the next batch.

Finally, we rolled the dough into twelve-inch logs, divided each log into eight equal portions, and shaped each portion into a ball. We finished placing them in greased round pans, covering them, and sliding them into the refrigerator to rise overnight.

Olaya looked at me and smiled. "You have come a long way, Ivy."

Wasn't that the truth. When I'd first met her, I'd been standing outside Yeast of Eden not knowing my future lay just inside. I'd been more than a little lost. Olaya, as they say, read me like an open book. She'd brought me into her kitchen, and I'd been by her side ever since. She'd introduced me to the tradition of long-rise bread baking; to the joy of digging my hands into a bowl of dough and kneading out the tension in my both my head and body; to the magic of bread.

I was forever changed.

"You've taught me well," I said.

She handed me a loaf of lemon poppyseed bread. "For you," she said. "Go home. It will all sort itself out."

I hoped she was right.

Chapter 19

The blacktop at Chavez Elementary was pulsing with spring energy. Tables ran along the perimeter, at least half swathed with pastel tablecloths and ribbon. One section was devoted to food, with some of the tables piled high with cupcakes, brownie bites, and the like. Another section was for the town's crafty people. Scented candles, fabric face masks, wooden handmade toys, and an array of other goods were being sold. The district had rented booth space as a way to fund the event, and the people of Santa Sofia had stepped up. Olaya had paid for the highest level of sponsorship, which meant the bread shop had a primo placement. There was not an empty spot by the time Maggie, who was close to graduating from Santa Sofia High School and worked most afternoons—and whenever else Olaya needed her—showed up.

Maggie brushed a strand of her dark hair from her face. She tightened her ponytail, then stood, hands on hips, waiting for me to direct her. We had an hour before the Spring Fling officially began, but moms, dads, and plenty of kids were already milling around.

Felix had come by earlier and set up the large rectangular table for our goods, but I'd sent him home. He'd been up since well before dawn. The rest of the day was in my charge. I'd draped the table with a pale green cloth and unwound a roll of wide burlap ribbon. Once the platters and stands of breads were set up, I'd arrange it artfully around the breads, placing a few decorative Easter eggs and Olaya's requisite skull cookies as the finishing touches.

"I unloaded most of the stuff from the van," I said to Maggie. "We just need to unpack it and set it all up."

"Gotcha." Maggie looked at me and did a double take. "Your hair."

I had a hairband on my wrist to pull it into a topknot, but I'd been waiting till the last minute. Even after being slept on the night before, my hair still looked pretty good after Gretchen's cut and style. "Oh yeah. I got it done yesterday. Trimmed."

"More than that," Maggie said. "It looks so good." She stretched her hand out toward me like she wanted to touch it but dropped it again. "It looks so soft. Perfect curls. Who did it?"

Instinctively, I patted my ringlets. "Gretchen at Soho Salon."

"Where's that?"

"It's in the historic district near—"

"Did you say Gretchen did your hair?"

Maggie and I turned to see a smiling woman standing just behind us. She was tall—close to six feet, I'd venture—and had short naturally graying hair in a sassy, flippy style. She was fit—I assumed from the outdoor exercise that had given her her bronze color. "Yes. At Soho."

"Pregnant? Cute as a button?"

"That's her."

She clapped her hands together. "I love her! She gets me. Gives me the short cut I want without making me look masculine."

"I need to try this Gretchen," Maggie said. "Sounds like my mom'll love her."

"Your mom'll love who?"

Once again we turned, this time to see Taehyun Chu, Maggie's boyfriend, walk up. He was a relatively new cameraman for a local TV station and the two had met when Yeast of Eden had been featured on a new food-centric show. Tae had dark hair, which he parted and swept to one side. His long sideburns and dark clothing made him look much older than he actually was. I'd placed him at twenty-five when I'd first met him, but he was only twenty. Still a few years older than I would have liked for Maggie, but Tae was a nice young man who treated her well.

Maggie lit up when she saw Tae, slipping her arm through his. "Ivy's hairdresser." She went up onto her tip-toes and kissed his cheek. "Hi, bube."

A faint blush tinted Tae's cheeks. If it was possible, it made him look even more handsome. He whispered something in her ear, and she giggled.

I reached into the bin of the knickknacks I'd brought and fished out the Yeast of Eden sign. It was the final touch to finish decorating the table. I held out one end of the banner to Maggie, but the very tall gray-haired woman who was Gretchen the hairdresser's biggest fan stepped up and took the other end, leaving Maggie to canoodle with Tae.

"How long have you been going to Gretchen?" I asked as we attached the banner to the front of the table. The Yeast of Eden logo was in the center of the banner. Artistic line drawings of a variety of breads were on either side of the logo.

"Oh, gosh, two and a half years, I guess?"

"So you must have crossed paths with a lot of her other clients," I said. Possibly Nessa Renchrik?

"Sure. Gretchen's a master at scheduling. Efficient with her time. She'll wash and style one client while someone else's color is processing."

I made a deliberate show of pulling out the framed photograph of Nessa Renchrik that I'd printed off the Internet. It wasn't the best quality, but it would serve its purpose. I found a spot on one end of the table and propped it up.

The woman, whose name I still did not know, watched me, then zeroed in on the picture. "What's that about?"

"Do you know her?"

"Oh yeah. She was one of Gretchen's clients. I saw her last week at the salon. I was coming in as she was leaving. You'd think she'd just run a marathon."

"What do you mean?" I asked.

"Her face was beet red. And Gretchen was worked up. She had to take a mini break before she did my hair. That is not like her."

A red flag shot up. "What day was that?"

"Friday," she said.

I pinched my eyes shut for a second. Friday. Nessa Renchrik had been to see Gretchen on Friday. Gretchen hadn't said a word.

"Why do you have her picture there?" the woman asked instead of answering my question.

I turned to look at it, thinking again how Nessa had had a knack for making more enemies than friends. "We're doing a little memorial for her today."

She started to respond but stopped when someone called, "Carol. There you are!" Another tall gray-haired woman with a short cut came up beside the woman who I now knew was Carol. The resemblance between them, from the bumps in their noses to the bows of their top lips to their height and build, was uncanny. Sisters. Maybe even twins.

Carol pointed to the photo of Nessa Renchrik. The sister looked at it, then met Carol's eyes in some sort of silent communiqué with raised eyebrows and dipped chins.

"There's going to be a memorial for her," Carol said.

The sister scoffed, derision dripping from her face. "Why?"

Carol turned to me, her eyebrows lifted now in a question.

I looked from one to the other. "We just thought it would be a nice thing to do for her kids."

Carol spoke, the same disdain as on her sister's face coloring her tone. "She didn't care about our kids. I don't even think she liked her own, so why should we care about them?"

Wow. I wasn't quite sure how to respond to that. Turns out I didn't have to, because Carol's sister flashed her a warning look.

Carol gave a nonchalant shrug. "Debbie has a little more compassion than I do."

So now I had the names of both sisters. What I didn't

have was why they had so much contempt for the dead school board president. I looked at Carol. "Evil?"

"Through and through," she said. "She claimed to be about equity and support for all kids? No. Just no."

"What do you mean she didn't like her own kids?"

"The boy, at least."

I closed my eyes and waggled my head like I was clearing out the dust. "I don't understand."

Carol looked down at me from her six-foot height. "I heard it from Gretchen. You know, hairdressers are like bartenders. They get all the good gossip."

I remembered what Gretchen had said about there being no secrets in a hair salon.

"She never wanted another kid. Then came the boy. What's his name?"

"Tate," I said.

"Right. Well, according to what I've heard, she got pregnant, but of course, being an aspiring politician, she didn't have any option but to keep the unwanted baby."

Debbie shook her head. "Poor kid."

I couldn't take what these women were saying as one hundred percent truth, but I wanted to flesh out more gossip. I lowered my voice to a conspiratorial level. "I heard that Tate might not be her husband's."

"Of course he's not. Have you seen him? That kid is Hispanic."

My heart dropped to the pit of my stomach. I hadn't gotten a close enough look at Tate, but these women clearly had.

"Which doesn't make a lot of sense, right?" Debbie said, bringing me back. "The woman never supported equity. Never cared about things being equal for all the kids in the district. I mean, a surfing club? How elitist is that, especially when this school doesn't have some of the basic technology the other schools have."

"She totally ignored Chavez," Carol added. "I haven't seen her here in forever."

Something clicked into place. "Are you a teacher here?"

"Fifth grade going on twenty-five years now," she said. She turned to her sister. "Debbie works at Richardson Elementary. Big difference in support, right?"

"Oh yeah. Nessa was at my school once a week like clockwork—"

"And here at Chavez maybe once a year. *Maybe.*"

I read between the lines. Chavez didn't have the *right* kind of kids.

"As long as the kids that looked like her"—Carol wagged her finger between us—"like all of us, succeeded? That's all she cared about. Forget about all the others."

"But you said her son—"

"People get off on having something they shouldn't."

Debbie nodded. "I saw her once with a guy. God, so long ago, but I remember his face. She was so mad. I thought her head might explode, and he kept trying to calm her down. I could hear him. He was breaking up with her, and it was like she couldn't believe he'd have the gall, you know? Like she was so much better than him, so how could *he* be the one dumping *her*?"

"When was this?" I asked after an exhalation.

Debbie looked up. Her lips moved and I knew she was counting back the years in her head. "Ten or eleven years ago?"

I swallowed down the nerves that flooded my system. Had it been Miguel Debbie had seen with Nessa? He had said he'd last seen Nessa—or Vanessa—when they'd gone to a bookstore. He hadn't said they'd fought, though. Had he told me the truth? My mind went to Captain York and his focus on Miguel. He'd told me, in no uncertain terms, that Miguel was one of his primary suspects and that I should be cautious. My head fogged and suddenly I realized why he was so convinced Miguel was involved in Nessa Renchrik's death. I did the math. Ten or eleven years ago Miguel had dated Nessa. Tate was around ten.

Was it possible . . . ?

Could Tate Renchrik be Miguel's son?

My head felt hot and icy cold at the same time. I was going through the motions, but my mind was not on the booth at the Spring Fling. Olaya showed up, took one look at me, and pulled me aside. "What happened?"

If something had happened, it had been ten or eleven years ago, between Miguel and Nessa. But had it? Did Miguel have a son? And if he did, did he know about it? I couldn't even say it aloud to Olaya, as if uttering the words would somehow make them a more real possibility.

"Nothing. I'm fine," I said.

She looked at me with wide eyes and skepticism. "You forget, Ivy, that I can see into your heart. I know you, and something is wrong."

I released the breath I'd been holding. She could, and she did. But that didn't make me ready to share. "I'll be fine."

The Spring Fling had officially begun. Groups of kids and parents had started arriving fifteen minutes before the official start time. Now it was noon and the place was buzzing. Olaya and I went back behind the Yeast of Eden table to help Maggie. There was already a line of people wanting to buy a hot cross bun, a triangle of star bread, or a slice of the van Dough focaccias. Carol and Debbie had ambled away to check out other booths. "We'll be back at one," Carol had said.

I'd raised one eyebrow at her in an unspoken question. Why would she come back if she despised Nessa Rench-rik so much?

"Curiosity," she'd said.

Maggie and Olaya handled the sales at the table, using gloved hands and bakery sheets to pluck the bread from the table and placing the items in small brown bakery bags. They reminded people to take one of the leaflets or Yeast of Eden stickers I'd set out on the table. Marketing the bread shop had become one of my tasks. I'd spent a month photographing all the different breads, the interior of the bread shop, and the exterior with its awnings and cute bistro tables, editing the photos, and putting it all together into a trifold brochure telling the story of the bread shop. We brought the marketing materials to every special event featuring Yeast of Eden's bread.

It wasn't that the bread shop needed the publicity. People already came from far and wide to experience the magic of Olaya's bread. It could cure a broken heart, breathe confidence into a person, or calm anxiety. It had been known to be a love potion, bring serenity, and whisk away remnants of grief. Olaya infused the bread she baked with herbs, the combinations and whatever magic she had inside of her fulfilling needs people didn't even know they had. Her reputation spanned California's coast, from San Diego to San Francisco, and beyond. What I'd included on the brochure and website simply told Olaya's story, focusing on her passion from a young age for traditional bread baking using the best possible ingredients and baking with love.

Once a person had Olaya's bread, nothing else would do.

As the bread on the table was depleted, I replenished it, piling up more star bread triangles, more hot cross buns. More slices of van Dough focaccias.

"Oh my gosh, look, Nick!" A woman pointed to the focaccia we'd made to look like van Gogh's *Starry Night*. Her eyes were wide and her mouth was open. "I need to buy that." She already had her wallet in hand and was handing over a pile of bills before Olaya had even told her the price, but their conversation faded away as I looked through the crowd. It was 12:55. The impromptu memorial I'd planned for Nessa Renchrik was five minutes away.

The blacktop teemed with people. Kids participated in a cakewalk. They skipped in a circle as music played, stopping when the song cut off. A man—a parent? A volunteer?—pulled a number from a plastic bowl he held and called out the number. A boy of about eight let out a whoop. He pumped his fist in the air and spun around, then did a victory dance by standing with his legs about two feet apart and bending his knees together, then out, together, then out. This kid was already hyped. He didn't need the sugar from whatever cake he'd won, but I knew he'd enjoy every last bite of it.

A small crowd had gathered around the Yeast of Eden booth. They'd come for the memorial, attendance bolstered, I was sure, by my posting about it on social media.

They were separate from the people lined up to buy bread. I glanced at Olaya, who gave me a nod.

I pulled off the purple nitrile gloves I'd been wearing, tossed them into the makeshift garbage box just under the table, and stepped out from behind the bread table. I cleared my throat and held one arm up to gather everyone's attention. "Thank you for coming," I said. "I didn't know Nessa Renchrik, but"—I gestured wide with my arm, encompassing Olaya, Maggie, and the table piled high with bread—"we wanted to do something to honor her for her service to the school district."

A low murmur spread through the crowd. I took a deep breath and surveyed them. Cliff Renchrik stood in the back. So Rachel had gotten him to come. Candace Coffey stood next to him. On the other side of the crowd were Margaret Jenkins-Roe, Jerry Zenmark, and Katherine Candelli. Joseph Patrick and Lulu Sanchez-Patrick stood side by side but hung toward the back of the crowd. Carol and Debbie had been true to their word. They'd come back, each with a caramel apple in hand. Next to them was . . . Gretchen. I blinked, surprised to see her here.

My gaze traveled to Terry Masaki. He held Hana in one arm and Mei held on to his other. Next to them was Dr. Sharma. She wore a sleeveless cream dress and beige shoes. It wasn't too professional and, at the same time, wasn't too casual. Next to her was the principal of Chavez Elementary, Mr. Davies, and the school's receptionist, Misty Jackson. People had come out in droves, but were they here to pay their respects to Nessa, or were they looky-loos, here because they couldn't tear their eyes away from the drama?

Then I saw the kids. Rachel and Tate worked their way

through the gathering of people until they were in front, looking at me with rapt attention. Rachel had a scarf wound around her neck, wore a gauzy skirt, and had a protective hand on her brother's shoulder. They had each other, which was nice to see.

"I spent some time last night writing down all the things Nessa did for the students and district during her time on the school board." It was true, I'd spent two hours hunting down information via Google and the *Santa Sofia Daily* website. The truth was, it had taken so long because her accomplishments were hard to find. It turns out there weren't all that many. She'd been one of those politicians who had worked their way into their positions without a lot to show for it. Somehow, she'd convinced her constituents that she was working hard for them.

"Nessa had big political aspirations," I began, glancing at Joseph Patrick. His expression revealed nothing. Whatever he'd felt about Nessa and the fact that he'd withdrawn his support of her was not revealed on his face.

As I continued speaking, I let my gaze linger on Tate. His hair was dark, while the rest of the family was blond. Rachel had green eyes, as did Cliff. Nessa's had been hazel, but Tate's were brown. He was slightly darker complected than the others. I looked at his face. Did he look anything like Miguel? Was it possible?

Once again, I found Cliff Renchrik in the crowd. Did he know Tate might not be his son?

I swallowed and set my mind to the task at hand. "Nessa Renchrik served Santa Sofia Unified School District with great commitment. She supported our other school board members, fighting for reading programs for the schools, providing nutritious lunches to the kids in the district, and starting a surf club to keep kids entertained and off the streets. According to some of the people who knew her best, this was one of her biggest passions."

I glanced at Jerry Zenmark. His eyes burned with anger. Would he ever get over the fact that Nessa had died and so they'd lost the surf club funding to technology for the poorest school in the district?

"Nessa leaves behind a legacy of service, and her loving family." I looked at Rachel and Tate. "Rachel, would you like to say anything?"

I knew I'd put her on the spot, but the offer had come from my heart. She and Tate both looked broken. Red-rimmed eyes. Sallow skinned. She looked over her shoulder, catching her father's eye. He gave a slight nod. Rachel turned and whispered something to Tate, dropped her arm from his shoulder, and made her way to where I stood. She looked at me with a sad smile and a nod before clearing her throat. "I-I miss my mom," she began, her voice cracking with emotion. "I-I guess it's weird to think that she won't be at my graduation, or my wedding one day." She looked at her brother. "She won't see Tate grow up."

I scanned the crowd. So many of the people here had seen Nessa Renchrik within twenty-four hours of her death. Nessa had gotten her hair done at Soho Salon by Gretchen on Friday, hours before the charity event she attended. Lulu Sanchez-Patrick had seen her there. Both Lulu and Joseph Patrick had been at the charity event, as well, and Joseph had met with Nessa the next morning to withdraw his support for her senate bid. Dr. Sharma and Principal Davies had been at the event. Misty Jackson had seen her at the elementary school. All four school board members had been at the Friday evening dinner, along with

Nessa. And Nessa's husband, according to Rachel, had seen his wife the morning of her death.

A new group of people approached the Yeast of Eden booth, standing at the edge of the gathered crowd. It was Guillermo Cabrera and his daughter. Of course they'd be at the Spring Fling. Their residence was just a mile or so from the school. The little girl was probably in third or fourth grade here.

I swallowed, scanning the people again. This felt like a planned gathering of all the people who'd had an ax to grind against Nessa Renchrik. Only Miguel, who had met with Nessa about her daughter's graduation dinner on Friday, wasn't here—the one person I was desperately trying to prove was innocent.

Joseph Patrick's gaze shifted from Rachel to me. He gave a slight nod, acknowledging me.

His wife, Lulu, looked at me, then quickly looked away.

Gretchen's mouth lifted on one side and she gave me a quick wave.

One after the other, the four school board members looked at one another. Candy then met my eyes. Even from where I stood, I could see her jaw tense.

The principal and the superintendent glanced at each other, as if they shared a secret; then Mr. Davies carried on the secret by looking pointedly at Misty Jackson.

A chill slithered through me. One of the people in this impromptu memorial crowd was a murderer.

My gaze sought out Guillermo Cabrera again. He had one arm on his daughter's shoulder as he nodded to me.

Cliff's attention was completely focused on *his* daughter. At one point, he found Tate in the crowd but quickly shifted back to looking at Rachel. He must have felt me watching him because he briefly averted his attention from Rachel to me, then back again. No acknowledgment. No emotion. No response whatsoever.

I looked at Tate with his big eyes. Tears streamed down his face as he listened to his sister speak about their mother. Rachel cleared her throat again. She looked at her brother and nodded to him. "I'm here for you, Tate. No matter what happens, I'm here for you."

I blinked, replaying her words in my head. *No matter what happens.* What did she mean?

Later, as I lay in bed going over the events of the day, I envisioned each of the people who'd shown up at the memorial for Nessa Renchrik. My brain was doing its own version of Michael Jackson's "Black or White" video, one face quickly morphing into another. Nessa, who I knew only through photographs, turned into Rachel, who turned into Guillermo, who turned into Cliff, who turned into Lulu, who turned into Joseph. On and on it went, ending with the remaining school board members, Gretchen, Carol and her sister, Debbie, and finally Guillermo's daughter.

It wasn't until I fell asleep that I realized it wasn't Guillermo's daughter at the end of my own little mind video. It was Tate.

They looked so similar.

I bolted upright. Oh. My. God. Tate and Guillermo's daughter. They had the same eyes. The same hair. The girl's complexion was a little more olive than Tate's, but otherwise, they were almost identical.

My brain processed the information. It flew in and out of my head like one of those screensavers where the words appear, then fade before another one appears.

Nessa had told Miguel she'd been through a rough breakup.

She'd had a heated debate with someone in the bookstore. A work acquaintance.

Sylvia's deportation.

Tate . . . and his look-alike.

There was a common denominator.

Guillermo.

Chapter 20

I'd called Olaya and Mrs. Branford as soon as I woke up the next morning. "Meet me at the bread shop."

"I am already here, Ivy," Olaya said.

I smacked my forehead with the heal of my palm. Of course she was. This was day two of the Spring Fling and she and Felix were probably elbow deep in more hot cross buns and van Dough focaccias. I told Mrs. Branford that I'd pick her up, and thirty minutes later the three of us were sitting around one of the cute bistro tables in the dining area of Yeast of Eden, Felix still working in the kitchen.

Every morning, the bread shop dining room was filled with people sipping coffee and eating a ham and Gruyère or a chocolate croissant. Every afternoon it was iced tea and some savory roll or hunk of bread. The bread shop had something for everyone. The bistro tables and chairs were put to good use.

Mrs. Branford wore a black velour lounge suit. She

was bright-eyed and bushy tailed. I wondered how many hours of sleep she needed, because day or night, rain or shine, whenever I called her, she was awake and raring to go.

Olaya, on the other hand, had on a subdued black-and-cream caftan and Birkenstocks, and her iron-gray hair was mussed. Her eyes looked sleepy, as if she hadn't gotten a full night's rest. A pang of regret passed through me. "Were you up late prepping more dough?" I asked her, guilt flooding me. I should have stayed later the night before to make sure everything was ready for today.

"No. Felix prepared everything while we were at the school yesterday."

"But you look so tired," I said.

A coy smile lifted one side of her mouth. I stared at her, my mouth falling into a surprised O. "Olaya Solis!" I said, while Mrs. Branford sniggered and said, "About time, if you ask me."

Olaya chuckled, pressing her fingertips to her lips. Her cheeks bloomed pink.

"H-how? W-who?" I asked. The woman worked nonstop and had ungodly hours. How did she have time to be dating someone without us knowing about it?

Mrs. Branford gave me a stern look. "We are old, Ivy, not dead."

I laughed, letting my surprise fade away. Mrs. Branford had recently rekindled a relationship with a teacher she'd worked with at the high school. Mr. Caldwell, room 315, had taught chemistry at Santa Sofia High School when Mrs. Branford had taught English. Now, every now and then, they, ahem, *studied* together.

Olaya held up a hand to quiet us down. "I have a friend, yes, but that is all I will say about it."

It was hard not to pry, but more pressing things were on my mind, so I was able to push Olaya's newly revealed love life to the back of my mind. That was a topic for another day. A plate of golden-brown pumpernickel rye rolls, each square artfully slashed, half topped with everything bagel seasoning, the other half with poppyseeds, sat in the center of the table. I'd taken one with the bagel topping, split it open, and slathered the insides with butter. Mrs. Branford tore pieces off the poppyseed roll she held. "You made these this morning?" she asked Olaya.

"I made the dough last night and baked them this morning."

I eyed her suspiciously. It was as if she knew I'd be calling and we'd need some comforting bread to eat.

She smiled at me and rolled her hand in the air in front of her, telling me to get on with whatever I had to say. "Coincidence. Now, why did you call us here this morning?"

I cleared my throat. "I think Guillermo Cabrera is Tate Renchrik's father."

Mrs. Branford stopped chewing.

Olaya's lips parted.

"That woman Sylvia's husband?"

"His little girl looks just like Tate. If he fathered them both . . ." I trailed off, letting the idea simmer. "Plus, it makes sense. She told Miguel she'd been through a breakup, but she was married. He saw her arguing with someone. This was ten or eleven years ago. The timing is perfect. What if she met him through their business and started an affair? She gets pregnant, but meanwhile, he falls in love with Sylvia, so Nessa keeps their child a secret and raises him as Cliff's."

Mrs. Branford resumed her chewing, swallowed, and said, "If her husband only just found out, that gives him a very strong motive."

Olaya looked skeptical. "Would he only have just found out?"

I'd thought about this. "Why not? If he didn't suspect the affair, why suspect the child wasn't his? Guillermo still worked for him. If Cliff knew he'd had a relationship with his wife, would he still keep him employed?"

"How would he have suddenly found out?" Mrs. Branford asked.

"The truck," I said.

They both stared at me, waiting for me to continue. "There was a truck parked at Sylvia's—Guillermo's—house. It's the same blue as one I saw pulling into one of Seaside Property's rentals."

Mrs. Branford cocked an eyebrow at me.

"Miguel and I followed Cliff one day. He went to a mansion overlooking the Pacific. An old truck pulled in after him. Someone was with him. What if—"

Olaya broke in. "What if it was his daughter."

I snapped and pointed at her. "Exactly! Maybe it wasn't the first time Guillermo had brought his daughter to work. What if Cliff saw the girl and realized the truth?" I snapped again and told them what Rachel had said about her parents arguing about Tate. Maybe he really had found out.

The three of us fell silent and munched on our pumpernickel rye rolls. Mrs. Branford spoke again first. "That is a lot of maybes."

My head was filled with what-ifs. It felt like it was a balloon ready to pop.

What if Cliff realized Guillermo was Tate's father?

What if Nessa had kept Tate a secret from Guillermo, but he realized he had another child?

What if Nessa blamed Sylvia for her breakup with Guillermo? So many years later, could that be the reason she'd worked to get Sylvia deported? Payback? Revenge?

Or . . . had Sylvia realized that Tate was Guillermo's son? She worked at the house. She would have seen the resemblance. That would be motive for Nessa to get rid of her. Nessa was in politics, after all. It was not beyond reason to think she knew people in high places. And if Sylvia had confided in Carmen, that would explain the removal of the longtime nanny.

Any or all of these things could be true. Cliff and Guillermo both had potential motives to kill Nessa, but had one of them met her at the district office boardroom on a Saturday afternoon and clobbered her with a chair?

I could picture Cliff showing up there, but Guillermo? He'd never been in that part of Nessa's life. If he were to kill her, would he do it somewhere else? Somewhere he had access to?

I buried my head in my hands. *What if* I was completely off track? "Too many maybes," I said.

Mrs. Branford finished her roll and reached for another, tearing off a piece and popping it in her mouth. "Let's recap the woman's actions on the day she died," she said after she swallowed.

I'd gone over Nessa's day in a play-by-play in my head. Talking it through aloud could help me clarify things. "Not just the day she died, but the day before. Nessa stopped by Baptista's that Friday and talked to Miguel. Plus, she left him a message. For whatever reason, that's the only thing Captain York is focusing on."

"If only this Captain York had been one of my students," Mrs. Branford said.

If only, indeed. She'd have paid him a visit and given him a good what for.

"He doesn't seem to be very logical, nor very thorough. Why is he so intent on Miguel being the guilty party?"

"That's a great question." I told Olaya and Mrs. Branford about someone parking outside Miguel's house and following him. "It's like York isn't even looking at anyone else. I believe he thinks Miguel is Tate's father."

Mrs. Branford pinched another bit of her pumpernickel rye roll but held it between her gnarled thumb and forefinger. "In my experience, people often take the easy way out. It sounds to me as if this Captain York zeroed in on Miguel early on, decided he was the guilty party, and now is doing what he can to make the facts fit his theory."

I dropped my hands, resting my forearms on the table, my roll abandoned. My appetite was gone, and not even Olaya's miracle bread could fix it.

"You will get to the bottom of this," Olaya said. She laid her hand on mine and squeezed. "Now. Let us go through the timeline."

I drew in a deep breath, gathered my thoughts, and began. "Friday. There was a charity dinner for an organization called Communities in Schools. Nessa got her hair done at the salon. Although Gretchen didn't mention that when we talked about Nessa."

Mrs. Branford had finished her second roll and looked like she was contemplating a third. Instead of reaching for one, she picked up her cane from the chair next to her where she'd laid it down and stood. "An intentional omission or an oversight?"

"Good question." I couldn't answer it, so I moved on. "Nessa placed an order at Baptista's and went to pick it up. That's when she saw Miguel."

"Did they have an argument?" Olaya asked.

"Not that I know of."

Mrs. Branford ambled around the dining area of the bread shop, gently swinging her cane. Her shoes squeaked against the black-and-white-checkered floor. "Miguel Baptista is as honest as the day is long. If he said there was no argument, I'd bet my house that there wasn't."

Olaya nodded in agreement. "Your man, he has no reason to hurt Nessa."

"She wasn't hurt," I said. "She was killed."

Mrs. Branford pshawed. "He has even less reason to have killed her."

"I know that, and you know that, but Captain York doesn't seem to care." My voice rose. This was what it felt like to be on the brink of hysteria.

Mrs. Branford came back to the table and stood behind her chair. "Who was at the dinner Friday night?"

I ticked the people off on my fingers. "All the board members. The superintendent and one of Nessa's campaign donors. His wife. Maybe the principal of Chavez," I said, but I wasn't sure about that. "Her husband."

"Apparently some of the board members were at odds with each other. Nessa was in the thick of it. She wanted funding to go to a surf club. Others wanted it for technology funding for Chavez."

"That means the board members who didn't want the club had a motive to stop her from voting," Mrs. Branford said.

"And the principal of the school so he could get his funding," I finished.

We contemplated this for a moment before I continued. "On to Saturday morning. Nessa had coffee with Katherine Candelli—" They both raised their eyebrows at me. "School board member," I said.

"About the same funding?" Mrs. Branford asked.

I nodded. "And she met with Joseph Patrick, the donor, who pulled his endorsement and funding from her campaign."

"Why?" Olaya asked.

"Apparently she had skeletons in her closet," I answered, using the very word he and Lulu had used.

Again, their expressions asked their unspoken question.

"She and her husband employed undocumented workers. Mr. Patrick couldn't support her because she wouldn't make it through the vetting process without it coming out. He's pro–immigration reform, but he said he wants it done aboveboard. Nessa couldn't fight for real immigration reform while she subverted the law."

"That is not a motive for him to kill her. Maybe for her to kill him," Olaya said.

Exactly.

Mrs. Branford tapped the rubber-tipped base of her cane on the ground. "It sounds to me like she had more enemies than friends."

"If she met with this man—the donor—the day she died, he could have done it." Olaya pulled off a piece of bread and pressed it between her fingers.

"She could have arranged to meet anyone without telling a soul," Mrs. Branford said. "The donor admitted to meeting her that day. Why would he do that if he was guilty of killing her?"

It was a good question. "And then there's Guillermo," I said, coming back to the reason I'd called Olaya and Mrs. Branford in the first place. "He has a solid motive if he found out Nessa's son was his and she'd been keeping it from him all these years."

"Excuse me?" We all turned to see Felix popping his head out from the door to the kitchen. "I have a question about the pumpernickel rye rolls," he said, beckoning to Olaya.

She nodded but held a finger out to Felix. He ducked back into the kitchen. Olaya stood and glanced at the clock on the wall behind the counter. "Ivy. We must be at the school for day two in one and a half hours. You will be ready?"

"I'm ready now." I looked at Mrs. Branford. "Let me run you home—"

"Heavens, no," she said. "I missed the event yesterday. I want to see the children playing. Many of their parents will have been my students."

I was glad to have her come with us. Her former students would spot her and come running. More business for the Yeast of Eden booth. "I'll bring an extra chair."

The last thing I did before helping Mrs. Branford into my car was text Emmaline. She and Billy were arriving back from the Costa Rica sometime today. She had resources I didn't. As soon as she landed, I wanted her to see the text and see what she could find out. Her honeymoon was over.

Chapter 21

It felt like Groundhog Day.

I'd worked with Maggie, who Olaya was paying overtime to work on a Sunday, to set up the table just like we had the day before. People milled around as we loaded the table with all the featured breads. We had more van Dough focaccias. More hot cross buns. More skull cookies. More star bread. And today, we had what felt like a million pumpernickel rye rolls.

Mrs. Branford sat on the edge of the padded folding chair I'd brought for her, biding her time until she saw a familiar face. She had her hands clasped around the top of her cane, almost like she was using it for balance, but I thought it was just so she wouldn't grab another roll or move on to the cookies. "Ever since Olaya and I buried the hatchet, baked goods have become my weakness," she often said.

That hatchet had been about a long-ago love triangle between Olaya, Mrs. Branford, and her husband, Mr. Branford. They'd come to an understanding with each other after I came into the picture, and it seemed that they'd both moved on—Mrs. Branford with her chemistry teacher and Olaya with her mysterious love interest.

Day two of the Spring Fling officially began at noon. Perfect timing for those families who attended church to go to service first, then come to the festival. My heart squeezed tight at the sight of little girls and boys in their Sunday best.

"Ready for one of those?"

I spun around to find Miguel behind me. "One of what?" I asked, though I thought I knew what he meant.

"A little rug rat of your own." He paused, adding, "Of *our* own."

My heart swelled. I smiled, but I knew it didn't reach all the way to the crinkles of my eyes. Miguel and I had talked about our future together, but this was the first time he'd mentioned something as permanent as having kids together. The weight of Captain York's focus on Miguel for the murder of Nessa Renchrik dampened the sentiment, though.

"It's about time," Mrs. Branford interjected from her chair. "The clock is ticking, you know."

I spun to face her. "Mrs. Branford!"

"Pshaw." She fluttered one hand. "The truth is the truth, my dears. You wasted many years apart. Now it's time to move forward."

Olaya raised one hand. "I agree."

The conversation was cut short when someone in the crowd called my name. "Ivy!"

"Dad!" I circled around the table and pushed through the line of people waiting to buy bread from Olaya. "I didn't know you were coming today," I said, giving him a hug.

"Unlimited bread, so why not?" he said, his lips quirking up into a half smile.

My dad did love Olaya's bread. When I'd first come back to Santa Sofia, I'd gone to Yeast of Eden nearly every day, making my way through everything she baked and bringing something home for my dad. He'd slowly come through his grief at losing my mother, and I thought the special bit of magic in Olaya's bread had had something to do with it.

"What would you like? I'll grab it for you," I said, but he shook his head.

"No, no. I'll wait in line. You go back to your work."

My dad was a stickler for the rules. Before I turned to go, I asked, "Any word from Billy and Em?"

"Billy texted from the airport last night. Dinner next weekend at the house so we can hear all about their trip," he said.

Oh, thank God. I couldn't wait to fill in Emmaline on all my different theories. She'd be objective and could take over, figuring out who had killed Nessa and putting a stop to Captain York's ridiculous idea that Miguel had had anything to do with it.

As if I'd magically summoned him by thinking his name, Captain York appeared in my line of sight. He looked right at me and gave a small nod. It took everything I had not to react . . . not to acknowledge him.

"Your dad's looking good," Miguel said when I went back behind the table and my dad got in line to buy some bread.

It was true. Every day, Owen Culpepper looked healthier than he had the day before. He was cycling again, and his skin glowed from being back in the sun. His salt-and-pepper hair gave him a distinguished appeal, and he was smiling again.

The line moved at a quick clip. Miguel left to find his sister, Laura, and his niece and nephew, while I used my purple nitrile-covered hands to bag the breads Olaya and Maggie sold. It was mindless work, so, of course, my brain shifted to thinking about the memorial for Nessa Renchrik the day before and everyone who'd shown up for it.

"Two rye rolls," Olaya said.

When I looked up again, York was gone and my dad at the front of the line smiling and chatting with Olaya as he pulled a five-dollar bill from his wallet. Once again, my gaze was pulled into the distance. Gretchen. She stood near the booth sponsored by a local coffee shop talking to someone, her hands on her pregnant belly, her floral sundress fluttering around her legs.

Why was she here? She didn't have kids yet, I thought, but then Tate Renchrik walked up to them and I realized who she was talking to. The ash-blond hair. The slight physique. It was Rachel. Instantly, my suspicion about Gretchen dissipated. She had done Rachel's hair since Carmen, the nanny, had taken her to the salon that first time. Carmen had been a constant in Rachel's life and then she was gone. Gretchen had told me that she wished she could help Rachel. Maybe she had become a constant for the girl, too. I hoped so, because Rachel needed all the support she could get.

Still, two words circled in my head over and over and over.

She lied.

She lied.

She lied.

Or had she just neglected to mention it?

Was there a difference? I made an instant decision. I

wanted to find out why Gretchen hadn't told me that she'd done Nessa's hair the day before she'd died.

By the time I looked back to the line, my dad had moved behind the table and was in an animated conversation with Mrs. Branford. They both had a love of books, so if I had to guess, I'd say they were talking literature.

Things at the booth looked under control, so there was no time like the present. I caught Olaya's eye. Her cheeks were flushed, but she was smiling and focused on each customer in line as if they were the only person in the world. I remembered the feeling of her attention the first time I'd spoken to her outside Yeast of Eden. "We are waiting for you," she'd said, as if I'd known her for years. She had a knack for making each and every person feel special.

"I'll be back," I called to her.

She gave me a nod and went back to her customers.

Only by the time I looked back to the spot where Gretchen had been a moment ago, she was gone.

As I hurried along the blacktop trying to spot Gretchen, Rachel, and Tate where they had been just seconds ago, I wondered how I'd ever managed to help Emmaline solve murders in the past. It had never been easy, but now, when it mattered so much to prove Miguel was innocent, I was at a loss.

I had a fleeting thought about Agatha Christie's *Murder on the Orient Express*. There were so many people who had grudges against Nessa Renchrik, and not enough clues to make one of them rise to the top of the list. What if they'd all done it, one after the other?

I dismissed the idea one second after I thought it. This

wasn't a book by the Grand Dame of mysteries. This was real life in a small coastal town. This was the murder, not of a beloved community member, but of a divisive politician. *Divisive and diabolical*, I amended.

Nessa had cheated on her husband—at least twice, but probably more than that.

I'd lay money down that Tate was not Cliff's son. That gave him a strong motive.

Then there was Guillermo. If he discovered that Tate was his son, could he have lashed out at Nessa? Keeping a child from his father. If he'd learned the truth, that definitely gave him motive.

Nessa had divided the school board by lobbying with Jerry Zenmark for the surf club. The other three board members wanted the tech funded, not the surf club. It didn't feel like a strong motive, but it was something nonetheless.

Nessa's push for the surfing club would keep Chavez Elementary from getting much-needed funding for technology. Could Principal Davies have killed her to guarantee the funding his students needed?

And then there was Joseph Patrick. Nessa had lost her biggest backer when he pulled his support.

A new thought hit me. *Could Nessa have had something on Joseph Patrick . . . or his wife?* When he'd met with Nessa, could she have tried to blackmail him into keeping his support of her? That would be a strong motive.

Gretchen's face drifted into my mind. I couldn't fathom a motive for her to kill Nessa, but I couldn't dismiss her, either. Once again, those two words echoed in my head. *She lied.*

My final thought was about Miguel. Captain York had him at the top of his suspect list for three reasons. One, they'd dated ten or eleven years ago. Two, she'd been in touch suddenly, coming by the restaurant. Three, she'd contacted him about being a sponsor for the Spring Fling. All this proved was that Miguel had known Nessa, but it didn't give him a motive.

Once again, as if on cue, York appeared. "Ivy," he said. In that one little word, I felt the man's unpleasant-ness.

I matched his tone. "Captain."

He adjusted his Santa Sofia sheriff's department hat and said, "Looking for your boyfriend?"

"No. Are you?"

"At the moment, I'm talking to you."

I felt my nostrils flare. "Why?"

"Why am I talking to you? Why not?"

"Look, Captain. I don't know why you think Miguel is involved in Nessa Renchrik's death, but he's not. And there are a lot of other people you should be looking at—"

"There you go again, butting into something you shouldn't. I've heard all about you. And let me tell you, you are not a deputy. You are not an employee of the county, in fact. You have no reason to be involved in this investigation—"

"I do if you aren't doing your job!" I snapped. "Miguel has—"

His eyes flashed red. "You need to back down."

There was no way that was happening. "What makes you think Miguel has anything to do with this? Because he doesn't."

He didn't speak for a few seconds and his eyes nar-rowed. Finally, he said, "Nessa Renchrik's son is not her husband's."

I had to fight to keep my eyes from rolling. "I know."

This caught him off guard. "You know?"

"Yes, and if you think that gives Miguel a reason to kill Nessa, you're wrong. First of all, Cliff would be the one to have a motive to kill Nessa since she betrayed him. And second, Tate is not Miguel's child."

He pulled a face, his lips twisted. "And I suppose you know who is."

"As a matter of fact––"

He held up a hand, palm out, and I clamped my mouth shut. "The Santa Sofia sheriff's department does not need your help to solve this crime!" he snapped.

I debated shutting my mouth and walking away, but my anger and frustration got the better of me. "If you're not considering all the possibilities, then I think you do."

He dropped his arms to his sides. I stared at his face, but I could see his hands clenching by his sides. Too late I realized that Captain York's hubris was fully in play now. He had something to prove and he wouldn't let me interfere in him making his case, no matter how wrong he was. He'd lose face if he let go of his theory about Miguel.

I spoke slowly enough to emphasize every word as I said, "Miguel is not the boy's father, and he no longer had a connection to Nessa Renchrik. He has no motive."

"What's going on here?" It was Miguel, coming up beside me. He put his hand on my lower back. A little show of protection from the big, bad Captain York. I appreciated the gesture. We were a united front.

Captain York spoke before I could. He was blunt with his question. "Is Tate Renchrik your son?"

Miguel balked. "Of course not," he said, his voice tight.

"Isn't that, in fact, why Nessa came to see you Friday night at your restaurant? She was finally coming clean?"

Oh wow. York had worked out a whole scenario in his head.

"She came to the restaurant Friday night to pick up an order for her kids. *Her* kids."

"Mmm-hmm." York was clearly not convinced. "And how are you so certain?"

I turned toward Miguel and let my hands slide down his arm, taking it from my back and clasping his hand in mine. There was always the possibility that I was wrong, but Tate and Guillermo's daughter looked so alike that I couldn't fathom that they weren't brother and sister. Why had York concocted this scenario in his mind and why couldn't he see another possibility?

Miguel leveled his gaze at York and spoke slowly. "I'm so certain because I never slept with Vanessa Arnold."

Whatever Captain York had been expecting, it wasn't this. He clamped his mouth closed and his jaw pulsed. If his case against Miguel was entirely based on the idea that Miguel had had an affair with Nessa that had resulted in a child, it was just derailed. If this were a game of chess, the captain had made a bold move, putting Miguel into check, but Miguel had come back stronger and just checkmated him.

Miguel stared at York without an ounce of fear. "Anything else, Captain?"

York inhaled, letting his chest broaden in an unspoken cockfight stance. "The truth always comes out," he said. It was a veiled threat, implying that Miguel was lying, but Miguel didn't take the bait. His eyes narrowed as he said, "It will. And it'll prove you're wrong."

Without another word, York turned on his heel and melted into the crowd.

At the same moment, I spotted Rachel and Tate and called to them. Rachel stopped and turned around, spotted me, and raised her hand. I held up my index finger so she'd wait. "I have to talk to her," I said to Miguel. "But are you okay?"

"I'm fine, Ivy. You go on. I have to catch up with Laura."

Miguel's sister and I hadn't spoken for years and years—from the time we were both still kids and Miguel and I broke up after high school. It had taken some serious conversations, but Laura and I'd finally mended our fences and it turned out that I liked her, quite a lot. I liked her kids even more. Andrea was in her terrible twos, though she was anything but terrible from my experience. And Mateo was an adorable toddler. They were just a year apart, so Laura had her hands full. If her husband, Sergio, wasn't here helping out with the kids, she'd need Miguel.

I stretched on my tiptoes to give him a kiss. "We're going to get to the bottom of this," I said.

He wrapped his arms around and pulled me in for a hug. "I know."

We parted and went our separate ways, him to find his sister, niece, and nephew, and me to check in on Rachel and Tate and find out where Gretchen had gone.

Rachel looked like she hadn't slept a wink the night before. She was thin to begin with, but it looked to me like she'd lost ten pounds since yesterday. The memorial for her mother must have really taken a toll—more than either of us had considered.

Tate looked the same. Innocent big brown eyes that didn't betray the emotions he was surely feeling.

I approached them at the same time Fernanda did. The replacement nanny. Once again, my heart ached for these kids. They'd both lost so much. I laid my hand on Rachel's arm in a show of support, smiling at both the kids.

Fernanda put a protective hand on Tate's shoulder. I hadn't seen her up close before. She had short curly hair that sat like a helmet on her round head. The features of her face were flat, her complexion dark, and she had pocked scarring on her cheeks. She wasn't short, but she wasn't tall, and she was pleasantly plump. I smiled at her. "Fernanda, right?"

She nodded but did not smile.

"She doesn't talk much," Tate said with a grin. Once again, I saw the resemblance between the boy, Guillermo, and his little girl.

Nessa, Nessa, Nessa, what did you do? I thought. If Cliff renounced this child for not being his own, Tate's whole world would fall apart—more than it already had.

"I talk just enough," Fernanda said, ruffling his hair. She had a slight accent.

I felt relief flow through me as I watched her interact with Tate. She may not have been with the family for very long, but I could see the affection she had for the boy.

It was Rachel who looked lost. "Are you doing all right?" I asked her.

She gave a helpless shrug and pressed her palm against her chest. "It feels like there's rope squeezing inside me." She looked at Fernanda, her eyes pleading. "I just want it to go away."

Fernanda gave her an encouraging smile. "It will. Give it time."

"You did a great job speaking yesterday," I said.

She exhaled audibly, blowing out through her mouth as if she could expel the anxiety coursing through her body. "Maybe."

"No, really. It was a beautiful memorial."

Fernanda nodded her agreement. "She is right. It was from the heart."

I hadn't realized that she'd come the day before. It was nice that she'd been a support for Rachel and Tate. "I thought I saw you with Gretchen," I said, glancing around. There was still no sign of her.

Rachel looked at me, her darkly rimmed eyes wide. "You know Gretchen?"

I patted my hair and smiled. "Saw her Friday for the first time."

"Looks nice," she said, though it didn't sound like her heart was in the compliment.

"Thanks." I acted as nonchalant as I could. "How did you find her? She's a treasure."

"I got a . . . mmm, what do you call them . . . a cold call?"

"You mean the salon called?"

"Yeah. No, Gretchen did because she was a new stylist trying to get clients."

That was interesting. Cold calling was an annoying marketing practice, but I'd never had a call from a hairdresser. "Sounds like it worked. You go to her, and your mom did, too, right?"

Rachel's lips twisted and her eyes instantly turned glassy. "I don't want to talk about it. Okay?"

"Sure, sure. I'm sorry, Rachel. Is there anything I can do for you?" I looked at Tate. "For you both?"

Rachel shook her head, tucking a wayward strand of

her hair behind her ear. "I have my family. We're fine." She added, "Thanks," almost as an afterthought.

"I know you do. Candy Coffey is there for you, too. Just don't be afraid to reach out if you need anything, okay?"

She gave a slight nod. I looked at Tate, noting how completely opposite he looked from his sister. His half sister. "You, too, Tate."

"Okay," he said. He looked past me, his eyes lighting up as they landed on someone. "Ruby!" he hollered, waving his arms overhead. He looked up at Rachel. "I'm going to go with Ruby and her dad."

Rachel turned paler. I wanted to grab her elbow and lead her to a chair where she could put her head between her legs. She looked seconds away from passing out, wobbling on her feet. "Okay," she managed. Her fluttery gaze followed Tate as he ran across the blacktop, dodging people.

"Are you okay?" I asked her.

Her nostrils flared and she exhaled through her nose. Her voice dropped to a pained whisper, her attention still focused somewhere behind me. "I don't know," she said.

I turned to see what she was looking at. My own breath caught in my throat. Tate's friend Ruby was none other than Guillermo's daughter. Which made Ruby, not just a friend, but Tate's half sister.

And from the expression on Rachel's face, she knew the truth.

"Rachel." Gretchen appeared beside me, her belly arriving first, followed by the rest of her. She snapped her fingers in front of Rachel's face. "Hey. Come on."

Rachel blinked, coming back to herself, and focused on Gretchen. "Sorry. I'm fine."

"I don't think you are, sweetie. Come on. Let's sit down."

I followed as Gretchen led Rachel to a bench along one of the school's exterior walls. Gretchen had a cross-body bag on and reached inside, retrieving an unopened bottle of water from it. She sat down next to Rachel, unscrewed the top, and handed it to her. "What's going on?" she asked.

Rachel closed her eyes and leaned her head back against the wall, her breathing ragged. "I can't . . . I don't know what to do. She shouldn't be gone."

She could only be talking about her mother. It didn't matter how many enemies Nessa had made during her political career; she was still Rachel's mother and the girl needed her. Gretchen, for her part, was true to her word. She was doing everything she could to help Rachel.

Gretchen slid her arm around Rachel's shoulder. "It's going to be okay," she said. "I promise you, it will."

Rachel squeezed her eyes tighter, fighting the tears that were sneaking out. "Okay," she managed.

For the first time, Gretchen looked at me, her eyes widening with recognition. "Ivy. Sorry. I—"

I held up my hand, stopping her. "No, it's fine, really. I just want to help, if I can."

Rachel slumped against Gretchen, laying her head on the older woman's shoulder.

I felt as if I was intruding on a personal moment between them. I mouthed to Gretchen that I was going. As I circled the blacktop, checking out the different Spring Fling games going on, anxiety bloomed inside me. Something nagged at me. The fact that Tate had run off with his father, who he presumably didn't actually know was his father? That had to be it.

Except . . .

I looked back over my shoulder at Gretchen and Rachel, the older blonde comforting the younger one. There was something about the two of them together. And then something Rachel said came back to me. She'd told me she had her family to take care of her . . . and here was Gretchen.

As if I'd turned on a radio show in my head, little snippets and phrases came back to me:

Ali, the hairdresser next to Gretchen's station, had said that Nessa Renchrik was terrible to Gretchen. She'd started to say something. That Gretchen, of all people—

I'd assumed she'd been referring to Gretchen as Nessa's hairdresser. But what if it was something else?

There are no secrets in a hair salon.

Something Candy said popped into my head next. I tried to remember exactly what she'd said: *My daughter and I both will be there for Rachel. For Nessa's children. Poor girls. Poor Tate.*

Who had she meant when she'd said "poor girls"? Her daughter and Rachel? Or could it have been Rachel and—

I yanked my phone from my back pocket, pulled up a search engine, and typed in *Soho Salon*. The website popped up and I scrolled through it looking for the names of the stylists.

My breath hitched. There it was. Gretchen Arnold. Oh. My. God.

I dialed Candy. She picked up on the third ring. "Hey, Ivy."

My blood pumped and pounded in my temples. I felt like I was so close to something. No time for small talk. "Hey. Listen. Quick question."

"Okay."

"This might be out of left field," I warned.

"*Okay*," she said again, drawing out the latter part of the word.

I inhaled, bracing myself for both the question and the answer. "Is Gretchen, the hairdresser Nessa went to . . . is she . . . ?"

The line went silent for a long moment. Finally, she said, "What?"

I looked over at Gretchen and Rachel again. Rachel was sitting up and they faced each other. Gretchen held Rachel's hands and looked like she was giving the girl a pep talk. Suddenly I saw the resemblance. The blond hair, of course. Their height. Their build. Beneath her pregnancy, Gretchen was slight. Just like Rachel. They had the same slightly upturned nose. If Rachel chopped off her hair, she'd look like a pixie, just as Gretchen did.

There was suddenly no doubt in my mind. They were sisters. "Did Nessa have a child—a girl—when she was younger? Before she married Cliff?"

"Yes," Candy said.

"Gretchen Arnold."

Candy sighed heavily. "She never admitted it to me, but the minute I saw them together, I knew."

A long-lost daughter, even if she was pregnant, had a pretty good motive to kill the mother who'd given her up.

Chapter 22

My head swam with the new information about Gretchen being Nessa's daughter. A daughter she'd given up. Gretchen had said she'd grown up in Kalamazoo. I'd been so wrapped up in Gretchen's story about doing Nessa's hair that it hadn't registered where Kalamazoo actually was. I Googled it, nodding when I got the result. Of course. Michigan, which was where Candy said Nessa had moved from.

I felt a tap on my shoulder and turned to see Emmaline—Sheriff Davis, aka Mrs. Billy Culpepper—standing there, her black skin sun kissed, the long, beaded braids of her hair pulled back into a hair clip, my brother standing next to her with a goofy grin on his face. I screeched and started to laugh. "Em! God, I've miss you!"

"What about me?" Billy asked.

"You and your husband," I said with a grin.

"I like the sound of that," Em said. "My husband. His wife."

Billy grinned. "Me, too."

I flung my arms around Em, reaching out to yank my brother into the embrace. "You guys. It's so good to see you."

Em extricated herself from my arms and stepped back. "I contacted a friend at ICE," she said, jumping right into the case just like I knew she would.

"And?" I held my breath. This point felt crucial.

Em nodded. "You were right. Nessa Renchrik had a friend there, too. She called in a favor. She wanted them both gone."

My heart dropped to the pit of my stomach. "Damn."

"Yeah."

The woman truly was evil.

I'd gone along thinking the political donor or the husband or the lover was the guilty party. Or even the long-lost daughter. But now my thoughts rearranged. I looked across the blacktop and caught another glimpse of Rachel. She knew about Ruby. She'd loved Carmen. What if those two things had converged and caused an unstoppable tsunami inside the seventeen-year-old girl?

I pulled my phone from my pocket, pulled up the Twitter app, and searched, finding the profile I was looking for. I scrolled through the tweets, my thumb pressing down to stop the feed when I found what I was looking for: *You're a liar. You've ruined my life.*

No one was tagged, but I had no doubt who it was written to.

My eyes turned glassy as I turned to Em. "I think I might know what happened to Nessa."

* * *

It didn't take long for me to find Rachel again in the Spring Fling crowd. I stood in front of her and took her hands in mine. "Rachel," I said, my voice soft and coaxing. "I know about Gretchen."

She stared at me, looking more like a walking skeleton than the seventeen-year-old girl she was. Her voice was scarcely more than a whisper. "How?"

"I just . . . put it together.

"Did your mom know you knew?"

The color drained from Rachel's face. "Gretchen didn't do this."

I hadn't been sure till that moment, but now I was. I spoke softly, taking her hand in mine. "I know. You spent the night at Ronnie Coffey's house the night before your mom died, is that right?"

She nodded, swiping at the tears tumbling down her face with the back of her hand. "My mom picked up dinner for me and Tate. Ronnie ate with us; then we went to her house."

"And Tate stayed home alone?"

"With Fernanda," she said.

"How did you find out about Ruby?"

She swallowed. Sniffed. "I drove Tate to her house . . . once. . . . Then I . . . I found her phone."

She didn't have to say any more. I knew. She'd taken one look at Ruby and seen the truth. A truth she'd verified with Nessa's missing second phone.

Someone called Rachel's name. We both turned to see Cliff hurrying over to us. I turned, standing next to Rachel. I wanted to give her as much support as I could, and I didn't know how Cliff would take the truth.

"What's wrong?" he demanded. "What's going on?"

Rachel looked up at him and started sobbing. "I'm sorry, Daddy."

Cliff suddenly looked scared . . . and as weary as his daughter. He swallowed. Stared at her. "Sorry about what, baby?"

It was as if his words sounded a silent alarm around the blacktop. Emmaline and Billy came up behind me. Gretchen appeared and stood off to the side behind Cliff. Tate was next to her. Olaya and Mrs. Branford, who had her arm draped through Miguel's, came up to the group and stood on the other side of Cliff.

"You can tell us what happened," I said to Rachel. The poor girl looked at Gretchen and Tate, then at her father again. "I-I can't."

Cliff put his hands on his daughter's shoulders, his gaze boring into hers. "What's going on? Tell us what?"

Rachel covered her face with her hands. At some point, she'd run out of tears, but it didn't look like that would happen anytime soon.

I saw Captain York in the distance at the same time he spotted me. I could see his face register the people I was with and his face twisted with anger. Seconds later, he stormed up to me, glaring at me, then at Gretchen and Rachel and Tate and Cliff. "What the hell is going on here?" he demanded, but his words breaking off abruptly when he saw Emmaline. "Oh. Sheriff. Didn't see you there."

"Captain," Em said. Even dressed in civilian clothes and fresh off a Costa Rican vacation, she exuded authority. Commanded respect. She held up her hand, one finger pointed, ordering him to be silent.

Rachel, poor girl, seemed completely oblivious about

anything happening around her. She looked up at her father, speaking only to him. "I'm sorry, Daddy," she said again.

Cliff was trying to stay calm, but his face had turned red and his hands trembled, revealing the emotions he was trying to bury for the sake of his daughter. "For what, baby? What are you sorry for?"

Rachel didn't answer his question directly. She was lost in her own head. She could only say what was in her heart. What she had to get out of her. "She took everything from me. From Tate."

Cliff's voice turned hoarse. "What do you mean? What did she take?"

I expected indignation from Rachel. Or some other visceral reaction. Instead, she was like a zombie. The tears still streamed, but the hysteria had receded. In its place was a vacant stare. "Carmen knew."

For a split second, Cliff's gaze shot to Tate. "What did Carmen know?" he asked Rachel, focusing back on her.

Rachel grabbed the front of the navy T-shirt she wore, pulled it up to her face, and wiped her nose. "She knew about Sylvia. About Ruby." She took a step closer to Tate, as if she could protect him from what she was about to say. Her voice dropped to an imploring whisper and myriad emotions passed over her face in a matter of seconds. She didn't want to say it out loud. She didn't want to give wings to her mother's indiscretions because of how it would change Tate's life. At the same time, she seemed to understand that it didn't matter. She couldn't keep it inside. "She knew about Tate. About what Mom did."

I expanded on what Rachel was saying in my head. Carmen and Sylvia were friends. Sylvia knew the truth about who Tate's father was. Of course she did. Guillermo had fallen in love with Sylvia. She was the reason the dalliance between Guillermo and Nessa had ended.

She'd told Carmen.

Cliff opened his mouth to respond but froze for a beat, then closed it again. His face took on a hangdog expression as he looked at Tate, then Rachel. It was clear he knew the truth.

"She had them taken," Rachel said. "She took Carmen from us."

"Do you know why, Rachel?" I asked. "Why did she have them taken now, so many years after—'

I broke off, not needing to say *after Tate was born*.

Her head wobbled as she nodded. "I-it's my f-fault. She h-heard me talking to Carmen after I saw R-Ruby."

Em's discovery that Nessa had a contact at Immigration and Customs Enforcement supported what Rachel was saying. If Nessa had overheard Rachel telling Carmen what she suspected, Nessa would have tried to stop anyone from knowing the truth. The best way to do that was to get rid of Carmen and Sylvia.

Cliff pulled Rachel into a hug, but she pushed herself away. She looked at Gretchen, then turned her red-rimmed eyes back to her father. "She took our sister."

Instantly, the color drained from Cliff's face. "What?"

Gretchen moved next to Rachel, grabbed one of her hands, and held tight. "It's okay, Rachel. It's going to be okay."

But Rachel shook her head so hard I thought her brain might start rattling inside her skull. She was at the breaking point.

I swallowed and steeled my nerves. Rachel was a child, after all. "How did you find out Gretchen was your sister?" I asked softly.

Cliff drew in a sharp breath. Tate's eyes had turned glassy. He looked from Rachel to Gretchen, his lips quivering. The little guy was only around ten years old. His world was falling apart.

Gretchen answered instead of Rachel. "I told her. My dad brought me here to see Vanessa—sorry, I can't call her my mother—when I was little. I knew who she was, and I knew she didn't want me. But when I found out she had other kids? *My* siblings? I wanted to meet them. To be in their lives. For them to be in mine."

Hence the cold call from Gretchen to Rachel. She'd orchestrated their first meeting. "Did you want to see Nessa again?" I asked her.

Gretchen shrugged, but her hand went to her belly. I thought I knew what she was thinking. She was having a child and wanted to know that her child wouldn't be anything like Nessa. "I wanted to ask her why."

For a second, I questioned what I thought I knew. What I thought happened to Nessa Renchrik. "Did you?"

She shook her head. "It was like this huge white elephant in the room. I think she knew who I was, but I couldn't bring myself to actually tell her and she never said anything."

"But she kept coming to you—"

She shrugged. "Like a moth to a flame, I think."

Gretchen had been abandoned by her mother. That certainly gave her a motive to have killed Nessa, but deep down I knew that wasn't what had happened. I turned to Rachel again. "Did you meet your mother at the district office that day?"

Slowly, Rachel nodded.

"No!" Cliff's whole body shook. "You were at Ronnie's—"

"I left early." She looked only at Cliff, explaining only to him. Imploring him to understand. "I called Mom and told her I knew the truth. She told me to come see her in the boardroom. I confronted her. I yelled at her. 'How could you abandon your own daughter? How could you keep Tate from his father? How could you send Carmen away? And Sylvia . . . ?'"

Captain York looked over my shoulder. His jaw pulsed. I knew before I turned that Miguel was standing there, listening to every word being spoken. The case York had sewed up against Miguel was coming undone before his eyes.

Cliff wobbled on his feet. I thought his knees might give out, but somehow, he stayed upright. He crossed one arm over his chest and scrubbed his face with his other hand. He looked at his daughter. Exhaled. Closed his eyes. "You killed her?" he finally asked, his voice so low I could barely hear the question.

"I-I d-didn't mean to. S-she started to . . . to . . . cho ⸺"

She broke off as she brought her hand to her neck.

My blood turned cold as another piece of the puzzle fell into place. It was spring. It wasn't hot, but it certainly wasn't cold, yet Rachel was wearing a long-sleeved shirt and had a scarf wound around her neck. Each time I'd seen her, she'd been wearing something similar. "Rachel," I said, coaxing her with my voice.

She raised her eyes to mine. Suddenly all I could see in them was her terror and pain. I nodded, directing my gaze to her scarf. Her eyelids fluttered and she inhaled, releasing the breath through her mouth. Slowly, she took hold of her scarf and unwound it. Around me were gasps. Someone said, "Oh my God," under their breath. I covered my mouth with my hand. Faded yellowish bruises marked her neck.

A strangled sound came from Cliff. "My God," he breathed out.

Tate's eyes went wide. "What's that? What happened, Rach?"

Cliff found his voice. "She did this to you?"

Rachel closed her eyes, breathing heavily as she nodded. She pulled up the sleeve of her left arm revealing another set of distorted and fading bruises. She spoke in scarcely more than a whisper. "I didn't mean to do it. I just wanted her to stop. I had to make her stop."

"Step back, please." Emmaline's voice came through the hushed horror of silence, strong and commanding. She gestured to Captain York to come forward. Moments later, they were escorting Rachel, Tate, and Cliff away from the festivities of the Spring Fling and to the parking lot. I knew Em would get the entire story out of Rachel and would do everything she could to protect her.

Chapter 23

When I'd moved from Austin back to Santa Sofia, I'd hauled all my photography equipment back with me. I'd finally gotten the second spare room in my house set up with a green backdrop for green screen, a white backdrop, side lighting, and everything else I needed.

Gretchen Arnold was my first official client in my in-home studio.

She showed up right on time, bright and early so we could capture the soft light of the morning sun. She looked ready to pop. She wore dark gray leggings and a white T-shirt, looking ready for a yoga class. She held up a burlap bag. "I brought a dress, too."

"Perfect," I said, my mind already planning different shots. "We'll take some inside in the studio, but also out in the yard. Okay?"

"I've never had professional photos taken," she said, "so whatever you say." She grinned and bounced on the balls of her feet. "I'm excited!"

I led her to my new studio space. I'd set up side lighting and had the white backdrop in place. I positioned a few cream-colored pillows on the floor and helped her down, setting them up so she could recline slightly. I positioned her, instructed her to reveal her belly, and set to work, moving around her to take close-ups of her hands shaped into a heart and laid on her bulging belly.

"How's Rachel doing?" I asked her after I'd taken at least fifty shots.

"She's hanging in there. Her dad has her seeing a therapist. She knows deep down that it was self-defense, but she killed her mom, you know, so that's going to leave some emotional scars."

"Did she tell you what happened?" I asked. I'd heard the lowdown from Emmaline, but I wondered how much Gretchen had known.

She looked suddenly melancholy. "No, but I knew something was wrong. She wouldn't tell me, though."

I helped her up and adjusted the settings on my camera while she went into the bathroom to change into the other outfit she'd brought. She emerged wearing a white eyelet V-neck dress. I led her outside. Agatha was stretched out on her belly in the sun, fast asleep.

Gretchen let out a soft, "Ohhh," followed by, "It's beautiful out here."

The vibrant green of the hydrangea leaves provided a backdrop for the spring flowers, which were in full bloom. It was early enough the lighting was still soft. Gretchen walked alongside the flower beds, the sunlight filtering though the leaves of the Japanese maples in the corner of the yard like lace. I snapped a few candids, glancing at the digital screen on the back of my camera to check how they were turning out.

"Ethereal" was the word that came to mind.

I offered her a glass of iced tea and one of the blueberry scones I'd made before she'd arrived, and we sat at the table on the little patio outside the French doors leading to the living room.

She took a bite of the scone and closed her eyes. "So good," she said after she swallowed. "You have a gift."

"Olaya Solis has the gift. I'm just learning."

She held up the pastry. "This is not the work of someone just learning."

I felt my cheeks warm from the compliment. I'd come a long way with my baking in a short time. I doubted I'd ever get to the level Olaya was at, but that was okay. My bread, and sometimes pastry, baking had become my favorite pastime. My neighbors, especially Mrs. Branford, loved my hobby since they were the beneficiaries of all the extras I baked. I certainly couldn't eat it all.

After a few moments of silence, I broached the subject I'd been wondering about. "You said your dad brought you here when you were little. To see your mom?"

"I think he thought if she saw me, maybe she'd come back to us." A veil of sadness fell over her. "It didn't work. My mother was not a good person. What kind of person attacks their own daughter?"

A monster.

I thought about all the machinations and manipulations Nessa Renchrik had under her belt. Having a child with Guillermo, but keeping Tate from him. Orchestrating the deportation of Sylvia and Carmen. Manipulating the school board vote for the surfing club. Her untimely death changed the outcome of that vote. Good for Chavez Elementary. Too bad for Jerry Zenmark.

"I'm glad you're there for Rachel. She's going to need you. Tate, too."

"Cliff introduced Tate to Guillermo," she said.

I'd been about to take a bite of scone but stopped midway and put it back down instead. "Wow. That must have been hard for him."

"I think he knew deep down. It almost seemed like a relief. Like he didn't have to wonder anymore."

That made sense. Wondering if your wife had had an affair was one thing. Wondering if she'd had a child with someone else and was hiding it was entirely different.

"They'll get through this," Gretchen said.

I hoped she was right.

Chapter 24

Miguel and I arrived at my childhood home, two bottles of wine in hand and a tureen of sausage, kale, and potato soup in hand. I hadn't gotten a chance to pick up bread from Yeast of Eden. We'd have to do without.

We joined my father, Billy, and Emmaline in the backyard. Miguel set the soup in the center of the table and uncorked the Sangiovese, pouring us each a glass. He raised his and toasted the newlyweds. "You got back in the nick of time," he said at the end.

Em lifted her beer bottle. "I'll drink to that."

"Are you keeping Captain York?" I asked.

"He's got a good track record," she said. "He was way off base this time, but I think he was trying to close the case quickly to prove his worth."

"Yeah, at the expense of Miguel," I said, frowning. I didn't like that Em was defending the guy.

"I can't discuss it," she said, "but suffice it to say that I'm handling things."

"Reprimand," Billy said.

Em didn't confirm, but she didn't deny. If York had to stay, I hoped she would be able to rein him in.

"What's happening with Rachel?" I asked.

"The DA is not pressing charges. They've deemed it self-defense."

I felt a weight I hadn't known I'd been carrying lift from my shoulders. "So, what happened?"

"It's just like she said. She was upset with her mom when she found out about Tate's biological father. She met her at the district office. Rachel says she told her mom she was going to tell her father the truth. That's when Nessa went off on her. Rachel says her mom threatened her, then, when Rachel didn't back down, Nessa attacked."

"Those bruises," I said.

My dad just shook his head. "Unbelievable."

"There are more on her back. Turns out the abuse wasn't a onetime thing. Nessa never wanted kids, according to Cliff. She wanted her political career more. She got pregnant and he convinced her to keep the baby."

"So, she took out her anger on Rachel?" My stomach churned with nausea. "What about Tate?"

"He's being evaluated," Em said.

"Cliff didn't suspect anything?"

"Apparently not."

Billy scoffed. "I don't get that."

"People see what they want to see, Son," my dad said.

Emmaline nodded in agreement. "Nessa would have killed her own daughter if Rachel hadn't fought back."

I sipped my wine, then said, "I saw Gretchen. She said Cliff has found a therapist for Rachel."

Em nodded. "She needs it, but she'll get through it. She's got lots of people rallying around her."

I knew that to be true. Candy had called to say she and her daughter Ronnie would do any- and everything they could to help Rachel. The girl had friends standing by.

My dad stood. "I'll get the bowls." He disappeared into the house, returning a few minutes later with them, as well as spoons, and a basket covered with a cloth.

Miguel ladled soup into each bowl as my dad removed the cloth covering the basket.

I stared. In the basket was a mound of rolls. Rye pumpernickel rolls, to be exact. The very same rolls Olaya had served Mrs. Branford and me the week before. The same rolls she said she'd made for the Spring Fling.

Olaya's glow.

My dad's chipper mood.

Olaya had said she was seeing someone.

Holy smokes. Was her secret romance with my father? *Owen Culpepper, you devil*, I thought with a smile.

Later, back at Miguel's house, Agatha curled up in the little dog bed Miguel had bought for her. We sat on the outdoor couch on the porch overlooking the vast darkness of the Pacific Ocean. "So, your dad and Olaya," he said after I filled him in on my suspicions. "Are you okay with that?"

I hadn't been sure how I felt until he asked the question. I only had to think about it for a split second before I said, "He needs to live his life. If they are making each other happy, then I'm all for it."

Miguel took my hand. "You never answered my question. About rug rats," he said.

"I've thought about it," I said, going for nonchalance, but this time my smile reached my eyes. Miguel was in the clear and life was good. "I want a few."

"With me?" he asked, squeezing my hand.

"Only with you, Miguel."

Recipes

Van Dough Focaccia Bread Art
bread art for the eyes and the eating

Yield: Makes approximately 1 large 10x14 or two
medium 9x6

(Recipe courtesy of The Vineyard Baker)
Total time: 4 hours

<u>Ingredients</u>

For the Preferment
1 cup bread flour
½ cup cool water
1/4 teaspoon instant yeast

For the "van Dough"
1¼ cups warm water
1½ teaspoons instant yeast
1 tablespoon extra-virgin olive oil, plus extra for dough
     shaping
3 cups bread flour
1½ teaspoons salt

Some Suggested Garnishes/Toppings
Olive oil
Salt and pepper
Garlic
Parmesan cheese
Sweet peppers
Scallions
Basil or parsley

Kalamata olives
Purple and red onions
Capers
Grape or cherry tomatoes
Carrots
Cooked beans
Nuts and seeds

Olive oil, salt, pepper, garlic, and Parmesan cheese make great additions.

Little sweet peppers make great flowers, fresh scallions or chives for stems, basil or parsley for leaves.

Kalamata or purple olives, purple onions, capers, small grape tomatoes and cherry tomatoes, red onions, carrots, cooked beans, nuts, and seeds all add beautiful color to your palette. You are only limited by your imagination.

Look at life through an edible lens. A walk in the woods, a visit to a museum, or just a walk through the grocery store or farmer's market provides wonderful inspirations.

Equipment You Will Need

I would encourage you to make this dough by hand in order to get a full understanding of the texture and process of making yeasted bread. For this you will only need:

a large mixing bowl

a whisk

measuring utensils

a bowl scraper or spatula

a small bowl or deli container for preferment

a kitchen towel or plastic wrap for covering dough as it rises

Other items, such as parchment paper, a baking pan, and a paring knife, are used as part of the vegetable prep and baking processes.

Directions

Step 1: Preferment

Preparing a day ahead is best; however, you could start this step 3–4 hours before making the actual dough if you forgot. Mix 1 cup of bread flour with ¾ cup of water and ¼ teaspoon of yeast, *mix well*, and leave covered in a bowl or container at room temp overnight. This long fermentation process evokes the deep nutty sweetness of the grain and lends itself to better textures.

Step 2: The "van Dough"

The next day:

Place 1 cup of warm water and 1 teaspoon of yeast in bowl; mix to dissolve. Add all of your prefermented dough and 1 tablespoon of olive oil. "Squish" this up with your fingers, breaking apart the preferment in the water mixture until there are no large chunks, then add the 3 cups of bread flour and 1½ teaspoons of salt.

Mix all ingredients together until the dough just comes together in a shaggy ball. It will appear lumpy and sticky. Make sure all the flour has been incorporated, about 6-8 minutes. Let it rest covered for 15 minutes. The next process of stretching and folding takes the place of classic kneading. It is helpful to set a bowl of water near your mixing bowl to dip your fingers in while stretching and folding this dough so dough won't stick to your fingers. You will stretch the dough over itself right in the bowl, turning the bowl and pulling the dough from the outer edge, then folding it over toward the middle until the dough becomes a smooth ball. Eight full turns in the bowl should be enough. Cover and rest the dough for another 15 minutes; repeat this process two more times at 15-minute intervals for a total of 3 sessions of stretching and folding. After the final stretch and fold, you will notice the dough transforms into a supple, smooth texture that moves as one uniform ball in the bowl. Next let the dough rest in a warm place well covered for 1 to 2 hours to proof or until it just about doubles in size. Now is the time to prep your veggies, herbs, and spices for your creative presentation while the dough is "on the rise."

Vegetable and Herb Prep

Use raw vegetables only. Cut colorful mini peppers in different shapes, long strips, or circles. Trim up your herbs; slice scallions long ways for stems, or use chives. Basil or parsley can be used for leaves. Kalamata or black olives can be chopped for flower centers. Purple onions provide brilliant color. Some cherry tomatoes can be sliced but should be laid on a paper towel to soak up some of the seeds and moisture before using. If you are using colorful carrots, slice very thinly. The exception to raw vegetables is mushrooms! These contain a lot of water. I highly suggest sautéing them a bit and then patting dry before using. Cut slightly thicker pieces for tomatoes and onions. Herbs have thin membranes and brown up fast; to maintain the green, dip your herbs in a lemon-water solution just before placing on focaccia and try not getting too much olive oil on them.

Come up with some creative ideas on your own. I've seen some people use beans, seeds, and nuts. All great ideas and they provide color as well as nutrition and flavor! Remember to keep in mind, some vegetables have varying amounts of natural sugars, and nuts have natural oils. Both will get darker in the oven as the focaccia bakes.

The Shaping of the Dough

Preheat your oven to 450° F; line a heavy-gauge sheet pan (12x18) with parchment paper and olive oil. Gently turn out the risen dough onto a lightly floured flat surface. *Gently* shape the dough into a fat rectangle, place this in the center of the pan, pour a generous amount of good olive oil on the top surface of the dough, and continue to stretch and dimple with your fingers until the dough is the desired size. Sort of like a cat kneading. *Do not use a rolling pin*; this will leave you with dense dough. The air bubbles are part of the overall character of focaccias. If your dough keeps shrinking back, don't fight it, let it rest for a few minutes; the gluten will relax and it will be easy to work with again. Be sure to leave a little room on the top, bottom, and sides of your baking sheet for baking expansion.

Placing Your Decorations on the Dough

Some helpful tools to have are your fingers, chopsticks, toothpicks or skewers, clean tweezers for the tiny things, and a finger bowl of water with a teaspoon of lemon juice for dipping herbs in to preserve their color while baking. When you place the veggies, herbs, and spices on the dough or "canvas," the billows will help to "lock in" with gentle pushing and poking. This prevents the garnishes from falling off while baking. Because bread art takes time and the dough will be rising while you are creating your bread art, it is nice to have a little idea of what you will be creating ahead of time. Feel free to sketch your ideas and take notes while you are creating and baking for future reference. Begin by placing your herbs and veggies gently in your chosen pattern on the top of your focaccia dough. When you are satisfied and everything is picture perfect, go back and press some of the veggies in so the dough is hugging them a bit. The dough should be supple and bubbly at the time. The art process takes about 30–40 minutes, which I find is just enough time for the final rise. If the dough's not soft and puffed up, just place it on the heated stove top for 15 minutes; be sure it is kept moist. You can spritz with a clean bottle full of clean water if needed. The dough should have puffy billows and be slightly raised above the top of the ridge of the pan.

Step 3: The Bake

One last check on the embellishments. Scan your focaccia bread art and gently tuck in any vegetables and herbs that may look like they are popping off. Add a sprinkling of salt and pepper. Lightly brush dough with olive oil, and sprinkle parmesan cheese on the edges, if desired. Carefully place focaccia on center rack in preheated oven. Bake at 450° F for 12 minutes. Check the bread in 10 minutes; if it is already starting to brown, turn the heat down to 375° F for the final 10–12 minutes. Notice if any toppings are popping off. This just means you have to tuck them into the dough a bit tighter next time.

Bake time is approximately 24 minutes. Remember every oven is different. Happy eating!

(We love looking at other people's creative master-pieces. Share your bread art on social media such as Instagram or Facebook. This is a wonderful way for sharing your beautiful creations and inspiring others. #Breadart #Focaccia and tag @vineyardbaker and @melissabourbon books.)

The Vineyard Baker's Frequently Asked Questions and Baking Tips

A Warm Place for Your Dough

Dough needs a nice, warm environment to activate the yeast. It will rise cold or warm; however, the time for cold rise is much longer. A good gauge is something we call the T-shirt test. If you can wear a T-shirt comfortably in your kitchen without feeling cold, it's most likely the perfect temperature for dough to rise. Some good warm spots are the top of your stove and the top of the refrigerator Just be sure the dough is well covered and does not risk drying out at all. A little olive oil rubbed on the dough ball will help as well.

Flour Recommendations

I recommend using a good flour like King Arthur bread flour in the blue bag. You need high protein for chewy interior texture and crusty exterior. All-purpose will work if you can't get bread flour. Try to avoid bleached flour. The package should say "never bleached" or "un-bleached"; hope this helps. (FYI: I do not work for the King Arthur company, just have always used their brand with consistently excellent results.)

Baking Tips

I can't stress enough that every single oven in every single house is different. Each one has its own quirks. Use the directions only as a guide, not the gospel. Your nose and your eyes will tell the real story. Using a very hot oven and a thick-gauge aluminum pan is essential to the quality of the overall texture and color. Thin aluminum disposable pans do not conduct heat well. Put oil on dough before veggies. Do not get too much oil on veggies unless you want darker colors. Do not precook any of the vegetables except mushrooms. Wetting the herbs in a bowl of water with a few drops of lemon juice helps to keep their color. Bake on high, 450° F, for 10–12 minutes, then turn down to 375° F for 10–12 minutes or until crust is golden brown. Involve all your senses in baking, especially common sense.

Don't Fight the Gluten!

As you stretch your dough into your desired shape you will notice it will become active and want to fight back. Simply allowing a few minutes of rest will give the gluten a chance to relax and make it easier to reach your desired shape and size. Be sure the dough does not dry out while resting. While there is no depth restriction, think of a regular pizza depth when shaping. Also keep in mind, while you are decorating your dough, it will be on the final rise. You can have it as thick as 1 to 1½ inches or as thin as ¼ inch, based on your own preference. Thinner will require less time in the oven and will be more of a crisp bread.

Prepare Ahead and Storage Tips

While fresh is always best, there are times that we need to prepare ahead:

This dough can be made up to three days in advance as long as you refrigerate the dough after the final mix in a rather large container with lid (it will rise in fridge). I do not recommend precutting veggies or herbs. This should be done as dough is coming to room temp from the fridge. Alternatively, you could bake the focaccias and freeze them by double wrapping and bagging as soon as they are cool enough. Reheat: Preheat 375° F oven and heavy baking tray, place frozen focaccia in tray, and bake for 6–8 minutes or just until hot.

About Me

I have been bread baking for over forty years. I am a "breaducator" at our local schools and library. The word "focaccia," derived from the Latin for "from the hearth," inspired me to create a decorative heart-shaped focaccia "From the Heart," and it was onward from there. I live on Martha's Vineyard, have four sons, and enjoy sharing good bread with good people. I hope you will, too. Be well, eat well, and happy baking. ~The Vineyard Baker

Miguel's Savory Sausage, Kale, and Potato Soup

Yield: Serves 4

Ingredients

1 tablespoon extra-virgin olive oil
3–4 Italian sausages (choose your level of spiciness)
3 celery stalks, cut into bite-sized pieces
3 carrots, cut into bite-sized pieces
2–3 turnips, cut into bite-sized pieces
1 medium onion, diced
2 cloves garlic, minced
4 cups chicken or vegetable stock
5–6 red potatoes, cut into bite-sized pieces
1 bunch of kale, leaves only, roughly chopped
1 tablespoon fresh thyme or 1 teaspoon dried
1 tablespoon fresh rosemary or 1 teaspoon dried
1 bay leaf (remove before serving)
Salt to taste

Directions

Preheat skillet over medium heat. Add olive oil.

Remove sausages from casings. Separate into chunks and cook in skillet until browned and cooked through. Drain fat and set aside.

Preheat a large stock pot or Dutch oven over medium heat. Add chopped celery, carrots, turnips, and onion. Sauté until vegetables have softened. Add garlic.

Add sausage, stock, potatoes, kale, and herbs. Simmer until potatoes are soft enough to poke through with a fork and kale is tender.

Salt to taste.

Olaya's Hot Cross Buns

Yield: Makes 16 buns

Ingredients

For the Preferment
½ cup milk
1 teaspoon sugar
1 tablespoon instant yeast
½ cup whole wheat flour
1 stick unsalted butter
1 cup low-fat milk
⅓ cup brown sugar
2 eggs, room temperature and lightly beaten
1 teaspoon cinnamon
¼ teaspoon ground nutmeg
3½ cups all-purpose flour
¼–½ cup raisins (optional)

For the Egg Wash
1 egg
2 teaspoons milk

For the Glaze
1½ cups confectioners' sugar
2 tablespoons milk

Directions

Creating the Preferment
Microwave milk until just warm. Add sugar, yeast, and flour. Stir and let sit at least 15 minutes until bubbly.

In mixing bowl, cream butter using the paddle attachment. Alternatively, whisk by hand.

Add milk, brown sugar, eggs, cinnamon, and nutmeg and mix until smooth.

Add the preferment and stir until smooth.

Add flour and mix until dough sticks together.

Turn dough out onto work surface and knead, turning and adding only enough flour to form a smooth ball. Dough should not be sticky.

Add raisins to dough and knead until raisins are evenly dispersed. (Skip this step if you are not putting raisins in.)

Form dough into a ball and let rise for 1 hour in covered greased bowl. Dough should be almost doubled.

Forming the Buns

Grease two 8-inch square or round baking pans. Divide dough into two sections. Punch one of the dough balls down, and turn out onto floured surface. Roll into a 12-inch log. Divide log into 8 equal portions. Shape into balls and place in prepared pan, evenly spaced apart. Repeat with second dough ball.

Cover each pan with plastic wrap and place in the refrigerator to rise overnight!

The next morning, preheat the oven to 350° F. With a sharp knife, make a cross on the top of each bun.

Create egg wash by mixing egg and the 2 teaspoons of milk, and brush buns. Bake for 25–30 minutes.

While buns are baking, make the glaze* by whisking together powdered sugar with 2 tablespoons milk.

Let buns cool for 5–10 minutes before drizzling glaze over top. Serve immediately.

*Instead of glazing the buns, if you prefer, you can serve them with butter.

Rye Pumpernickel Rolls, Recipe adapted from King Arthur

Ingredients

For the Dough
1½ cups warm water
2 tablespoons vegetable oil
2½ cups all-purpose flour
1¼ cups pumpernickel or rye flour
2 tablespoons cocoa flour
1 tablespoon brown sugar
1 tablespoon wheat gluten (optional, but helpful to develop elasticity with rye bread)
2 teaspoons onion powder
2½ teaspoons instant yeast or active dry yeast
1½ teaspoons salt

For the Topping
1 large egg white
1 tablespoon molasses
1½ tablespoon water
2 tablespoons everything bagel topping or poppy seeds (optional)

Directions

For the Dough
Combine all ingredients together. Mix until combined, then knead with mixer (or by hand) for 6–8 minutes. Use a greased surface if kneading by hand. The kneaded dough will be shiny and a little bit sticky.

Cover and let rise in a warm spot for 45–90 minutes. Dough should be close to doubled.

On a greased surface, divide dough into 16 pieces. Shape into rounds.

For the Topping

Whisk together egg white, molasses, and water. Brush tops of the rolls and dip them in seeds, if desired. Place the rolls on a parchment-lined baking sheet.

Cover with greased plastic and let rise until almost doubled in size, approximately 45 minutes. Meanwhile, preheat oven to 375° F.

Create a slice down the center of each roll.

Bake for 15–20 minutes. The rolls are done when the internal temperature is 190° F on a food thermometer.

Can't get enough of Ivy and the Yeast of Eden crew?
Don't miss the previous books in the Bread Shop
Mystery series:

KNEADED TO DEATH
CRUST NO ONE
THE WALKING BREAD
FLOUR IN THE ATTIC
DOUGH OR DIE

And keep an eye out for more
coming soon from
Winnie Archer
and
Kensington Books.